TELL IT TO
THE MARINES

TELL IT TO THE MARINES

Amy J. Fetzer

BRAVA

KENSINGTON PUBLISHING CORP.
http://www.kensingtonbooks.com

BRAVA BOOKS are published by

Kensington Publishing Corp.
850 Third Avenue
New York, NY 10022

All Kensington titles, imprints and distributed lines are available at special quantity discounts for bulk purchases for sales promotion, premiums, fund raising, educational or institutional use.

Special book excerpts or customized printings can also be created to fit specific needs. For details, write or phone the office of the Kensington Special Sales Manager: Kensington Publishing Corp., 850 Third Avenue, New York, NY 10022. Attn. Special Sales Department. Phone: 1-800-221-2647.

Brava and the B logo Reg. U.S. Pat. & TM Off.

ISBN 0-7582-0808-1

First Kensington Trade Paperback Printing: December 2004
10 9 8 7 6 5 4 3 2 1

Printed in the United States of America

Contents

HOT CONFLICT

One

Panama

Gunnery Sergeant David James "DJ" McAllister leaned back against a sunbaked stucco wall, and from beneath the well-worn Panama hat, he scanned the area. The sun was low in the sky, glaring and red.

In front of him, the narrow street curved down the mountainside in a line of odd-sized buildings, half-abandoned, each more cracked than the last. Toward the bottom, tourists strolled past shops, though most were closed at this hour for after-dinner siesta. A couple of kids raced by on bikes, barely noticing him in civilian clothes.

Uniforms, MP5 assault rifles, and black ops gear wouldn't do for this mission.

Hell, he looked more like a drug dealer waiting for a sale in loose black slacks and a printed shirt.

"In position, Gunny," came through the earpiece.

DJ motioned to his left. A fellow Marine stationed a few yards away moved in a little closer, DJ watching his six. Between them was an old tin warehouse once used to store fruit for transport to the city. Somewhere in one of the apartments across the street were a couple of CIA operatives, watching, perched like birds on a wire. His gaze slid along the rusted walls of the warehouse, hoping for movement, a sound.

He was still having trouble wrapping his brain around the fact that she'd been kidnapped. But that it happened in his "backyard" told him this was fate, that he'd never escape her. Even when he'd tried his damnedest to forget her.

He almost felt sorry for her kidnappers.

Mary Grace Heyward was a force to be reckoned with: beautiful, educated, and to say she was opinionated was lukewarm. Mad, she had a mouth that could peel the skin off the best of men. DJ included.

He and half the U.S. intelligence community here had been searching the trail from the posh hotel in Panama City for two days. She'd been snatched right after a reception for the U.S. Ambassador. Why he and his wife of twenty years had Mary Grace down here to plan the wedding-vow renewal ceremony was clear. The ambassador's wife was her older sister. Why Mary Grace was taken was still a bit of a mystery.

"I got a sighting," came through DJ's earpiece. Another Marine was in the rear, moving through the dense forest backing the warehouse. "It's her. Red hair, lavender suit. Gagged, tied to a chair. She looks asleep." DJ prayed she wasn't dead. "Three men, armed and looking mighty impatient, Gunny. One's on a cell phone."

"Translate?" DJ said. Impatience riddled him as the Marine repositioned himself closer. He had listening equipment that would pick up her breathing.

"They're going to move her. Shit. They want to send on her finger to push the ambassador along."

DJ cursed, fear nibbling at his spine. These guys were playing hardball.

"We need Intel." This from the CIA birds in the apartment.

"Get it yourself some other way," DJ snapped softly, not glancing up to the room he knew was lined with surveillance equipment and a couple of soft-handed analysts. "She's not staying there a moment longer just so you can gather what you should have known!"

That the kidnappers had planned and executed this with stealth and precision warned DJ that they were not dealing with idiots. He pushed off the wall, walked in front of the tin building, then slipped between it and the neighboring structure. The ground was overgrown with weeds and flowers, the space too narrow for quick movement. Each step brought the stench of decaying animal feces as he edged the perimeter. He inhaled deep, making himself accustomed to it. Then he ditched the hat and drew his weapon.

"Markus, get high." Sergeant Steve Markus was sniper-trained, and could pick dirt off a bug's ass at three hundred yards, but this was a no-kill zone. They needed the kidnappers alive and had to get her out of there without much notice. No telling how many sympathetic rebels were hiding in these mountains.

"Aye, aye, Gunny."

"Intel? Make yourself useful and trace the call."

"You're a real prick sometimes, McAllister, you know that?"

"Yeah, yeah, just do it." DJ kept low, the bank of windows above him bleary with dirt. If the warehouse wall wasn't tin, and wouldn't make one hell of a noise, he'd brace himself between the two buildings and work his way up for a look-see.

Then he heard a short, harsh scream, high-pitched and muffled. Don't fight them, he silently begged.

"Heads up, got a door opening."

DJ stopped short of coming around the edge, heard the hinges scrape.

"One guard, one Uzi."

DJ peered around the corner, saw the guard light a thin cigar. He backed up to speak. "Bates, Camden, get ready to go in. Markus, spot me." He edged behind the kidnapper, and when he was within reach, he snatched the machine gun by the barrel and as the man whipped around, he popped him in the throat. It crushed his larynx, stripped blood from his brain, and he went down on his knees without much sound.

Camden rushed in, gagged and dragged him into the forest as Bates picked up the Uzi. The door was still open. DJ snatched the cigar, puffed on it to make like the man was still near, then peered, his gaze skipping past Mary Grace to the other two. With hand signals, he identified the enemy's location. Bates advanced opposite him.

DJ gave a three count, then slipped around the edge of the door.

Head bowed, Mary Grace's cheek burned from the slap, her eyes watering. A shadow to her right caught her attention and she lifted her head, afraid the man was going to make good his promises. What she saw was a one-man wrecking machine in a flowered shirt. DJ. His weapon out, his back against the open door, he scanned the room, and when he saw her, blue eyes pinned her to the chair. If she wasn't tied, gagged, and highly ticked off at being kid-. napped in the first place, Mary Grace would have laughed at the sheer irony of it all. Why did it have to be *him?* For a slivered moment, he just stared, so intense, so raw, Mary Grace felt her whole body tighten with an inescapable punch of need and emotion.

She wasn't surprised he could still do that with a look, and right now, was damn grateful for it.

Her gaze flicked to the two men a few feet away. DJ put his finger to his lips and moved on silent feet toward them.

He had one little gun, they had machine guns. What did he think he could do?

Then he did it, hitting so hard and fast she almost didn't see it.

He clipped one in the throat, the second in the solar plexus. Both buckled, choking for air. Then, with double-fisted hits to the back of the neck, DJ sent one to the ground. The Marine behind him dispatched the other with equal speed.

"Well. That was fun," a Marine said, aiming his gun at the kidnapper.

"We're not done yet." DJ kicked the weapons out of reach, then picked up the cell phone as his teammates secured the prisoners. "The line's still connected." He covered the receiver. "Shit! That'll alert someone nasty." Markus came in and he tossed the cell to him. "Give that to Intel, see what they can find. Let's make this exit quiet—no telling who they were talking to on that cell or how far away they are."

He searched the prisoners, ignoring her.

"Yo, DJ! Hurry up and untie me!" she shouted from behind the duct tape gag. It sounded like bad humming.

DJ faced her, his gaze moving over her in a clinical "inspecting for injuries" look, bypassing her porn queen position: thighs spread, ankles tied to the chair legs. Her skirt was hiked so high she felt a draft, and humiliated, she gave him her best glare.

"Bet that look sends men running home to Mama, huh?" he said, pulling up his shirt enough to holster his weapon and reveal a kevlar vest underneath.

Suddenly he touched his ear, all three men looking at each other as if listening to God. DJ cursed, motioning to the other two. Collecting weapons, they hurriedly dragged the unconscious men out the door.

"Untie me!" she shouted again and knew darn well he understood her. But he didn't, and instead, he fiddled with the ropes cutting into her wrists and ankles, and lifted her from the chair. Then the man had the unmitigated gall to toss her over his shoulder like a sack of feed. Air punched out of her lungs at first impact, then again and again with every quick step he took out of the warehouse.

"Jesus, Mary Grace. Put on a few pounds lately?"

She twisted on his shoulder and glared murderously at him. He smirked, cupped her behind, and kept moving. *The man always had more nerve than smarts,* she thought, conceding temporary defeat, and slumped. She couldn't breathe; her head was pounding with all the blood rushing between her ears, and never mind that this was the most unladylike position ever.

DJ stopped between the buildings, set her on her feet, then whipped out a knife and cut her bonds. She groaned, but before she could pull the sticky tape, he yanked it off.

"Ow!"

He covered her mouth, backing her up against the wall. "For once in your life, keep quiet!" He looked left and right. "Those three aren't the only men after you."

Her eyes flared and when he let her go, she huddled close to him, rubbing circulation back into her arms and legs and trying not to gag on the smells lingering in the humidity. She noticed the tiny, flesh-colored earpiece in his right ear—then she let herself notice the rest. Black hair, chiseled profile, he was still heart-stoppingly handsome and packed with a sexual energy she'd never found in any other man. Ever. Not even with her late husband. Just being this close made her hands itch to touch him, and never mind that her body was doing a happy dance. *It's been so long since I felt that,* she thought. To hell with the kidnappers. She laid her hand lightly on his arm.

DJ's gaze flew to hers, locking hard, her wide-eyed stare grinding right down to his bones and making him nuts in all the wrong places. He didn't want her to look at him like that—not now, not here. The situation was too dangerous to get sidetracked.

Then, "Be advised, late arrival," came through the earpiece and DJ focused.

The hollow rumble of an engine moving into the warehouse sounded like thunder. Doors slammed, footsteps, and their pissed-off Spanish crystal clear as the men passed toward the back where they'd found her.

Mary Grace made a tiny sound, and DJ looked at her, mouthing, "Let's go." He scooped up his hat, moving through the alley toward the street. He stopped at the edge as the warehouse door went down.

DJ felt Mary Grace press up against his back, every inch of her defined. "Intel! Intel?" he said just above a whisper.

"We're packing out."

"Like hell you are! Where's the fucking car?"

"Behind this place."

Great. It was supposed to be parked in front. DJ muttered something about national security in the hands of idiots and looked at Mary Grace. "We have to run to that building, get inside and to the car in the back."

"And if we can't?" she whispered back. *If they shoot us?*

He shrugged. "I'll improvise when we get there."

"That's your *plan?*"

"Best one I got right now."

He checked the area, and with her, took off across the street to the apartment. He shoved through the doors, overtook the hallway toward the back of the building. He stopped for a second, glancing around. They were trapped, no exit. Then he kicked in the last door. A woman inside screamed and hurried into the corner.

Mary Grace apologized in Spanish, but DJ headed straight to the nearest window, then shoved it open. He glared at the screaming woman. She shut up instantly.

He grabbed Mary Grace close. "It's a short drop. Get going."

She looked down, eyes wide. "Oh, no no *no!*"

He didn't give her a choice as he scooped her up and put her legs over the sash, almost dumping her out.

Mary Grace grabbed the window frame. "DJ, that's too far."

"It's only nine, ten feet. Where's all that southern backbone?"

"Back in South Carolina in my panty drawer."

They heard shouts and footsteps. "*Now,* dammit!"

"Okay, okay, I'm going." Mary Grace closed her eyes and jumped. She landed fine, but her high heels stuck into the ground, toppling her backwards on her butt.

DJ dropped to a crouch beside her. "You just gonna sit there?" He yanked her to her feet, pulling her along toward a car.

Mary Grace gaped at the vehicle, reaching for the handle. "This isn't a car, it's a go-cart." His shoulders wouldn't fit in it!

"It runs. Get in." She did. Already inside, he started the engine and was pulling out when a bullet hit the side window. It shattered over her head. She yelped, ducking.

"You okay?" He ground the gear, jammed the gas, and the little car lurched forward, sliding on the steep incline. When she didn't respond, he grabbed her shoulder and shook. "Are you injured?"

"No." She brushed glass out of her hair as the car bounced along at an amazing speed, and Mary Grace held on for dear life. "You call this a rescue?"

"Nag, nag, nag," he said calmly. "We're still alive."

He turned right, then left, then right twice more, speeding up the hill. The car moved faster than she'd expected, hitting every rock and dent in the road.

Mary Grace swore she lost a filling back there. "Where are we going?"

"Haven't a clue." He reached under the seat and handed her a radio. "Turn that to 12 megahertz and say, 'Op one.' "

She obeyed, repeating it.

"You have to put your finger on the button."

She flushed and did it again.

"Now let *go* of the button to hear."

"Be more helpful next time." She repeated the transmission.

"Op two to Op one," came through instantly. She held the radio out like it was infected.

DJ grabbed it. "The gang is hot on my tail, guns blazing."

"No backup. Intel took the other ride."

Fucking cowards. "Then steal one!"

"Will do, Op one. Base is coming for the first team, but you have to lose those guys. Get out of sight, ASAP. Will contact at oh-seven-hundred tomorrow."

"Shit." DJ confirmed and handed her the radio. He was on his own.

"What did all that mean and why are you still driving so fast? There's no one behind us."

"Yes. There is." He turned the car so hard she slammed into the door.

Then she saw it, a dirty black truck barreling after them.

"Man, I wish they'd give up. I really didn't want to shoot anyone today."

She glanced back, seeing only men and weapons. "Don't stop on my account."

"What the hell did you do to these guys?"

"Nothing."

"Try that on someone who *doesn't* know you."

She shrugged, brushing the glass off her clothes. "I bit and kicked."

"Scratched and clawed, too, I'll bet."

"Yes, well, a good manicure *is* a woman's best weapon."

He scoffed, amused, shifting gears and hauling ass. "What did they say?"

"They wanted me to pay for what my husband did."

He scowled. "But Paul's been dead for three years."

"I caught that discrepancy, too." *And I hope he's rotting in hell, the cheating bastard.* No one knew that. No one. And Mary Grace wasn't going to share her humiliation with anyone. Especially DJ.

"They had to have said more." DJ glanced in the rearview mirror, saw the ride close in. Christ, they were a determined bunch.

"Nothing about why they took me." She slapped a hand on the dash when he swerved to avoid a dog. "And my Spanish is a little more than passable."

They were going to send her back in pieces—the fact that they hadn't blindfolded her told DJ they never intended to trade her for a ransom. But he didn't point that out. She looked scared enough and he wondered if they'd brutalized her, but didn't have time to ask. He'd want to turn around and do some damage if they had.

He drove for another mile, cut right, took a dirt road, then slid the car behind a stand of trees. He killed the engine and motioned for her to hunch down in the seat.

Mary Grace slid to the floor, yet DJ remained as he was, dumping the hat on his head and looking like he was taking a nap, his eyes slitted. It was painfully quiet—no truck, no people—just the hot, humid wind coming through the shattered window. Without much movement, DJ cocked his weapon, his finger on the trigger. Then his gaze flicked to hers.

"Hello, DJ."

His lips quirked. "How's it going, Mare?"

He was the only one who called her that. She wouldn't let anyone else. Even her late husband. "I didn't know you were stationed here."

"Two years." DJ just looked at her, thinking that even dirty, with bruises on her jaw, her pinned-up hair falling and still stuck with dead flowers, she was still beautiful. And got to him. DJ wanted nothing more than to pull her into his arms and go from there. She'd probably beat the shit out of him if he did. Yet the past two days made him realize that the *thing* he had for Mary Grace had never died. Though he'd tried his best to kill it.

It just wasn't easy to see the only woman you ever wanted in the arms of another man. Even if DJ had pushed her there. Even if neither of them deserved her.

"Just what is it you're doing in Panama?"

"If I tell you, I'll have to kill you."

"How very bad-ass of you to say." Mary Grace rolled her eyes. "And still playing it close to the vest, I see."

He stared out the window, not wanting to have this conversation. He'd kept his feelings for her locked up tight for years, and he wasn't about to break his silence now. "Makes life easier."

"For you, maybe." A tense, bittersweet silence stretched between them, gazes locked. DJ read a jumble of emotions in her eyes—curiosity, pleasure, and lastly, a sadness that ripped at his heart. "I almost wish it wasn't you, DJ," she said softly.

A sigh deflated his chest. "I know." They'd been on the edge of something for years. The edge of desire? The edge of need? All he knew was that being near her for however long would lay nothing but a straight shot to mind-blowing temptation in front of him.

"But I'm glad it was a familiar face."

He offered a half-smile, yet as she pushed a loose strand

out of her view, her hand shook almost violently. DJ realized while this might be commonplace for him, it wasn't for her.

She exhaled slowly, then said, "I didn't think I'd get out of there. Thank you." She stared at his profile. "I know what it took for you to do this."

She had no idea. Mary Grace was the one big regret of his life. She'd been an ungodly craving under his skin since he laid eyes on her. But he'd never let her know that. She'd been young and wild, and the only person to offer friendship to a kid from the low side of town. She'd ignored his rebellious mean streak, his hand-me-down clothes, and brought him to her life, her house. He'd never wanted to lose that, so he never once touched her the way he wanted. Which was to explore every delectable inch of her.

DJ shifted on the seat, propping his elbow on the window as if the inches of distance would make a difference. It didn't. The erotic images played hell on his mind and to distract, he popped out the earpiece.

"Too far out of range—we have the radio." He opened the first couple of buttons of his shirt, then pulled out a thin black wire with a flat little box on the end.

Mary Grace sighed, resigned to the change of subject. What did she expect? For DJ to admit his feelings for her, feelings she knew he had? A man didn't look at you as if he knew what you looked like naked and not feel *something*. Every time she got this close to him all she wanted was to feel his mouth on her, his hands on her body, but he used to be her best friend and he'd made it clear years ago that's all he wanted with her.

Mary Grace wanted to believe he was lying through his teeth, but that was her fantasy, not his. She smoothed her hair, rubbing the bruises on her jaw. "What now?"

He peered over the dashboard. "We wait."

"For them to come to us? That's not a good plan."

Under the Panama hat, he arched a brow. "What would you suggest?"

"Confront them?"

"I'm trying *not* to cause an international incident."

"Kidnapping me isn't?"

"You're the sister-in-law of the ambassador, not the president."

"True enough. But still, I'm an American citizen kidnapped by right-wing fascists, or whoever they were."

"That gets you four Marines. And this is touchy—we're in the middle of cocaine country."

Fear skated across her features. "I always wanted to visit there, but it wasn't on the tour maps."

His lips curved. "Toss a coin in any direction, you'll hit a factory." All the way to Colombia, he thought, then frowned. Since Panama had no military, only a national defense force, the ambassador was brokering a deal with the Panamanian government to let DEA in to help stop drug movement into the U.S. He'd bet his best pair of combat boots that was why they'd snatched her. For leverage.

"The ambassador and his wife are back in the country, by the way."

She sighed hard. That cut short their second honeymoon to Barbados. "So much for the renewal wedding of the century going off without a hitch."

"I think they'll forgive you." He started the car, motioning her to get up as he pulled onto the road. He drove fast, but not at the teeth-cracking speed he had before.

He reached across to the glove box, pulling out what looked like a Palm Pilot. He punched in codes with his thumb. The little glowing screen lit up. A soft, blinking tone that sounded like a submarine ping filled the car.

"And that is?"

"A GPS."

"I don't speak Marine, DJ."

"Global positioning system. Tells me where we are by satellite."

"And that would be?"

"Coming up on the lake. And a safehouse."

"Why not just go back to Panama City?"

"It's a hundred and fifty miles away." Her eyes flared with shock. "And those men are still looking for us. This car isn't exactly hard to spot in the hills."

They passed a man leading a donkey with a horse cart. "I see what you mean."

"We'll have to hide out till it's clear." He checked the GPS, then slowed the car. "We'll ditch the ride and walk."

Though she'd been tied to a chair for two days, and would have loved to walk to get blood in her muscles, she had a feeling DJ wasn't talking about a short stroll in the woods.

He pulled the car to the left, under some trees, then turned off the engine. "Out."

She climbed out, and he opened the trunk, removing a black pack and a duffel, then a murderous-looking machete. Without explaining, he dislodged something from the engine, then cut some branches and covered the car.

He shouldered on the pack, picked up the duffel, then nodded to the north. "That way."

She looked. "In case you didn't notice, DJ, there isn't a road."

"I'll make one." DJ pushed past her and started hacking a path into the woods.

"My, my, sir," she said with a deep Carolina accent, "I didn't know you were so handy to have around."

He paused, glanced back, and gave her one of those long, studying looks that turned her knees to jelly, and said, "It's been three years since I've seen you, Mare—a lot has changed."

"With me, too, DJ."

DJ's brows knit for a second. That sounded more miserable than pleased. Was she still mourning Paul? "Then we won't lack for conversation tonight."

Tonight?

She moved behind him like a recently resurrected zombie, thinking about the prospect of spending the night in the jungle, alone, with the one man who'd stolen her heart—and had never given it back. Nor given up his in return.

Two

Her feet were killing her by the time they hit the base of a mountain. She grappled for footing, grabbing roots and branches and trying to keep up. "DJ, I'm not used to this. Stop!"

"Toughen up, brat, and get your pampered ass up here."

"So that's how it's going to be, huh?"

"Yeah, make those thousand-dollar shoes work for you."

"Go to hell, Marine. They're forty-dollar, dyed-to-match-for-one-occasion cheapies, and for your information"—she latched on to a branch—"there isn't an inch of me that's feeling the least bit pampered."

He smiled down at her, holding out his hand. "You were expecting the Hilton?"

She slapped her palm in his and he pulled her up. "I was expecting to be dead." She let out a tired breath and straightened her stained jacket.

His expression went suddenly dark, concerned. "Did they hurt you?"

Her green eyes turned cloudy. "Nothing I couldn't handle," she said, moving past him.

He grabbed her arm, forcing her to look at him. "Do I need to go back there and put someone in a hurt locker?"

"Hurt locker?" She laughed to herself. "I can only imagine what that means, and I think you did fine with that chop to the guy's throat. He went a lovely shade of purple rather quickly."

He wasn't amused. "When I saw you tied up like that, I wanted to rip them apart." He touched her jaw, the bruises dark and in the shape of fingerprints. She grasped his hand, holding it for a second.

She was touched. It had been so long since anyone cared about her like this. "I'm flattered, and like I said, it was nothing I couldn't handle."

Mary Grace didn't want to dip into that ugly well right now. The threats and mental torture were real enough. She wished they'd just stuck her in a room and left her to come up with her own worst-case scenarios, but they hadn't, keeping her near, mauling her, and letting her hear everything they wanted to do to her. It made her wish she'd flunked Spanish.

DJ stared into her eyes for a second, assessing, judging, but he'd noticed the hollow look just then. Did she think after all this time she could put something over on him? "Come on, let's keep moving—it's not far."

"Good, because I haven't slept in two days and I'm about ready to ask a monkey if he wouldn't mind a houseguest."

Smiling, he swept his arm around her lightly and guided her to the left. Mary Grace resisted the urge to sink into all that muscle and man, and was grateful when the ground leveled out. She moved away and followed him.

"Here we are."

It was a shack on stilts tucked in the side of the mountain, barely visible unless you were right beneath it. "Are you telling me this was intentional?"

"We train in the jungle—it's used as a command post."
He shrugged. "Sorta."

Mary Grace followed him up the stairs. He pulled over-grown vines out of his way enough to duck under them, holding them back for her, then moved onto the porch and through a door. She was right behind him and with the sun setting fast, it was pitch black inside.

"Stay there till I get us some light going."

She waited nervously and he moved in the dark as if he knew exactly where everything was. In moments, a soft white glow of artificial light filled the space from what looked like a small camping lamp. He set it on a table where he'd dropped his gear.

Mary Grace looked around. There was one cot flanking the back left corner, a trunk beside it, and a table with two wooden chairs in the center of the room. Other than that, the place was barren except for the dead leaves and dirt.

He unzipped the duffel and handed her a bottle of water.

Mary Grace broke the seal and drank, then plopped in a chair.

"You wouldn't happen to have food in there, would you?"

"Yeah." He tossed her an energy bar. She tore into it, biting off a chunk. It tasted awful, dry. She couldn't eat it fast enough.

"Whoa, take it easy, you'll get sick."

"I think I'm beyond that." She kicked off her shoes.

"I'm going to check the perimeter, set some traps."

Her brows rose as she chewed.

"Don't leave here without me for any reason—that includes going to pee."

She took a swig of water. "And here I thought we weren't going to get personal."

He stilled, his gaze snapping to hers. "Me and you, Mare, we've been personal for a long time."

"There's a gap in there, DJ."

"You were married."

"And that mattered?"

He couldn't answer that. He didn't have an excuse she'd understand or one he wanted to get into right now. "Look, I have a job to do. And today, you're it."

"You're changing the subject."

"God, you're quick."

"I'll just keep needling, you know I will." At his pained look, she just smiled and took another drink, pulling the pins out of her hair. "However . . . as cold and evasive as being your current *assignment* sounds, I'm very glad you're the smart one with the gun."

He flashed a quick grin. "That's because no one in their right mind would give *you* one."

"I can shoot. What southern woman can't?" She dropped dead wedding flowers on the table and finger-combed her hair.

"Shoot, sure, but aim right? Tell that to Bo Ridely's cat."

She smiled as the image of the cat shooting up ten feet in the air, shrieking because it had been too close to the target and too stupid to be afraid.

"There's water, some soap, a tin cup if you want to clean up."

She looked down at her clothes, her hands. "I'm not sure that will do the trick."

"There's some clothes, too—they'll be big, but take what you need."

"Clothes?" She pried in the duffel. "You were so certain you'd find me?"

"I wouldn't have stopped till I did."

Her gaze snapped up and something in her eyes went soft and liquid. DJ turned away from it. Yet Mary Grace stayed there, frozen, in the middle of shaking out a pair of black pants as he left her. No, he wouldn't have quit. DJ felt somehow responsible for her, a big brother type maybe, though brothers didn't look at her the way he did.

For a second, she wondered if fate was being cruel by sticking her with him, or offering her a chance to open a new door between them. Was she ready to risk a longtime friendship and the very real possibility of losing him completely? DJ had made himself clear years ago, but what about now?

Shaking her head as if it would shake loose some answers, she pulled out the items, snitching another energy bar, then washed her face and hands with lukewarm water. It didn't do the trick, except to cool her off a bit, so she took off her jacket, then shimmied out of her torn hose. She still felt grimy, and considered her actions for about two seconds as she slipped out of her blouse and skirt, glancing at the door briefly, then got busy cleaning up.

A little egotistical part of her wanted DJ to catch her like this, but her upbringing said that would be just downright slutty. Her mama raised her better than that. Or so she'd like to think. She worked fast on getting two days' worth of kidnapper ick off her, then balled her panties up with her ruined hose, deciding going without was better. She felt close to human as she stepped into the black pants.

DJ froze in the doorway, his gaze ripping over her bare back and narrow waist as she pulled on the pants. He got enough of a look to know she wasn't wearing a stitch under them. It was going to make him an idiot. Christ. Like he needed *more* fantasies? He hadn't thought of her in the daylight for years. Night was another matter. She crept into his dreams like a ghost, haunting him with the near-kiss they'd had when they were much younger, the innocent touches that soothed and excited him at the same time.

She was dangerous. But a little voice reminded him this time she wasn't married, wasn't the wild little rich girl from the big house on the two-hundred-year-old plantation. And he wasn't the kid from the tough side of town anymore. The path was clear.

DJ was willing to risk his life for a fellow American, but he wasn't sure about his heart. Losing himself in Mary Grace would leave irreparable damage. Especially if he wasn't sure about her feelings. She'd take his soul. He sure as hell didn't want to ruin a twelve-year-old friendship because of his lust. He was wise enough to know that you didn't mess with a good thing.

But then she reached for her lavender bra, drawing him out of his stupor, and he caught a glimpse of the curve of her bare breast. His body locked, and he mashed a hand over his face, wanting to rush over and pull her into his arms. Her back to him, she fastened the clasp, then reached for a dark tee shirt.

"You'll make a fashion statement in that with purple high heels," he said, and she jerked around, yanking the shirt down.

"I didn't hear you." How long had he been standing there?

"I'm supposed to be swift and silent." He moved to the table, and from the bags, unloaded all sorts of things. She had no idea what they were.

Mary Grace tucked in the too-big tee shirt that had to be his. It reminded her that he was so different from Paul, always had been. Her late husband was so average compared to DJ. He practically screamed raw power. While Paul was a financial wizard, he could barely mow the lawn without getting into trouble. Yet DJ had just dared gunmen to rescue her, and she took him in like a drug.

Built like a brick wall, he was just the kind of man a girl wanted in any tough situation. Even before he was a Marine, he wasn't the kind of guy others messed with. But then, DJ didn't have a weak bone in his body. If he did, he never showed it, not even to her, as if he had to keep his guard up all the time.

She understood that. He'd been raised in a rough neighborhood, without a mother, and when he was younger, had a chip on his shoulder she took great pleasure in knocking off sometimes. She smiled to herself, thinking of the young man leaning against the wall, his thumbs hooked in his belt loops, his gaze hooded by locks of dark hair. But she knew he'd been watching her any time she was near, and almost daring herself, she'd approached him and introduced herself.

All he said was, "Yeah, so?"

"You've been watching me."

"That get your rocks off, princess?"

"Are you always a jerk or is there a nicer guy hidden in there?"

Then he'd smiled and Mary Grace was knocked over by how much it changed his appearance. "Somewhere," he'd said.

"I want to know him."

His expression turned bitter then. "Why? Need a new charity case?"

She got angry. "If you think that, McAllister, then you really are just a jerk." She'd left and he'd laughed at her, telling her to "stop by again when you get the nerve." She found him the next day and they hadn't been separated much after that till she married Paul.

"Hey, Mare."

She blinked, brought sharply to the present.

He frowned. "Where'd you go?"

"Nowhere in particular. Booby traps set?"

He eyed her for a second. "Yeah. Enough to alert us if anyone tries to approach."

"Who would? No one knows we're here, right?"

"Never can tell. We've found enough debris in here before to know someone else besides the Marines knows this shack exists."

"That's not comforting."

He lifted his gaze, setting his gun on the table. "I won't let anyone hurt you. And I'll get you back to Panama City in one piece."

"I know you will."

He unbuttoned his shirt. "Just do what I say, okay?" He pulled it off, then unstrapped the dark kevlar vest. The Velcro ripped loudly, but Mary Grace felt like a kid about to get a whole lot of candy when he worked it over his head.

Her gaze moved over his chest, the ripped muscles, then—"My God, DJ, how'd you get those scars?"

He shrugged and didn't even look down. "I'm a Marine."

"But that's a bullet hole."

"See, I always knew you were slick." He hung the kevlar on a chair.

She came to him, stopping him from putting the shirt back on. He went still as glass as her fingers fluttered over the scar on his shoulder, then down to the one near his waist. She moved to look at his back. "Oh, God."

"The exit hole is always bigger," he said as if it mattered. "I know they're ugly."

"No, they're like . . . badges of your survival." She moved back around and touched the bullet hole again. "Why didn't you call me?"

"I was in Afghanistan."

"I would have found a way to be there for you."

He smiled down at her, amused and tense when her fingers slid over his skin. "I don't doubt it. And pissed off the Al Qaeda while you were at it." When her fingertips skipped over his nipple, he inhaled sharply and grabbed her hand. "Next time I get shot, I'll call you."

She yanked free, then, with both hands, shoved at his chest. He didn't budge. "Don't say that! I swear sometimes I don't know what goes on in that head of yours."

"What are you getting so worked up about? It was a year ago."

Her head jerked up, and he was stunned to see the tears in her eyes. "Because I care about you, you idiot!"

DJ felt riveted to the floor. She was prone to emotional displays—what woman wasn't?—but even he could feel the tremor racing through her.

Her back to him, she took a deep breath and let it out. "I shouldn't give a damn about you. Isn't that what you want? No one to care too much so you don't have to give anything back? I guess I should get it through my head that you don't think of me as your friend."

"I don't."

She flinched. Then she turned—her glossy eyes knifed him. He groaned, moving toward her, but her deadly expression stopped him.

"You get a new perspective when you're at death's door." He struggled with his words, wanting to tell her she was the first and only person he thought of then, but something made him couch it. "I wanted to tell you, just hear your voice, but I know you—you'd have made yourself crazy. You'd already buried a husband—"

"This has *nothing* to do with Paul's death," she cut in.

"My decision did. You'd lost the man you loved, Mare." He swallowed over the sudden knot in his throat, a reminder that she'd loved someone else. "And I didn't want you going through even *thinking* that again."

"I'm supposed to be touched by your concern?"

"No, just understand my choice."

"I understand you better than anyone. But you didn't call when you came back, either."

"I got shipped off again."

"And that's no excuse." She crossed the small room, standing directly in front of him, her hands on her hips and spoiling for a fight. "Don't do that again or I'll have to put you in a hurt locker."

His smile was slow. "Yes, ma'am."

She primly pulled his shirt closed and fastened the buttons. Suddenly he tipped her face up, staring into her green eyes. "Just so you know, we're more than just friends." Then he pressed his lips to her forehead.

Mary Grace closed her eyes, absorbing his scent, the warmth of him so close. She wanted to move in closer, lay her head on his shoulder and be held. But she knew he wouldn't want that.

And his next words said as much.

"Now, go sit and I'll make us some real food."

He turned away, and diving his hand into the pack, he pulled out dark brown plastic packages.

She eyed the package. "I think *real* is debatable if it's stuff in those."

"MRE, meals ready to eat." He sliced open the pack, moving so quickly Mary Grace knew he'd done this a thousand times. In a few minutes the small shack was filled with the smell of beef in a heavenly sauce.

She slid into the chair. "I'm impressed." He gave her a heavy tin cup full of food, and a fork.

Then he prepared another. "I'm better in a kitchen than with this."

"Yeah, sure, since when?"

"I live alone—it was either learn to cook or it was take-out for the rest of my life."

"No women wanting to cook for you?"

He glanced up, his expression going mysterious enough to prick her jealousy. "Once in a while, but I'm not around enough with Recon."

"Anyone waiting at home now?"

"No."

The single word was so harsh, Mary Grace wondered what he was hiding. A broken heart?

"Do you remember the first time you came to my parents' house for dinner?"

He groaned, stirring. "I try to forget."

"It wasn't that bad."

"Food was great, but your dad looking like he wanted to cut my throat wasn't."

"He thought you'd be a bad influence on me."

He snickered to himself. "Proves he didn't know his daughter very well. You were the bad seed."

"I beg your pardon?"

"Who rolled the judge's house?"

"You bought the toilet paper."

"Who got tossed out of a night club for dancing on the bar?"

Mary Grace blushed. "You rescued me then, too."

"I had to—you were about to strip for all those men. Then you thanked me by puking all over my car."

"I cleaned your precious Mustang."

"The smell lingers."

"Your dad's kept that car in great shape." He frowned curiously at her. "I look in on him when I'm in town."

DJ was more than a little touched. "Thanks. I appreciate that."

"It's what friends do, DJ."

"Now you're just nagging."

"Told you I would."

"So aside from getting wounded and not telling me"—his look said "give it a rest"—"where have you been for the last, say, three years?"

He ignored her dig. "Everywhere." He sat, propped his feet on the table, tipped back the chair, and started eating.

"I want specifics, and forget that 'if I tell you, I'll have to kill you' stuff. I swear not to breathe a word." She finished her food in record time, and looked over the extras in the MRE. She decided on crackers and the most disgusting-looking soft cheese. She squeezed the pouch, licking her fingers.

DJ watched her make a mess of the crackers and cheese, not bothering to tell her the extremely high fat content in that stuff. "I've been all over the world. Philippines, Japan, England, Afghanistan, Iraq, Kuwait, Bahrain, Morocco . . ."

She looked up, sucking cheese off her finger; for a second he watched her finger slide out of her mouth.

". . . Africa, China."

"My, my, you have been busy. The last time I saw you was at Paul's funeral."

"I'm sorry about him."

"It was an accident. But he'd talked about you a lot—I think he missed you."

"No, he didn't."

She blinked at him.

"He was my friend because you and I knew each other."

She shrugged. "I guess."

"No guessing. He tolerated me."

"He was a bit of a snot."

DJ didn't want to pry but it was the way she talked about her late husband that gave him the feeling there was something missing from that last statement.

She swiped her mouth and took a sip of water, shifting in the hard chair. "I've missed you."

He met her gaze across the table. "Me, too." *More than you'll ever know.*

"Mama asks about you every time I talk to her." His gaze flashed to her, his eyebrow lifting. "She has a soft spot for you."

"I wouldn't know why."

"Sure you do. You shared tea with her when she was sick. If you could sit through her going on and on about grafting roses and the advantages of a good compost, then you're a king in her book."

DJ smiled to himself, digging into his food. Her mother was always outside on the "back forty," as he liked to call it, wearing a straw hat and big gloves, shoveling horse crap and compost when she could hire someone to do it for her. When she was ill once, he'd done it for her. That was the tea afternoon.

He glanced up as Mary Grace yawned so hard her eyes watered. "Go to bed."

"Don't have to tell me twice." She left the chair and lay down on the cot. Then she sniffed, staring at the mattress. "Ew! I'm not even going to contemplate what's been on this thing."

"Probably a wise move." He took a light thermal blanket and tossed it over her.

She lifted her sleepy gaze. "Thank you."

"You already said that." He tucked her in like a child, wanting to kiss her, but not trusting her reaction. Christ, he'd never been unsure of anything, except with her.

Her lids drifted closed. "Itz zokay," she slurred. "You're still my hero."

His chest tightened painfully, and he simply stared down at her, his arms practically aching to hold her.

A hero.

Not if she knew the erotic thoughts racing through his mind right now.

Three

DJ sat in a chair between Mary Grace and anything coming through the door, his gun within reach. But his attention was on her, her restless fits of sleep. He touched her shoulder to wake her, and she winced, whimpering.

His heart ached and his anger rose. What the hell did they do to her?

Tears cked out from the corner of her eyelids, little moans escaping, and DJ moved to the cot, sitting on the edge, shaking her gently. She tried getting away from him, batting blindly, and he grabbed her back to keep her from falling off the narrow cot. Her skin was clammy, her eyes moving rapidly behind her lids. She looked in pain.

He rubbed her back, her arms, whispering that she was okay, safe. But it didn't do much good.

Then he pulled her into his arms, holding her tightly even when she fought him, and whispered close to her ear, "You're safe, Mare—it's me, DJ. Relax, baby." Nestling her against his chest, he kept talking, understanding her dreams, how the torture came in the calm of slumber.

Suddenly she inhaled sharply and whispered his name on a moan.

"I'm here." She let out a long, tired sigh and relaxed

against him, sniffling and trying not to let him know it. "What happened with those guys?"

"Just what you'd expect."

"Mare," he warned.

Her fingers dug into his back and she struggled for a moment to get the words out. "They threatened to cut off selected appendages. They took a lock of my hair first."

"How did they get you this far from the city?"

"Drugs, I think. I remember a pin-prick, then nothing more till they brought me into the warehouse."

He didn't want to, but he had to ask. "Did they rape you?"

"No." She met his gaze. "But you saw the position I was tied in. One of them . . . he'd kneel between my legs, grind on me—" Shame swept over her upturned face. "He put his hands up my skirt anytime he got bored. Last time, I bit him and he smacked me around, then gagged me." Her lip trembled and she breathed deeply. "I don't think anything would have stopped him if you hadn't arrived when you did."

His features sharpened and he gently pressed her head to his chest, cocooning her in his arms. "I won't let anyone hurt you, Mare."

"God, I'm more tired than I was before."

"Those kind of dreams wipe you out."

"You, too?" she muttered into his chest, not wanting to move a muscle now.

"Sometimes, yeah."

"About what?" She loved the feel of his chin on the top of her head, the safety of his arms.

"Getting shot, losing my men, battle." He shrugged. "The usual."

She half smiled, burrowing against him.

"Try to get some sleep." He eased her down to the bed, covering her again. "We'll be traveling fast before the sun is up." To someplace less isolated than this hut. When he made to move back to the chair, she grabbed his hand.

"Don't go. Stay close."

"I'm right here."

"Please, DJ. On the cot. You might not need me, but I need you."

DJ fell apart inside and slid in beside her, half sitting, his shoulders braced on the wall, and her head on his chest. She flung her arm across his stomach, snuggling to his side.

"Thank you." She was asleep in moments.

Yet DJ remained awake, his fingers toying with a lock of her hair. His gun was on the trunk within reach, his ears tuned to the sounds of the Panama night. But it was finally feeling her in his arms, warm and soft, that gave him such contentment. He knew that it wasn't just his overpowering lust for her driving him crazy. It was who she was.

God, he'd missed her so damn much, he thought, squeezing her for a second. She didn't have to be right in front of him to know that. The woman was in his blood, under his skin. But one step in the wrong direction and he could lose her completely. Lose what they had. He wondered if it was worth it just to end this torment.

His mind drifted to more immediate matters. He'd been trained to go without sleep, food, and water for days, and he knew those kidnappers wouldn't give up. She was a witness. Without her testimony they had nothing—no note, no visual capture, no witnesses. They could claim to be holding her because she lacked papers or something. Anything was possible in this country. He didn't dismiss that they'd try to kill her just to make a clean sweep of the whole crime. He looked down at her, brushing her hair back and curling it behind her ear. She nuzzled his palm, and stole another piece of him.

DJ knew without a doubt—he'd die before he let that happen.

* * *

A faint, artificial glow from the lamp painted the hut when Mary Grace woke abruptly. For a second, she felt trapped by his heavy arms, then relaxed and realized the arm surrounding her back was stretched low, his hand cupping her behind.

"I'm here," he said softly, patting her.

"Ah, DJ. Your hand is on my butt." *Inside* the loose trouser. His broad palm was warm on her skin and oh-so-delicious.

"Yeah, and your boobs are pressed to my side. Turnabout's fair play." He closed his hand over hers, which was firmly planted on his inner thigh.

"Oh."

He chuckled to himself, sliding his hand out of her pants and laying it on her hip. "Just because we're friends doesn't mean I'm immune to the woman."

"That's nice to know." Really nice, she thought. "Have you slept at all?"

"I'm on watch." He opened his eyes to check his watch. She wasn't really shocked to see a gun in his right hand.

"So this is really a sympathy hug with a little groping?"

"Only way to keep you still. You wiggled a lot."

"Been a long time since I've slept with a man."

DJ looked down at her, aching to pull her on top of him and explore the rest of those curves. "I can't imagine why. You're a beautiful woman."

She pinkened in the dark, her hand smoothing up his chest. He was rock-hard with muscle, and a little tense. "Picky, I guess." And lots of distrust.

"No one measured up?"

Her expression turned soft and sad. "Not in a very long time."

He clasped her hand, stilling her touch. "What are you not telling me?"

She broke eye contact, unwilling to admit her marriage

had been a first-class joke, and leaving an imprint on her self-worth she'd been trying to shake ever since. "Nothing. Time to get moving?"

DJ scowled in the dark as she left the cot. He could read her so easily—the sudden leap of tension in her body, the way she wouldn't look at him. He'd get to the bottom of it soon enough, he decided, swinging his legs over the side and rubbing his face. His groin ached, and knowing it was obvious, he gave up on willing the damn thing away, and stood.

Mary Grace stretched, then righted her clothing, offering him a wan smile as she finger-combed her hair. That was the first time he'd had his hand on her like that, so intimate yet casual.

He packed up the gear, except for a couple of things on the table and a bottle of water, then told her to stay put— he was going to break down his booby traps. "Eat something. Sun's almost up. And we need to put some distance behind us."

He was gone maybe three minutes, long enough for her to eat an energy bar and see that he'd left a disposable toothbrush with paste already on it. When he returned, he held the radio and what looked like a grenade.

"Have some rope?" She pulled out the waist of the pants. "Ten steps and they'll be around my ankles."

"That's an amusing image." He slipped off his belt, putting it through the loops. He leaned close and whispered, "My pants look cute on you."

"Ha. I have no shape in these things."

The belt wasn't small enough and he flipped out a knife and cut a new hole. He secured it, his gaze shifting to her. "Trust me, you do."

A blush stole over her face. "That's because you were playing with my ass last night."

His blues eyes seemed to cut right into her soul. "If I played, you'd have known it."

The man had just too much power, she thought. "Yeah, yeah." They used to tease each other like this years ago, before Paul, before the Marines. She tried not to read anything into it. "Where do we go now?"

"We try to get as close to Panama City as possible without running into anyone we don't want. Which is just about everyone. I can't let anyone know I'm a Marine or that you're the ambassador's sister-in-law."

She nodded, wetting the toothbrush and brushing her teeth. She looked around to spit.

"Spit it on the floor, or out the door."

Her look said, "I don't think so," and he laughed softly when she swallowed it.

"You're too well-bred for the jungle. Need to use the bathroom?"

"Yes," she said with feeling.

He gathered everything up, and with a last glance, they headed out. Below the cabin, DJ stowed the packs in the jungle, then escorted her to a secluded spot. He turned his back, handing her a small plastic pack of TP over his shoulder. Mary Grace was blushing when she came back out. He cast her a side glance, amused.

"Well, that was a new experience."

"I'll bet, considering your idea of roughing it is a hotel without room service."

She tipped her chin up. "I can handle it."

"Never doubted it for a second." He hefted the pack and she took the duffel, slinging it on her shoulder. They walked a few yards when DJ turned back to make sure she was there. She was walking a lot easier and she showed him the heels of her shoes, broken. The sun was up by the time they arrived close to where they'd left the car. Mary Grace sat behind him on the ground while he used the binoculars to watch the car and the area.

Then he checked his weapon, slipped it into his waistband. "Ready?"

She nodded, a nervous tickle churning her stomach as they moved out into the open. Quickly, he stowed the gear and replaced the part in the engine, then started the car. He pulled onto the road, his gaze darting in every direction.

"You're nervous," she said.

"No, cautious."

"Same thing. Your men didn't find them, did they?"

"No. These guys went underground, I'm thinking. They'll surface, but you can't be seen till they're apprehended."

"At all? No contact, no nothing?"

He shook his head, constantly checking the mirrors.

"What about my sister? She'll be going crazy."

"The ambassador knows you're alive, and with me."

"That will calm Frances, at least." At his curious glance, she added, "She's a drama queen, and lives to worry over something."

He drove for a couple of miles before he said, "Why a wedding planner, Marc?"

She shrugged. "Actually, I'm an event planner—I do award ceremonies, corporate parties, but mostly weddings. And it's fun seeing people happy on the most memorable day of their lives."

Suddenly her wedding day exploded in his mind. He'd stood at the back of the church as she walked past him, hesitating for the briefest moment before she went into the arms of another man. She'd looked incredibly beautiful, a perfect silhouette in white, and so far from him. He didn't wait for the "speak now or forever hold your peace" moment, and left, afraid he'd ruin her day.

"That can't be all you've done lately."

"If you want to know about men in my life, then just say so."

"So?"

She smiled. "No, there's no one right now. Though I

have dated a few, they were more high-maintenance than I need. Ego stroking," she said when he scowled. "I don't think I want to get married again for a while, if ever."

"Why?"

Mary Grace looked at her hands, not wanting to tell him what Paul had done to her, how bad a choice she'd made in a husband.

DJ scowled. She looked suddenly miserable and ashamed, and he was about to press the issue when the car crested a hill. "Damn."

Her head snapped up. Ahead a four-by-four looking car blocked the road, and three men stood near—with weapons.

"Oh God. Who are they?"

"Drug cartel, I think."

"Oh, shit."

"Yeah, my thoughts, too." He stashed his gun between the seats, but if these guys found his satellite phone in his gear, they were done for. They'd know he was U.S. military and kill him for it. God knows what they'd do to her then. "Don't talk." DJ slowed the car, pulling out a brown envelope.

A man moved on either side of the car, one in front. "Papers."

DJ offered them. The man looked at them briefly, then said in Spanish, "Where are you going?"

DJ frowned as if he didn't understand and the man spoke English. "Panama City," DJ said.

"Get out."

DJ obeyed, moving slowly, trying to look helpless. "We're just tourists." The man nearest him patted him down, taking his wallet. DJ's military ID wasn't on him. Standard procedure for covert ops.

The man on the opposite side of the car was staring intently at Mary Grace. Then he ducked, eyeballing her. "It's her." He reached for the door handle, demanding she get out.

Mary Grace slammed down the lock, scooted away, and ducked down. "DJ!"

DJ reacted on instinct, grabbing the machine gun and driving his forearm up into the man's face, then whipped around, aiming at the others. "You get over with your buddies," he said in clear Spanish, then he told them to drop their weapons.

One at the front of the car held his out, letting it dangle. DJ aimed at his head. "Make no mistake, I *will* shoot." The man dropped it.

A raggy-looking man near Mary Grace gave him a cocky look and pointed the barrel at the window glass—at her head. "So will I, *tourista.*" He took a breath, then tightened his fingers on the weapon—a sign he would fire—and DJ had no choice.

He double tapped him, then swept the barrel toward the other two and stared down the business end of a pistol. DJ fired before they could.

Mary Grace flinched with the reports, her face buried in the car seat, and prayed DJ wasn't hit. She chanced a look and yelped as one man fell against the car, sliding down and leaving a trail of blood. *Oh God.* She sat up and saw DJ take back his papers and wallet, disable the weapons, then drag the bodies off the road. He came to her side, opening the door and pulling her out.

"Come on, we're taking their car."

Leaning against the open door, she blinked up at him, breathing hard. "Oh God, oh God." She looked around at the blood trail, then up at DJ.

He gripped her arms. "Look at me." He shook her. "Look at me! We have to get moving—someone could have heard the shots."

Mary Grace nodded, straightening. "What do you want me to do?"

He was suddenly very proud of her. "Clear everything out of the car, everything."

She stripped the car of any signs of their presence as he grabbed the gear. "Done," she said, and he hurried her into the other vehicle. He pulled away fast, speeding down the unpaved road.

"I never saw anyone shot before."

"He was going to kill you."

"I know, I know, I heard him."

"You all right?"

"Fine. Fine." But she wasn't. She was trembling and he reached over, grasping her hand. She clutched back tightly.

"I'm scared. I mean I wasn't really that scared before, but just so you know, now I am."

"Anybody would be. Breathe slowly, Mare." He brought her hand to his lips, kissing her knuckles. "Come on."

She let out a long breath. "How big is this thing? My kidnapping, I mean."

"Bigger than we thought, apparently." DJ reached behind her seat, his hand moving past the radio to the Sat Com phone. He handed it to her, telling her how to get a flash signal, and he made contact, relaying the events. He had to hide her, quickly.

While DJ talked to his command, Mary Grace stared numbly out the window. The road cut right through the jungle, so overgrown the sunlight barely touched the ground. Anyone or anything could pop out and they wouldn't see it coming. He hung up.

"Were they after me? Is that why they stopped us?"

"I don't think so. I think they were looking for a bribe to let us pass but one of them was on the lookout for you. Your face has been in the local papers. I'd like to have questioned him, but . . ."

"I'd be dead."

"I wish you hadn't seen that."

"I didn't, really. I had my face courageously down in the seat and my eyes shut."

He glanced, a little relieved. "We need a place to stay,

one that will be out of the way, but near enough to people so it will raise alarm if they try anything."

Mary Grace rooted in the glove box, pulling out an old, water-stained map. She located their position, then followed the path. "There's supposed to be a hotel, small, on the southeast side of the lake, about seventy miles from Panama City."

"Outstanding—that'll do."

She gave him directions. "Let's hope it's still there—this map is five years old."

DJ drove without stopping, circling back once to see if they were being followed. The jungle gradually thinned, the dense, vincy land giving way to plush hills and homes. Really big, expensive homes. It was like driving into a different world—luxurious, manicured. Wealth.

"God, will you look at these estates! Hard to believe a few miles away people are living in tin shacks."

"The house that drugs built." He nodded to one home that sprawled over an acre. "Though some people come here to retire, the cartels have no problem throwing their drug money around and rubbing it in the nose of the authorities. We, however, need a little slice of poverty so we don't draw attention."

She agreed. "Your job must be really hard sometimes."

He didn't look at her. "Sometimes."

"I mean, pulling a trigger can't be easy."

"Lately, it's easy to tell who the bad guys are. But I shoot to protect my life and yours."

"I have no problem with that, believe me."

He squeezed her hand again, then withdrew to handle the wheel. They drove further into the little city, passing shops and grocers, slowing for traffic. People didn't pay them any mind and Mary Grace's fear ebbed.

"It's two streets down," she said, then frowned when he pulled in front of a shop that sold handbags. "Looking for something in a light alligator to match your boots?"

"Yeah, this mismatched ensemble is just driving me nuts." She was smiling when he left the car, told her to keep his gun close, then went inside.

Mary Grace didn't touch the Beretta stuffed in the console and watched the crowd move around her, her nerves jangling when anyone came close. Thank God DJ returned in short order. He carried a large suitcase and put it in the back.

"I can't bring a military pack in without raising a red flag," he explained, then drove to the next block, slowing in front of the hotel. "It's dingy enough," he said, ducking to see the three-story, stucco-and-tile inn, then driving past. There were enough non-locals to blend in.

"If they have a shower, I'll be happy."

"You *are* getting kinda ripe."

She gave him a playful shove. "We're not stopping?"

"Not just yet." He pulled the car around to the side, and killed the engine. Then he switched his gear into the suitcase, packing in the empty pack, then drove around the block and parked near the hotel.

"Show time." He grabbed the case, and locked up. He checked them in as husband and wife, glancing at her as if waiting for her to protest, but she simply smiled and whispered close to his ear, "Regardless of the, you know— that's exactly where I'd want to be."

Something sparkled in his eyes just then, a dark, heated look that turned her inside out all over again. They took the elevator, and DJ pulled her close, away from the other guests. She could feel his gun pressing to her side, a reminder of the danger surrounding them, yet she had never felt more safe. When she looked up, he winked, pressing his lips to her temple, then ushered her out of the lift and to their room.

Inside, he dropped the gear and programmed the SAT COM phone instead of the radio.

"Why use that now?"

"Anyone in the area with a radio can tune in to the same music, and I'm giving locations—vague, but still, we have to be careful."

He talked, mostly in a mishmash of code and abbreviations, and Mary Grace was more than a little mesmerized by him. He was calm, in control, from the moment she'd seen him. Did anything faze him?

She glanced around, not really shocked by the small size of the two rooms. There was nothing more than a sofa and coffee table in a nook outside the bedroom, and she went to investigate the rest. "This place is actually very nice, DJ." She came out of the bathroom holding a mono-grammed robe. He didn't seem to care, packing up the SAT phone and hiding it.

Done, DJ glanced around, finally noticing the rather romantic décor. His gaze zeroed in on the bed he could see through the open door, big, high, and mounded with fluffy comforter and pillows. His gaze flicked to her. She wore a feline smile that made his muscles lock, and he wondered if he was reading it right.

"I have to go out." Her expression fell. "Stay here—no phone, no standing near the windows. And I'm locking you in." He closed the curtains, darkening the room. "Don't get into the shower till I get back."

"Why?"

"If anyone tries to break in, you won't hear them coming." He handed her a loaded gun. "Keep this close."

She stared at the handgun, turning it over in her hands. "They would have killed us today for no reason, and no one would ever have found our bodies."

Fear trembled in her tone, and he came to her, grasping her upper arms. She lifted her gaze. "But they didn't. We're alive and safe." She simply nodded. "I won't be gone more than a half-hour."

She forced a brave smile, but inside she was terrified to be alone. "I'll be fine, and in case you pass any nice stores, I'm a size nine and a stylish babe."

His lips quirked and he kissed her forehead, then headed to the door.

"And don't forget shoes. Seven-and-a-half."

He paused, his hand on the knob. "Anything else, princess?"

She eyed him, her smile devilish. "Are you brave enough to buy lingerie?"

DJ's gaze swept over her, long and slow, and he heard her breathing quicken deliciously. His clothes on her shrouded her figure, but the memory of seeing her years ago in a thong bikini was still alive and kicking. DJ knew what lay beneath. Rich curves and valleys, full breasts, and long, sexy legs he wanted wrapped around him.

"Can't be any harder than buying C-4 off the black market."

She laughed, throwing a pillow at his head, and he reached for the knob, thinking that being locked up with her was going to be either pure hell or pure pleasure.

His vote was for the latter. And his body cheered a quick hot ooh-rah to that.

Four

Mary Grace was a wreck.

This wasn't like her. She'd already dealt with a cheating, lying husband, his death, and in her work, faced every possible bridal crisis all the time. What could be worse?

She stopped short.

"Killers trying to put your lights out? Running through the jungle?" she murmured, looking around. *Hiding in a hotel and praying no one found you?*

A second later, the doorknob jiggled. Her heart shot to her throat, and she rushed for the gun, pointing it, her finger trembling on the trigger. It opened slowly.

"Put it down, Mary Grace," DJ said before he came around the edge.

She sagged, lowering the weapon and flipping the safety.

DJ entered, loaded down with packages. But at the look on her face, he kicked the door closed, dropped them, and rushed to her. He pried the gun from her, laid it aside, then gripped her shoulders. "What's wrong?" She was trembling.

After a false start, she blurted, "Nothing. I'm just edgy, I guess." She plopped on the small sofa. "I feel like a complete idiot right now."

DJ smiled gently. "You were kidnapped, threatened, brutalized, and shot at. Give yourself a break."

She kept seeing that guerilla pointing the gun at her head. So carelessly, so willing to pull the trigger. "How do you do it?"

"I've had training. And I don't have time to be afraid, so I just block it out."

"Well, that's nothing new," she said without thinking.

He reared back, arching a brow. "I have a feeling we're not talking about fear in combat." He folded his arms over his chest and simply stared. "If you've got a bone to pick, then have at it."

"Oh, like that makes you receptive?" She gestured to his "bully in the school yard" stance. "You look like you're daring anyone to get past that wall. That 'I don't need anyone, baby, so don't bother,' attitude might work great for the Marines, but not with me."

"Do you have a point?"

She met his gaze, rising to the challenge. "Yeah, why are you avoiding what's going on between us, DJ? Why haven't you ever tried to kiss me?"

His eyes flared. "You always go right for the jugular, don't you, Mare?" He lowered his arms.

"It's a refined skill. Well?"

"Well . . . we're just friends. And you were married."

"Not for three years, and not last night."

He scraped his hand over his mouth. "I don't want to ruin what we have."

"Which is two people dancing around an old friendship? Oh wait, you did tell me you didn't want attachments, marriage, kids, just be *friends*." She slapped her forehead. "How could I forget that? It was about the time you practically shoved me at Paul."

"You went," he snapped. "And he made it clear I was a third wheel."

Her eyes flared hotly. "Why, that little . . . what'd he say?"

"He reminded me that the two of you were cut from the same cloth. And I was a bad plaid."

"And you believed it," she said, deadpan.

DJ shrugged. "He was raised like you, wanting for nothing, same friends, same country club membership."

"So you thought I was better off with *him*? And when has your background and mine *ever* made a difference?" Her hurt look slayed him, her soft voice pricking his hide. "And I resent your using it as an excuse."

"That's how it was then," he ventured.

She hopped off the sofa, moving restlessly. "No, you let it be that way. You let me know very clearly that we'd be no more than pals, and then you made yourself scarce so I'd have no one."

"Are you blaming me for your marriage?"

She looked at him sharply. "Oh, for pity sake, no. I made the choice. I'm mad that he tried to ruin the only relationship that meant anything to me."

The only? His heart picked up pace. "Didn't you love him?"

"When I married him, yes." But it was just second best, she thought.

When? "How about after?"

"That's not the point." Her expression turned cool, isolated, and she moved toward the bathroom.

But he caught her. "Oh no, you don't. You opened this can of worms. What do you mean?"

She hesitated, the humiliation of her marriage riding up her spine like an ugly spider. How could she admit to the one man who truly mattered that she was a failure? That she couldn't make a marriage work for even six lousy months? Paul went to another woman for sex, and to her that meant she lacked basic feminine skills to keep him home.

DJ caught her chin, forcing her to look at him, and in her beautiful liquid eyes, her expression, he saw her private torture, the pain. "Talk to me, honey. I'm the one person you can trust with your secrets."

A single tear slid down her cheek. Her breath shuddered hard. "It was a mistake. I'd filed for divorce. We hadn't lived together for over a year. In fact, he was coming to see me about the settlements when he was killed."

His features went taut. He'd had no idea. "What happened between you two?"

She pulled free. "Irreconcilable differences."

He blocked her path, his thunderous look bearing down on her. "What did he do?"

"You're so sure it was him."

"Hell, yes."

That softened her posture, her mood. "Six months after the wedding I discovered he was sleeping with another woman. Well, from what I saw, they didn't actually *sleep*. He did that with me."

"Tell me you didn't see them having sex," he said, his anger for her cresting in his tone.

"In full Technicolor." Her stomach turned violently at the memory.

"Oh, man."

"I was surprising him with a picnic lunch." She sneered to herself. "How Suzie Homemaker is that? I walked into his office, and found my new husband screwing a colleague like he was some porn star." She shook her head, dismissing the image of Paul, half-dressed and pounding into the woman. "It doesn't matter. He couldn't deny it. Then he said it was really all my fault."

DJ's expression turned deadly. "The bastard. You don't believe that."

Her shoulders moved with doubt. "He went to her, didn't he?"

"He was a prick."

"I have more creative names for him."

With both hands, he brushed her hair back, cupped her face. "A man who truly loved you would never do that to you—tell me you know that?" She nodded, but DJ could tell she wasn't convinced. He wanted to dig Paul out of the ground just to beat the living shit out of him for this. "Why didn't you saying anything to me?"

She moved away, breaking his hold and folding her arms. "Isn't it obvious? It's humiliating. I couldn't keep my new husband in my bed and off other women. I'd married the wrong man, one I never truly loved, while—"

She clamped her lips shut, staring at the floor.

"Marc?"

A noise punctured the silence and she flinched. "The phone."

"Let it ring," he said.

"It's the *satellite* phone."

Groaning about bad timing, he turned to answer it, frowning when she moved away. "Where are you going?"

"To take an obscenely long bath."

DJ watched her slip into the bathroom, wondering what she was going to say before the call interrupted them. He put the phone to his ear.

"All clear, Gunny," came through clearly.

"What?"

"We got 'em. I'm looking at them right now. Snagged and gagged."

"Outstanding work, Marine. Excellent." DJ rubbed his mouth. "Did you learn why they took her?"

"Mistaken identity. They thought she was the ambassador's wife. Easy to do—Miss Heyward is a younger version of her sister."

Aside from the red hair, Frances and Mary Grace didn't look all that much alike to him.

"When are you bringing her in?"

DJ's gaze moved to the bathroom door. He heard the

water running in the tub and she stepped out to grab the robe she'd left on the bed. Across the room, she met his gaze, looking wild and beautiful. And wounded. He couldn't take his eyes off her.

"Gunny? When can we expect your arrival?"

"Don't. And don't reveal this location."

He heard a deep, knowing laugh from his Staff Sergeant. "Gotcha, Gunny. Your back is covered."

DJ cut the link and resecured the phone.

"Did they find them?"

He stared her in the eye, knowing this was his one chance; if he let it go, he'd never get it back. Aside from their circumstances, DJ knew one thing for sure. Fate put him and Mary Grace together. The past few minutes of conversation had erased a distorted past, and opened a new door. One he'd wanted to swing wide open for as long as he could remember.

It was his chance, his last one. To step through and win the woman he'd loved for nearly twelve years.

"DJ? Did they capture them yet?"

"No, they didn't," he lied, and laid the phone down.

She sighed tiredly, turned her back on him, and closed the bathroom door behind herself.

DJ dropped to the bed, then flopped back, knowing exactly why he'd lied through his teeth, and hoping that later, she'd understand.

Mary Grace came out of the bathroom, toweling her hair dry and talking to DJ. When he didn't answer, she looked up and smiled. He was asleep on the bed, looking as if he'd fallen there and just conked out. She tossed aside the towel and crawled onto the bed and sat beside him, watching him sleep. He'd been awake for two days, she realized.

She stared at his profile, not touching him. He'd waken easily, and he needed some rest. She slid to her side, thinking his reaction to her confession had been so knightly, defending her so doubtlessly. But she knew that either her late husband was a habitual adulterer before she'd married him, or she pretty much sucked in bed. It hadn't been that good anyway, she thought. *Another feeble attempt to soothe your ego?*

Why hadn't she confronted DJ years ago? She couldn't find a reason that made sense other than she'd adored him, wanted him, but while he'd flirted and teased her for years, he never dared take it a step further. Was he as afraid as she was that it might ruin an old friendship? Or was he afraid she wouldn't be receptive?

She was mulling that over when her gaze fell on the store bags practically covering the dresser. She wanted to see what he'd bought, but was so relaxed, she couldn't keep her eyes open.

DJ woke to Mary Grace sitting on the bed beside him, eating half a sandwich. Instantly he was awake. "Where did you get that?"

She gestured to the tray on the coffee table. "Room service."

"Dammit, I told you not to use the phone or answer the door!"

"Don't wig out—I signed for it with an illegible signature, then I held a gun to the waiter's crotch and told him never to speak of this again or I'd shoot off his *cojónes*. He was pretty compliant." She took a bite, grinning.

He shook his head wryly, then sat up, took her sandwich, and devoured it in two huge bites.

She blinked. "Good thing I ordered a lot more."

He shook his head. "Shower first."

"Yeah, you are kinda ripe."

He covered her face with his hand and shoved. "Smart-ass." He left the bed, stretching, then gathered clean clothes.

"I found a chess set."

He smiled. They'd played chess on his dad's back porch, teaching each other. "Best two out of three?"

"If you're lucky."

He started for the bathroom, then stopped short. "You didn't like the stuff." He gestured to the store bags.

"Never looked at them, I fell asleep right beside you."

"Shame on me—I didn't even notice."

Something clouded her eyes just then. DJ realized her late husband's infidelity had left an indelible imprint. DJ was going to do something about that. How and when, he wasn't sure.

"You were tired, you're forgiven." She slid off the bed, giving him a glimpse of bare legs all the way to the top of her thighs. DJ dragged his gaze away and went into the bathroom. Ice cold water was the only thing that would help him right now.

While he showered, Mary Grace investigated the contents of the bags. He'd gone way overboard with bath-and-body products and some makeup. She opted for shorts and a tee shirt. But it was the lingerie that gave her a start. First, it fit perfectly, and it was luxuriously decadent. Sheer lace and satin. When she heard the water shut off, she went to the door, rapping softly.

He peered, a towel around his waist, the gun in his hand.

She reared back. She didn't know he had it with him. "No danger, I just wanted to say thanks and, well, it fits."

"You're still in the robe—how would you know?"

With a devilish smile she opened the robe, showing him the pale mint-green bra and panties.

He choked. "Jesus."

"You've seen me in a bikini, DJ."

"*That* is nothing like a bathing suit." His gaze never left her breasts cupped in the mint lace.

"You bought it. What were you thinking?"

He pulled his gaze to hers. "That you'd look good in it."

"And?"

His gaze rode over her with the power of touch. "You'd look better without it."

Her eyes flared, then she turned back toward the clothes, letting the robe slip off and fall to the floor. "You're still staring."

"No, I'm drooling." His gaze lowered to her sweet behind, then back up to her face. "Mare?"

"Yeah."

"You have the sweetest ass I've ever seen."

She smiled over her shoulder, reaching for the tee shirt. "Is that all you have to tell me?" Her gaze lowered to his groin.

DJ smirked, knowing he was rock-hard, then closed the door, laying the gun down before he accidentally shot himself. He had to get some control, or he'd do something stupid like throw her on the bed and devour her whole.

Why not? a voice said. She was provoking him. But he didn't want to screw this up, or scare her, because his need for her, to dive in and experience everything there was with her, had been bottled up for so long. He dried, shaved, and dressed in jeans and tee shirt. When he left the bathroom, she was dressed, sitting cross-legged on the sofa, the chessboard set up.

"So what are we betting this time?"

She looked up, a smile breaking over her face. "It's certainly not going to be the phantom raider running through the boys' locker room with a bag on my head."

He chuckled, grabbing a plate and picking up a sandwich. "You were so damn gullible."

"And you locked the exit door. I was mortified."

He chuckled to himself. "I was leaning on it."

She threw a potato chip at him. "At least I hadn't agreed to run naked or something."

"Now *that* I would have stopped to see."

Her gaze flashed up, a little shy, and he stared as if he could see beneath the clothes and lace and satin.

"I like it when you look at me like that."

"What way is that?" he asked, though he knew good and well.

"Like you want to peel me like a grape."

He just grinned.

She arranged a chess piece, then slid to the floor, gesturing to the seat on the sofa. "So what's the bet?"

His eyes danced devilishly. "Winner decides."

"A man who lives dangerously. Beware—I could ask you to dance."

His look went sour. "That would be your mistake, then." DJ made the first move.

"You're trying to lose," he said twenty minutes later when he'd won the first game.

"Oh, no I'm not. I want control." She grabbed his hand, taking a bite of his sandwich, then made her move.

He played her again, and she won.

Mary Grace sanded her hands together, then reset the chessboard.

"We should have cards—this is taking way too long and I want my prize," he said.

"Cocky Marine." Ten minutes later, she said supremely, "Checkmate."

DJ gaped at the chessboard. "You cheated."

"Skill, skill, darlin'. I whipped your butt—admit it."

He leaned back in the sofa cushions as she came to sit beside him. "So what's your poison?"

"Kiss me."

His gaze sharpened instantly. "Come here."

"I won—you come to me."

He leaned, looming over her, one hand braced on the back of the sofa, the other by her hip. Her scent filled his head, weakening him.

His palms went clammy, his heart pounding like a sledgehammer, and he felt like he did with his first parachute jump, a leap into the dark unknown. Suddenly, he wanted to remember this moment, how beautiful and vulnerable she looked, how her liquid green eyes held him in a tiny prison, her breathing quickening the slightest bit. She was like a narcotic, and he'd been addicted to her since he was a street punk. Time and age had only fermented his feelings.

"Are you sure?" he said, a breath from her mouth. "Crossing this line will change everything."

Her eyes softened, and she touched the side of his face. "This isn't up to you or me, DJ. Never has been. It just *is*." The anticipation was killing her, making her skin flush, and when he leaned, his mouth pressing to hers ever so softly, she made a little sound of triumph and pleasure. *Oh, yes.*

DJ felt her body shimmer as his tongue slid lightly over her lower lip. Her breath tumbled into his mouth and he drank it, sensations spiriting through him with lightning speed, a primal need driving down to his heels. His muscles tensed, then softened for her as she responded, and every inch of his skin ached with excitement, his groin thick and painfully hard.

It sent him over the edge, his tongue probing and slipping in and out, doing what he'd dreamed about for years. He moved in closer, took possession, wrapping an arm around her and drawing her off the sofa, then leaning back and pulling her across his lap.

His mouth never left hers, and his grinding need took him from tasting her to eating, to devouring, pent-up hunger—years of it, unwinding like the fuse of a bomb waiting to be lit.

Mary Grace wanted more, couldn't get enough of the unchecked power sizzling between them. Her hands were all over him, molding him, and she gasped for breath. Between her thighs flushed with heat, his lush mouth kissed her the way she'd dreamed of, with passion and possession, as if in a single touch he had her surrender. And he did.

She sank her fingers into his hair and curled toward him, gripping his shoulders and urging him to take more. When his hand slid up her bare leg, across her hip to her waist, her muscles jumped. She brought it to her breast, and he squeezed, deepening their kiss.

"Oh, man," he said against her mouth.

"I knew, DJ," she said, divinely breathless. "I always knew it would be like this."

"You shoulda said something." He nipped at her throat, trying to catch his breath. "I didn't let myself think on it too long."

She held him back. "Why?"

He swept his hand over her hair, his look so tender and loving, tears burned her eyes. "From day one, I was damn grateful you were my friend. As much as I wanted more, I couldn't ruin that." He kissed her almost reverently. "When I finally realized I'd never get you out of my system, out of my mind, I'd lost my chance."

"Oh, DJ." A tear fell and she kissed him, softly, a melding of mouths that stamped her claim.

And he marked his, suddenly devouring her mouth with a power that tipped her head back, that had her clawing at his shoulders. He had to touch her, feel her pleasure, and whipped his hand under her shirt, his palm warm on her cool skin. Her muscles flexed and he felt as if he were holding on to pure energy.

"I need to touch you."

She laughed lightly. "You are, and it feels so good."

His hand closed over her breast under the shirt, and she arched into his palm, but it wasn't enough. He needed to sever any thoughts of the old friendship that hovered between them, to shatter one to create another.

Now.

His hand slid down her belly, fingers deftly flipping the button and sending down the short zipper. She kissed him wildly, untamed and luxurious, and as his hand slid inside her shorts, she convulsed as if cut loose from a cage.

"Oh DJ, oh my God."

He smiled, watching her writhe, needing to see all of it. When his hand dipped beneath her panties, smoothly parting her, she gasped and clutched him, burying her face in his shoulder.

"Look at me."

She lifted her gaze and he smiled at the glazed look in her eyes.

"Everything's changed, baby." Before she could do anything, he slid one finger inside her.

five

Gazes locked, he plunged, then introduced another finger. "You're so wet and slick," he murmured.

"For you. Oh DJ, don't stop." She hadn't felt like this, ever—nothing in her past compared to feeling him touch her, his strong fingers intimately bringing her closer and closer to a climax. Her senses sharpened, her body screaming for more.

He circled the delicate bead, and her hips rose to greet his touch—short, wild pumps—and DJ's gaze flicked down her body spread across his lap. She was lithe and long, her thighs open, her hand pushing him to play more. He smiled, taunting her, teasing her flesh, and she gasped. His gaze snapped to her face.

"I want to see you come. I want to feel it." He flicked and rubbed, and she ground into him, her body pawing his fingers, and DJ loved her soft eyes, the way she bit her lower lip. She stiffened, her fingers digging into his shoulders as the explosion rippled up her body. He experienced every tremor as if she were inside his skin: her muscles flexing wildly, her gasps for breath. She choked on his name as he toyed and manipulated her till the haze of pleasure faded.

"Enough, enough," she moaned, and fell bonelessly back

on the cushions. For a long moment she didn't say anything. She couldn't—her breathing was too fast to speak. "I don't know whether to be embarrassed or thrilled."

"No longer pals, huh?"

She looked at him, her smile spreading slowly. "I'll say." She kissed him, holding him close.

"I've felt you come on my hand . . ." He looked her dead in the eye. "Next time it's my mouth."

Her body jumped to life again, her skin tingling in a straight shot up to her breasts. She wanted him inside her, untamed like the DJ she knew.

"I'm so game for that." She hopped off his lap, taking a step away, then pulled off her tee shirt. DJ sat there, hard as a rock as she tossed it in his lap, then shimmied out of her shorts. His gaze landed on her butt, tight and sweetly round inside light green satin. He wanted to bite it.

She glanced back. "You coming?"

He left the sofa, and when he came around the doorjamb, she was releasing her hair from the clip. He came to her, slipping his arms around her from behind. She was in front of the mirror and Mary Grace met his gaze in the glass.

"You're so beautiful." She blushed, and DJ realized that she hadn't had a compliment in a long time.

She stared at their reflection, his bare arms across her paler skin. He was a head taller and so much bigger. She felt delicate and protected as he bent and kissed her throat, one hand slipping to her back and releasing her bra.

"I've wanted to do that for years." He pushed it down, kissing her shoulder, then sweeping it away. In the mirror she watched his hands cup her breasts, his thumbs circling her nipples. "I've had dreams of this."

"Oh yeah?"

"Of stripping you down to your skin."

"Then what?"

"Lots. I'm playing with an eighteen-year-old imagination, remember."

"Ah well, that would be quick and rough."

He chuckled. "I've learned control over the years."

"I haven't had anything to lose control over."

He arched a brow, his gaze shifting to meet hers in the reflection. "I'll change that."

"Anyone ever tell you you're arrogant?"

"Yeah, for other reasons. But this is the first time I've made love."

Her heart swelled, almost breaking. He tipped her head back and kissed her, then nibbled a path over her shoulder, down her spine. He was patient, content with nipping and licking her flesh. She wanted to touch him, do things to him, but he was intent on her pleasure. She felt cherished and wanted, beautiful and sexy. He told her so—how he'd get hard every time he laid eyes on her. That he'd never thought about her till at night when his guard was down. He tasted the swell of her behind, dipping between her thighs. Her legs buckled. He left no part of her skin untouched, as if he wanted to wash away any memory of another man.

And brand her as his.

She wanted it, years of hunger simmering to the surface.

Then he turned her, burying his face in her smooth belly, holding her tightly. She plowed her fingers into his hair. "Come to me, David James," she said, and he looked up, smiling. Lifting her as he stood, he pressed a knee to the bed and laid her down, her hair spreading like liquid copper over the pillows.

He stripped off his shirt, his fingers hovered at his belt, and she realized he was trembling. It touched her, this big man being so unsure, and she came up on her knees to him and laid her head on his chest, his arms circling her.

"Talk to me."

"I want this to be good."

"I don't have any doubts." She tipped her head back. "And we have lots of time to get it right."

He smiled, bending to lavish her mouth, and he knew. He loved her. He'd never let himself think that, but he'd known anyway. He'd loved her with his soul.

Then her hands slid around to open his belt, his zipper. "A little eager?"

"Get naked or I start without you."

She moved back to watch him strip. He had a body to die for, all sinewy muscle and ropy strength. She couldn't resist touching him, and she moved close, splaying her hands over his chest and urging him to the center of the bed. On their knees they kissed and touched, her fingers sliding down his hip, shaping his tight behind, then slipping around. Slowly she wrapped his erection, and he groaned, cupping her ass and pulling her to him.

"I don't want to go slow and soft, DJ. I'm on fire. I want you inside me. I want to feel every inch of you. Tell me you have condoms."

He leaned to reach into the suitcase and dumped a handful on her head. "Part of my gear, believe it or not."

"You'll have to tell me later why you need those in combat," she said a little jealously, then ripped open the packet. He tried to take it, but she held it out of his reach, a devious smile on her face. He arched a brow.

She climbed into his lap, his arousal heavy between then, and rolled it down, licking his mouth, his nipple, his throat.

He gripped her hips, dragging her closer. "I'm about to explode."

"Do that inside me," she whispered hotly, inching up, guiding him, and with her gaze trapped in his, she eased down on him.

DJ suddenly cupped her face, searching her gaze. "Mare." He swallowed, his throat tight with the knot of emotion.

Mary Grace could see it, felt the joy of it, and her eyes burned.

They shuddered hard as he filled her completely.

"Oh, honey," he groaned, his big body quivering helplessly.

"I know. I know." Her voice cracked, a tear slipped past. She pressed her lips to his, tenderly, sweetly, and he wrapped his arms around her, holding her for a long moment, his face buried in the curve of her throat.

Mary Grace felt as if she'd made a long, torturous journey and was finally home. "Love me, DJ."

"Aw, Mare, that's so easy to do." He gave her hips motion, each savoring the feel of their bodies meeting and parting. They rocked, but the soft tempo didn't last. He wanted to eat her alive, climb inside her skin and feel her cloak him.

He cupped her breasts, thumbing her nipples, bending her back to suck on the tender tips as she plowed her fingers into his hair, feeling where his lips met her skin, wanting to remember every touch, feel every taste.

Leaning toward the mattress, he braced his hand on the headboard as he left her completely and drove home. She wouldn't be still, trapping him with her legs, her hands mapping wildly over his skin, then reaching low to cup him.

He groaned and thrust a little faster, a little deeper. "I can feel you gripping me, honey—oh, man."

She arched to him, spread brazen and bare beneath him, and DJ stared into the green eyes of the woman who'd stolen his heart and watched her rapture unfold. She stiffened, bowing like a silken ribbon beneath him, his name on her lips as she quivered with a bone-shaking climax. Her fingers dug into his chest. Then he shoved once, twice, and let it take him, extravagant, pulsing ecstasy tearing through him.

He let out a deep groan, clutching her to him, and she choked on a sob as the last ripples shimmered through them like hot glass.

"This is where we belong," she whispered softly, and he heard tears in her voice.

DJ scraped his hand over her head, kissing her temple. "I've been trying to get here for years."

She smiled against his shoulder, and David James McAllister held her to his heart, never wanting to let go. Now that he had her, he wouldn't.

They played chess on the bed, finishing the room service meal. This time DJ won all three matches.

"Name your poison," she said, her look playful as she hopped off the bed.

His mouth practically watered at the sight of her in the lacy bra and panties. "I can make you come before room service arrives." He checked his watch. "Which is in about two minutes."

"I'm a high-maintenance woman." She removed the tray and set it near the door.

"Not in my hands."

She grinned. "Then where's the challenge in that? Not that I'm balking at the idea, mind you."

"How about I don't lay a hand on you?"

Her brows shot up. "Not possible. You have great hands."

When she strutted back into the bedroom, he shut the door, then backed her up against it.

He didn't touch her, his hands braced flat on the door. He lowered to her breasts cupped in lace and he slicked his hot tongue over her nipple. She moaned softly. His motions deepened, grew stronger as her nipple peaked through the fabric. With his teeth, he pulled the lace down and her pert nipple spilled into his mouth.

He latched onto it, sucking hotly, and she arched.

"More?" he said.

"Oh, yes. Definitely."

"We have a minute-thirty."

Just hearing that heightened her anticipation, drenched her in heat. DJ nibbled a path over her belly, aching to touch her, needing to, but it was so erotic to have only his mouth on her body. He moved lower and with his mouth, covered the soft delta shielded in satin, his wet tongue and lips kneading and probing. Her fingers sank into his hair.

"Take them off!" she begged.

"No."

Someone knocked at the door. "Come in," DJ shouted.

"Oh, no!"

They heard the chink of the service cart.

"He's right outside—can you hear him?"

With his teeth, he caught the panties, pulling them down. He pushed his tongue deeply, slickening her, and she spread her legs wider.

He clawed the door, his body so tight he could barely stand it. He wanted to shove into her, feel her just as she climaxed, and when he found the tender nub, he flicked it rapidly, then slowly circled. She bowed, and flexed, her scent filled him, warm and erotic with forbidden pleasure. He could hear the servant on the other side—so could she.

"Okay, you win, touch me!" She slapped her hand on the dresser, coming back with a condom.

Instantly, her panties were off and he lifted her, wrapping her legs around him. For a second he fumbled with his zipper, then impatiently, she helped him, rolling down the condom.

"*Now,* DJ—oh, please hurry!"

He thrust upward, impaling her, and she cupped his face, whispering, "Harder, baby."

And he gave, gripping her hips, his own thrusting like a piston, making the door rattle. "He's right outside. Listening to those delicious cries."

When she clamped a hand over her mouth to smother her shrieks, he laughed and thrust in long, smooth strokes till she begged for heat and speed.

"DJ. Honey, I'm—"

"I know."

She climaxed in a luxurious, almost violent pull, bucking against him, clawing his shoulders, her mouth devouring his.

It ripped through him, blinding him to the moment, to the hard, fast thrust into her body, the slick, wet fist of pleasure trapping his erection and draining every ounce of strength he had left. He arched, soul-stripping pleasure grinding through him and into her. He held her, fused to her, his lungs laboring, his legs threatening to buckle.

Someone rapped on the door. DJ lifted his head.

"Senor? Is everything all right?" came from the other side of the door.

"Wonderful," she gasped, cupping his handsome face and kissing him. "You are just so bad."

DJ grinned, shifting to open the door a crack. Mary Grace yelped and begged him not to, but he casually handed the man a tip. The bellman frowned curiously, trying to look inside. DJ leveled him a dark stare reserved for prisoners of war, and the kid departed.

"I'll have to think of something to get you back for that," she said.

"Sure, any time." He lowered her legs, and left her body.

"Oh, you can count on it." She staggered to the bed, falling face first. "My legs are numb," she muttered into the pillow.

He lay down beside her, pushing her hair back to see her face.

"You're more amazing than I'd ever imagined," he said, his expression serious and gripping her heart in a tight fist.

She knew she shouldn't be stunned. He was much more vocal about his feelings, but she was having a hard time adjusting to the man who'd kept them locked up and pushed her away for years. Because now he wasn't holding anything back from her.

She leaned enough to kiss him, saying nothing, not needing to.

"You know . . . you make the sweetest sounds when you're coming."

She turned red instantly, all over. "They're new—I'm still trying them on for size."

He smiled. "I'll make sure they fit. Too tired to play?" His brows wiggled and she laughed. "Or dine on room service again?"

She pushed him on his back, straddling his thighs, and bent to him. Her tongue snaked over the moist tip of him, and he slammed his eyes shut.

"*Dining* is such a descriptive word, you know."

DJ went rigid, not believing he was up for more so quickly, but then, he was with Mary Grace. He had years to make up for, hundreds of fantasies to fulfill. Aside from the one he was fulfilling now.

Twenty-four hours had passed since they entered the room. No one called, no contact, and while Mary Grace was curious, she didn't let it overshadow her seclusion with DJ.

She toyed with his bare chest, her chin propped there, her body stretched over him like a warm blanket. They'd slept little, made love a lot. In the shower, in the parlor. On the floor. She was sure the hotel staff was going to come busting in, they made so much noise. Which was her fault. She learned she was rather vocal at times.

DJ toyed with her nipple, loving when her breath caught. "What are you thinking?"

"I'm thinking that if I'd known it would be this good and so much fun, I'd have attacked you long before now."

"No regrets?"

"Not a one."

They were quiet for a moment. Mary Grace was wondering, where they would go from here.

"I have something to tell you," he said, after a deep breath.

"Okay."

"You might not like it."

"Then you'd better spit it out now."

"They found the kidnappers."

She blinked, rising up a little. "When?"

"Yesterday." She sat back, her expression angry, and he thought, *Oh, shit.*

"David James McAllister, why didn't you tell me? The honest-to-God truth, and this had better be the last time you hide something from me."

God, she was almost intimidating, he thought, but he loved her temper. It made her look wild and seductive. "I didn't want to leave here."

"Why? To sleep with me?"

"Hell, no. Well, yes, dammit."

"Honest-to-God truth," she warned, with a deadly look.

He drew a long breath, then looked her in the eye. "You remember the call I got the other day?" She nodded. "You were about to say something before the call. What was it?"

She didn't have to think back, she knew. "I'd said that I'd married the wrong man, one I never truly loved."

"While—" he prodded.

Raw pain skipped across her features. "While the one I wanted didn't want me."

"Oh, hell."

"Well, you did say it."

"That was years ago. I was what? Twenty?"

"You never made your feelings known till last night."

"I know, I know." He scraped a hand over his mouth. "But I'd lived in that town for years, raised there, stuck there. I was afraid I'd never see anything but the county line or never have an adventure."

"Did you find the adventures?"

"Yeah, more than I wanted sometimes."

"So are you about done?"

He met her gaze, searching her pretty eyes. "I can't leave the Marines."

"I didn't ask that. I never would."

"What do you want?"

"To be with you, DJ." He broke eye contact, she forced it back. "I love you."

His features went taut.

"I've loved you for years. But if you don't want more than this, say so now."

"You think we can go back?"

She shrugged, feeling so fragile, her heart so tender. She was scared, really scared.

DJ realized she thought he'd say this was it, and leave her. He pulled her to him and rolled, pushing her to her back. "How can you even think I'd let this end? My God, Mary Grace, I've loved you since you called me a jerk to my face." Her lips quivered. "I loved you when I pushed you away. I even loved you when you married another man. But the instant I saw you tied to that chair, I fell hard for you all over again. My heart hurts, I've tripped so many times."

Tears spilled into her hairline.

"I can't live without you. I did it for too long, and I won't."

Her smile broke free, and DJ felt it light his heart and

lift it. He kissed her long and thick, wrapping her tightly in his arms.

When he drew back, she was warm and breathless. "Marry me?

She blinked.

"Marry me, make babies with me. We've already got strong roots—make new ones with me, Mare."

She stared for a long moment, cupping his strong jaw, pressing her mouth tenderly to his. She didn't have to think, and whispered, "Yes. Oh, yes!"

"Ooh-rah!" He kissed her hard, crushing her in his arms.

Mary Grace cried and smiled and rained kisses all over his face. He chuckled darkly, savoring the moment, wanting to start their life right now.

"How should we celebrate?" she asked.

He nudged her legs apart. "I'll give you two guesses."

A few months later.

In dress blues, DJ escorted his wife out of the base chapel, pausing for her to get a load of the uniformed Marines lining either side of the walk.

"Okay, that is so impressive," she whispered, her eyes tearing.

"Attention!" a Marine shouted. "Preee—sent swords!"

A dozen staff non-commissioned Marines in dress blues drew their gleaming swords and crossed the tips. Mary Grace smiled brightly, looked at DJ. Her heart stuttered every time she did and knew he was hers, forever.

"Ready?"

"I love you, DJ."

He kissed his ring on her finger. "I love you, too, darlin'."

They walked under the arch of the swords, and when

they passed the last, a Marine whacked her on the behind and shouted, "Welcome to the Marine Corps, Mrs. McAllister! *Semper Fi!*"

"Ooh-rah!" she shouted back, laughing, falling into DJ's arms. Over his shoulder, she saw her family and DJ's father, her friends and his, smiling and waving. She looked up at her husband, sinking into his Nordic blue eyes, and knew she'd treasure this moment all her life. It was more than their wedding—it marked the new beginning.

Though she'd found her true love when she was just a girl—a bad boy with an attitude—it took a daring rescue by a U.S. Marine and one special night to bring him into her arms.

Right where he always belonged.

Hot Landing Zone

One

Under the cover of a moonless night, Gunnery Sergeant Jake Mackenzie signaled to cut the engines. The two black Zodiak boats drifted on the rolling waves to the shore and when they were close enough, six Marines rolled over the side into the water, pulled the rubber boats onto the beach, then hurried silently along the shore toward the target. A few yards upshore, a small ship rocked wildly at the end of a floating dock. Over his head, the sky flashed with lightning, threatening to unleash one hell of a storm.

Jake knelt behind a palm tree, and sighted through night vision goggles to match the satellite photos to the stronghold. That didn't look like much of a terrorist compound. Instantly, he corrected that. Bin Laden lived in caves. Hussein in a hole in the dirt. Why couldn't Kali live in something left over from Blackbeard?

The elements had eroded an ancient stone wall to a pile of sinking rocks circling the north side toward the water and docks. Beyond it, a jumble of thatched and tin buildings made from castoffs were scattered enough to offer cover, yet backed by rocky cliffs.

Easy in, easy out. All they had to do was locate the package.

He scanned the area, noting the guards, weapons, and the barrels grouped in the distance. Likely fuel or something just as explosive in there. They'd kidnapped a scientist. Reason said they were forcing Dr. Katherine Collier to create something no one wanted out in the open.

His job was to get her out, and destroy any WMDs. Spooner was already under the docks setting charges. Jake planned to blow them back to the dark ages. Not that they weren't far from it now. Yet his concern was the center structure: cinder block, fairly new, and flanked by guards trying to keep dry.

She should be in there. If Intel was right.

But then, Jake never trusted analysts. They were guessing. Jake wanted to be sure.

He looked to his left to see if Spooner was done and saw the man slither out of the water onto the beach. He hurried to his teammates, spread out and under cover of sunburned vegetation. Outstanding.

"Number one?"

Jake knew they were impatient to assault. "Stand fast. We have to control this situation. Don't let this fort fool you. These guys aren't lazy or stupid. They got her this far without detection."

Which meant they'd kill anyone in their way.

"No one move without my signal." Jake glanced at his counter, checking the time remaining. "We have one hour to make it off this island." And hightail it to the pickup before unfriendlies found them. Or the storm hit.

A bone-jarring scream scratched across the night like a knife driving into solid metal.

Jake's eyes flared, stark against black, tiger-striped painted features. He swore and focused the night vision goggles. The cry was definitely female. Christ. They had no reason to hurt her. She was useless to them dead.

Guards turned to stare at the cinder building.

"West end, at the corner," Jake said, then noticed the men near the barrels walk, stop, then turn. Each paused at a precise spot, never getting close. "Riggs and Miller, take out the guards on the forward perimeter of the main building. Fletcher and Cook, when the guards are down, you cut the generator. Spooner, get to those barrels, find out what's in there, then set a timed charge. We'll blow it when I have the package."

"Roger that, Number one."

"Make it a big one." His tone was low, a growling promise of revenge.

Moments moved like water in the sand as Jake waited for Riggs and Miller to approach the compound from the land side, making a wide sweep to avoid detection. None of them wanted to tangle with more than they could disarm. Some C-4 meatballs and all hell would break lose. It was the cover and distraction Jake needed to locate and retrieve Collier.

He hoped she was ready for this.

Jake signaled, and crept forward.

Wind churned trash and island debris, the rain stinging his neck. Waves foamed and angrily slapped the shore. Hell of a night for a rescue, he thought, but it would cover noise. Not that he was planning on making much.

Crouched low, Jake raced into the open toward the north wall. He flattened back against the stone, listening for the sentry's footsteps on the other side of the wall, waiting for distance. Once the guards were out of commission, he had a straight shot to the only door he could see.

He heard grunts through the ear mike.

"Two guards down," men reported.

"Three and four down," another said.

"Path is clear, Number one," Spooner said. "I'm circling to the barrels."

"Roger that. Fletch, Cook, wait for Spooner before cutting the power." Jake snapped a look around the edge of the stone wall, then jerked back. Shit.

"Be advised. Land side, beyond the buildings, about fifty men under cabanas and armed. Let's not invite them. Watch your six," Jake said, moving forward. Someone would notice they were minus a couple of guards any minute. And then there was Kali to deal with.

Katherine stumbled back, falling to the nearest chair.

Her ears rang. Pain simmered through her jaw and up to her eyes, making them water. She rubbed her face and worked her mouth, surprised she wasn't bleeding. She lifted her gaze to Kali, a short, narrow man with gorilla features and empty eyes.

"I told you—"

Kali pointed the gun to her forehead. "*Soon* is not good enough, woman."

Katherine closed her eyes, the cold metal reminding her that reason didn't work with this man.

"Mr. Kali, these chemicals," she gestured to the canisters, "are unrefined, and rushing the process of separation will create a catalyst of insurmountable—"

He nudged her head with the gun. "You have one day." He held up a finger in case she forgot how much that really was. "One day to complete the formula . . . or you die."

Terror bled up her spine, seizing her breathing. He meant it. He'd already shot one of his own men for falling asleep on post. If she didn't do what he wanted, she was a useless tool. Expendable. Then he'd find another way to get what he wanted.

If she gave him a formula, she was still a liability, a threat to his organization.

Any way she looked at this, Katherine knew she'd die.

Stalling was the only thing keeping her alive, and she didn't know what she was waiting for. No one knew she'd been kidnapped out of her cab on her way to the Hong Kong airport. The instant she'd been snatched at the stoplight, she'd been blindfolded, drugged, and tossed in a van. She'd never seen the outside of this building. Was she still in China? All she knew was sand, salt air, and a lab that was more like high school than the research labs she was accustomed to having at her disposal.

It was a trade. Her life for a volatile chemical weapon created with easily purchased supplies that made it virtually untraceable. And she was running out of time.

Kali was still waiting for her answer, and she nodded. She wasn't going to say she'd try—she'd have to do it.

Kali's smile was oily as he holstered his gun and left her.

The guards near the door smirked. Other than the two of them, Kali, and occasionally a Malaysian chemist who popped in to check her work, she had no idea how many people were here. She didn't doubt they were all armed— even the chemist wore a pistol. Yet the burns on his hands said he wasn't very good at his career choice. Nor could he tell if her formula would actually work. Her notes were real, but complicated enough to satisfy her captors. Till now.

Her hands shook as she rubbed her face, then pushed out of the chair and went back to the table. She picked up a pen and clipboard, studying the computer screen showing her latest test experiment. Rain beat the tin roof, loud inside the lab. Wind shuddered through the gaps in the doors.

In some infinitesimal way, she was actually flattered that they'd kidnapped her.

Considering the grand scope of movers and shakers in the science community they could have stolen, she was *very* small potatoes. No . . . minuscule. Not even enough for hash browns.

Honestly, she thought, disgusted with her latest brain binge. The mind is definitely the first to go. And she supposed the never-ending hours locked away from light, and no sleep made her a touch philosophical. Or perhaps it was just the lack of hope? She'd clung to the notion that *someone* would come busting through the door any second, but lofty laurels had a way of giving out from under you when you least expected it.

No one knew she was trapped in Kali's personal war with the rest of humanity.

The two guards watched her, each leaning against the wall cradling poorly treated machine guns, the door between them. One stared intently, everywhere except her face, and when he approached, she snatched up a vial of blue liquid and threatened to throw it. Chuckling, he backed away, taking his position by the door with his partner, a fat, big-eyed man with disgusting eating habits who emitted bodily noises at regular intervals.

A knock rattled the door; she heard Arabic, and the guard eyed her for a second before he opened it.

A split second later there was soft double thump. A hole bloomed in his forehead, then his chest. The second guard stared as his friend fell to the floor, then shouted a warning and swung around the doorjamb to point his rifle out the door.

He fired.

Katherine flinched.

Then the guard stumbled back, clutching his throat. Blood fountained between his fingers. Katherine froze as he tottered, tripped, then fell to the floor. He hit the lab table. Chemicals spilled, caught the burner. Flames rushed across the table toward the computer.

Then the power went out.

But Katherine couldn't take her eyes off the door. First she saw the muzzle of a rifle, then a big man in black slipped around the jamb. He wore bug-eyed goggles, his head moving with the swing of his rifle, a beam of light with it. Then he pointed the barrel at her. Katherine backed away. He pushed up the goggles, then pulled up a Velcro strip on his shoulder, showing the U.S. flag.

"U.S. Marines, ma'am. We've come to take you home."

Katherine's legs nearly folded.

He held out his hand. "Come on."

She rushed to him.

Jake looked out the door. A guard ran toward his position and he fired, then spoke, the throat mike relaying to his team. "Riggs, Miller, get to the boats and lay down cover fire. Fletcher, we're coming out. Spooner, get the hell away from those barrels." Jake turned to look at her, but she was moving back into the room. "Doctor Collier! We have to go now!"

"But I need my notes."

He stepped in, grabbed her arm. "Leave them!"

"No! I can't." She broke free. "You don't understand—"

A door to the rear burst open. She ducked under a table as Jake sprayed the wall and door with bullets. Two men fell out the door, facedown.

Collier just stared at the dead men, their faces a foot from hers under the table.

"Now!" Jake shouted, and she flinched, banging her head, then grabbing up her notes and stuffing them in a leather satchel. "Spooner, get into the water. We'll pick you up. Wait for my signal to blow charges."

She crawled out, throwing the long strap over her head and under her arm as she came to him. Jake glared down at her. "You trying to get us killed?"

"Of course not."

"Then follow my orders and we'll get out of this, you got that?"

"Yes." Her voice trembled.

Jake ignored her fear and said, "Stay behind me and keep up." He stepped out, then pushed her ahead of him, turning constantly and firing his assault rifle at anyone close. Men raced from inside the walled compound, firing blindly, killing some of their own. Jake ran, pulling Collier with him. "We're out. Spooner, now, now!"

"Fire in the hole," came through the earpiece.

Jake threw her to the ground as the explosions ripped across the darkness, several rapid blasts in deafening roars. Barrels shot up into the air like rockets. Half the building went with it. Jake rolled off her and pulled her from the sand. "Go down the beach. There's a boat. Get in and stay low." Jake moved backwards. "She's heading to you, Fletch. Spooner?"

"In the drink. Come get me." Jake glanced to see Collier jump into the boat.

The entire area was lit like a carnival with chemical fire, and Jake laid down cover fire till the boat engines roared to life, sending up a curl of water as they banked. His men shouted for him, and Jake rushed into the sea, diving into the Zodiak, then repositioning to fire at the shore.

Kali was there, shouting and motioning to the ship as he ran toward it.

"Blow the ship, blow the ship!" Jake ordered.

It went up in seconds. Wood shattered into the sky, yellow fire spreading up the dock. Fuel ignited. Kali shrieked wildly, kicking the sand and shouting orders even as debris rained down on him.

Riggs steered the other Zodiak away to pick up Spooner.

Katherine's heart was in her throat, and she struggled to catch her breath as seawater washed over her. Slopping her hand in the water, she swiped her face and peered at the land, glad to see it growing smaller. Her rescuer was on his knees, sighting down the rifle and firing.

"Marine," she said in a timid voice.

"Not now, Doc, stay down." Kali was in his sights.

"But aren't those rockets?"

His gaze jerked to hers. She pointed.

The walls of a thatched hut had fallen away, a missile launcher beneath.

"Incoming! RPGs! Increase speed, increase speed! Now! Now! Now!"

Fletcher gunned the engine and swells of water fountained, giving away their position.

Jake heard the blast a second before he saw it. He looked in time to see Spooner being dragged into the boat. "Split up, split up!"

They steered apart. But it was too late. The missile hit near the Zodiak, the spiral of water tossing their craft and sending Fletcher over the side. Jake lunged for him, but the current swept him away.

"Riggs! Fletcher's in, Fletcher's in!" Jake moved to take control of the craft.

"We're on it, Gunny." The other boat doubled back, and Jake pushed theirs farther west when he saw Fletcher grab the towline and sweep himself into the rubber boat.

Jake threw the throttle forward, trying to outdistance the rockets. Kali wasn't going down quietly. The sky turned white with smoke, the rain beating it down and filling the Zodiak.

Too much water.

They were low and slow.

Another rocket fired.

Time froze for a moment. Jake watched the rocket shoot straight across the water toward them. He zigzagged the craft to avoid the strike.

Then knew he couldn't.

He shouted at Collier to jump. But she was frozen in terror, her gaze on the incoming rocket, and Jake dove for her, pushing a life vest to her chest. Then he wrapped his arms around her as he rolled over the side into the water.

The rocket hit.

The vibration ripped through the water, tearing them apart and churning massive waves. The break hurled them farther from his team. Then there was no sound except the rushing bubble of water, the violent crack of lightning.

Jake broke the surface, searched the black water for Collier, saw a flash of white and struggled to reach her. She was facedown, her arm caught in the life vest. Jake treaded water furiously, turning her over. She choked and coughed, then a wave hit them and she went under.

Jake's pack was bringing them down and he released the straps, then struggled to get her arms in the vest. She came up in a wild panic, clawing for him. Securing the straps of the vest, he held her till she got her bearings, her head above water enough to breathe.

She looked him right in the eye, and Jake could almost taste her fear. "I'm not gonna let you die, Doc!" he shouted above the storm.

She nodded shakily just as a huge wave curled behind her and crashed over them. Jake held onto the life vest straps as they went under, then burst through the surface, and towing her, he swam farther out to sea to avoid the big waves.

It was their only choice.

The tropical storm had turned into a nasty little typhoon. And there was no rescue ship in sight.

Christ.

Where the hell was the Navy when you needed them?

Two

Jake stirred as salt water rushed over him and into his mouth. He coughed and spit, pushing up on all fours. Dry land. Then he realized two things: he still had his rifle, and his hand was on something soft. He blinked through the stinging haze and looked.

It was Dr. Collier's surprisingly firm behind.

Quickly he checked her pulse, then stood and lifted her off the beach, carrying her out of the sun. She didn't rouse, looking like a cross between a sex goddess and a librarian. Most of her brown hair was still in a bun, and though her clothes were practically shredded, her purse strap was still wrapped across her chest. So much for her precious notes. Laying her down, he stepped back.

She looked like a drowned rat. Her shirtsleeve was torn at the shoulder, her skirt lining falling down past her knees, yet Jake would be a zombie not to notice that God gave her breasts to make a man drool, and an exotic taste in lingerie. Warning himself not to go there in any way, Jake checked the area for snakes, then went back to the shore to see what he could scrounge.

The pickings were pitiful.

A pack that wasn't even his and the life vest, torn but usable. He still had his emergency med kit in his war belt, magazines, and a canteen with a few ounces of fresh water, which would last maybe a day. He patted down the pockets of his LBV, the load-bearing vest still filled with ammo, binoculars, but the close combat communications radio was cracked, wet, and, well, useless at this range anyway. The Zodiak boat—what was left of it—was flat and floating with the roll of the waves. No motor, no patch kit, not even an oar left. He was surprised it was here. Then again, they were lucky they had survived the explosion, let alone that storm.

Jake stared out over the water, hoping his men got to the ship.

Nothing but blue horizons greeted him in all directions. Something dark floated in the water a few yards out, and he waded in, scooping up two grenades. Excellent. Securing the pins more tightly, he brought them back to shore and searched through the pack, then fell back on his rear.

His com radio was trashed, too, not that they were in range. His throat mike was gone, torn off in the storm, he deduced. He popped out the earpiece and flicked it into the water. And no Global Positioning System that would at least tell him where they were and give his command a chance to zero in on their location. Which meant there was no way for anyone to find them and know they were still alive. They'd drifted during the night and with the wild currents, they could be anywhere between Malaysia and Indonesia.

Jake was hoping it wasn't near Vietnam.

Christ, what a fucking mess.

He gathered up what was left, tossed it in the boat, and dragged it off the shore to where he'd left the doc. She still hadn't moved. Just as well, he thought, or he'd lay into her for getting them into this. If she hadn't gone back for the stupid notes, if she'd kept her yap shut and obeyed his orders—hell. They were stuck, and considering it was restricted airspace, there wouldn't be a rescue chopper or plane without a lot of diplomatic channels. And a boat, well, maybe he could hail a passing fishing boat if he was lucky.

Jake never counted on luck to work his way. Stripping off the LBV, his kevlar vest, war belt, and his wet camouflage shirt, he checked his pistol, groaning when water spilled from the barrel. He tossed it on the deflated boat, grabbed the machete that was still secured to the pack—thank God for small favors—and left Dr. Collier, chemical genius of the century, sleeping.

He went to scout the area, though he knew there couldn't be life on this pissant scratch of sand. Yet, right now, all he needed was water.

Katherine stirred, scowling at the taste in her mouth as she coughed hard. I've drunk the entire ocean, she thought, then realized she wasn't floating anymore. Grateful for the feel of solid earth beneath her, she dug her fingers into the sand, afraid to open her eyes. She did, and saw the thick green canopy of trees swaying above her. A warm, fragrant breeze passed over her skin as she sat up slowly. Her stomach rolled, her head suddenly pounding. She remembered the explosion, how the water shook with the force of it, remembered the Marine taking her over the side of the rubber boat. Shifting to her knees, she stared out at the horizon, then stood, walking to the shore.

Beautiful crystal blue water—for miles.

And miles.

She was alone. Oh God.

What happened to the Marines? Were they killed?

She walked a few feet, sheer panic threatening to unleash. What did she know about surviving alone? On her best day, she could microwave something to eat, but here? There was nothing. She faced the land. It rose to a peak, the forest thick with palm trees and dense underbrush.

Rocks were scattered as if tumbled from a truck. I bet there are creatures in there, she thought. Dangerous ones.

She sank to the ground. *I'm alone on a deserted island.* Tears burned. *Don't fall apart. Don't.* This is better than Kali and his threats, she told herself. Someone will come looking, right? Katherine moaned. She hadn't expected the Marines to come for her. A search party on the high seas was really out of her realm of thinking. And she was a pretty broad-minded woman.

Katherine climbed to her feet, too aware of her inabilities right now. She didn't particularly care all that much for the beach in the first place, preferring the creature comforts of her house, her lab. Moisturizer.

"Well, you wanted to lose a few pounds," she muttered. "Now's your chance."

Good God. She was already talking to herself—out loud.

A rustling noise startled her and she whipped around toward the woods, moving left, then right, unsure what to do and praying it wasn't a wild boar, then wondering if they could swim.

Then *he* stepped out of the dark forest.

Tarzan in a tight black tee shirt and pants.

And combat boots. A Marine.

Katherine was so thrilled to see him she ran and threw herself into his arms. "Oh, thank God. I thought I was alone."

Jake stood still, unmoved by the soft, shapely woman pressed against him. When she looked up, he arched a brow. "Alone? How'd you think you got from the water to the shore? Didn't the gear beside you give you a clue?"

She stepped back. "What gear?"

He inclined his head.

She looked. "Oh." Her face flushed.

"Yeah, *oh.* Some rocket scientist," he said bitterly.

"Chemical."

"Whatever." He started walking.

"You don't have to be rude."

He stopped, and Katherine nearly plowed into his back. He glared down at her like she was some bug, clearly more than a little annoyed at their situation.

"Lady, we are stuck here because you didn't obey my orders. Because you had to have your notes and that bag!"

Her shoulders went back, her chin up. "But it was important."

"No, it wasn't. Would have been blown to hell in that fire."

"I couldn't risk that."

"Why the fuck not?"

She reared back. "Excuse me, do you always speak with that much trash in your mouth?"

"Only to people who risk my life."

"Isn't that your job?"

His gaze thinned, like mean little coals. "Yes."

"Then stop complaining." She marched past him toward the gear.

He stared after her, stunned. "Complai—? I wasn't complaining! I was stating a fact."

"Facts are backed up by data."

"Fact." He started toward her and she turned, froze. He was like a giant bearing down on her. "If you hadn't gone back we would have gotten away without being hit with rocket-propelled grenades."

"They would have fired them anyway. I heard them say they would if anyone got close."

"Fact," he went on as if she hadn't spoken. "I could have radioed the potential threat and the command would have dropped a bomb on it. Or sent in Marines to take prisoners and offer cover fire."

"I hardly think so. The U.S. would have been diplomatic and left it up to the local government to deal with it."

Jake ground his teeth, wanting to shake her. "Not with a terrorist."

She thought for a second. "Perhaps."

"No *perhaps* about it, lady. Kali was Al Qaeda cell."

She paled. "Oh."

"Fact three, seconds matter. That mission was timed till you stalled. So, Dr. Katherine Collier, brain trust, is being stuck on this rat hole island instead of sitting on the rescue ship—*data* enough for you?"

Katherine had never had anyone speak to her like that. With so much anger and resentment. Honestly, it wasn't as if she'd forced him to come get her.

"I will concede that point." It was just plain wise to do so. He was bigger than she was.

"Good."

"But not the others." She quickly walked away from him.

Jake scraped his hand over his head, itching to wring her pretty little neck. And right now, she looked ridiculous walking the beach in heeled shoes. He shook his head, disliking her more than he did five minutes ago.

"What was so damn important about that satchel?" he said when he was near.

"Nothing, it's the notes inside. When they took me, I had them with me. They searched me for weapons but didn't read the notes. They couldn't understand them anyway." She sat, opening the satchel and pulling them out. They were still legible.

"And?"

"And it was a cure, Marine."

"Jake, Jake Mackenzie."

She looked up, then swiped her hand on her skirt before holding it out to him. "Dr. Katherine Collier—pleased to meet you."

Jake stared at her hand. What the hell did she think this was? A cocktail party? He ignored it. "A cure for what?"

She lowered her hand, embarrassed. "It's an antidote. For the very chemical bomb Kali wanted me to make."

"Did you make it?"

She looked up. "Of course not. What do you take me for?"

She didn't want to know the answer. She wouldn't like it. "You looked like you had a lab."

"Yes, crude as it was, and I was stalling till I could think of something to get myself out of there."

"You were on an island—where did you plan to run to?"

"Oh." She frowned a little. "An island? . . . Really?" She shrugged. "I was drugged and blindfolded in Hong Kong, so I wouldn't know. I was on my way back to the U.S. when—"

"I know how they took you, Collier—that's why my team was there."

She looked up at him, squinting, and he had a feeling she wore glasses sometimes. "How *did* you find me?"

"That's classified."

He wasn't being very cooperative. "Why did they come? I'm nobody."

That was a little humbling, Jake thought. "You were giving a lecture to half the defense departments of five countries, that's why."

"Well, at least I made some impression."

She was flipping through her notes, uninterested in the fact that the Chinese and Americans were finally working together to find one chemist.

"What were you hoping for, money for funding?"

"No. I was offering the cure to all of them."

"Why?"

"So they would be safer against chemical attacks, why else?"

"Seems to me you could have made a ton of ging-wah off of that."

"Ging-wah is money?"

He nodded.

She tipped her nose up a bit. "Saving lives with this is more important. It just might save your life, Mr.—"

"No mister—Gunnery Sergeant Jacob Mackenzie. Marine Force Recon."

Well—*that* was impressive. "Well, Jake, this," she tapped the notes, "was the presentation I'd given the heads of defense and their chemists. And as it's the antidote, it also contained the formula from which the chemical weapon can be made. So you see, if Kali had it, he could produce the weapon he was forcing me to create. Without my help."

Jake just stared at her, wondering how they could pack so much brain into such a little woman. And why the egghead didn't have the common sense God gave a rock. Once she'd made the weapon for Kali, he would have killed her on the spot.

Jake turned away.

"Where are you going?"

"Firewood."

"Oh, good."

"For a signal fire."

"You think they will look for us?"

"Yes." Not for long, though.

"You don't sound certain."

"I am." He put conviction in his tone. Hell, he didn't want to scare her. God knows what she'd do then. She'd breezed past eighty pounds of gear right beside her, for crissake.

"What are you not saying, Jacob?"

He faced her, deciding she needed to know the situation. "We floated in a typhoon. For over eight hours, I'm guessing. While we're damn lucky to be breathing, we could be anywhere."

"You don't know *where?*" Her voice rose a notch.

"No, I don't. Near Borneo, Sumatra, in the Java Sea."
He shrugged. "Still in the China Sea." He hoped. "Near
the shores of Vietnam." Her eyes flared at that. "This island could be one of the Anambas Islands—there are
thousands, most unnamed." Which meant unmarked. He
waited for that to sink in.

She licked her lips. "You don't have a map?"

"Lost at sea like most of my gear, Doc."

"Katherine, please," she said primly. "How long can
we survive here?"

"A while. We'll have to. We don't have a choice."

"What about food, water, shelter?"

Jake heard the fear in her voice, and didn't like that it
pierced his hide. He tried to understand it. Accept it.
"We'll survive, Collier. I'll make sure of it."

She started to get up. "What can I do to help?"

"Nothing. Stay put and don't wander off." He started
down the beach.

"Why stay put?"

He looked back. "Because I haven't checked the area
for wild game, people, snakes . . . and you're a little out of
your element." His gaze dropped to the shoes she still
wore. Badly stained and matching her skirt.

Katherine took off her shoes, inspecting them, and
made a face. "These were silk."

Jake turned away, shaking his head. "And don't touch
anything." Oh yeah, this was going to be a real picnic.

Katherine watched him walk away, a little nervous. The
man was all brute force and muscle. Dark hair, liquid
brown eyes, and a cynical impatience in his tone. Like she
was the thorn in his paw and the lion wanted it, and her,
gone. She supposed he'd rather be on the island alone, not
thinking about what a burden she must be.

But he was the only thing between death and survival.
He was a Marine, so he had all those skills, right? Didn't

they drop them into nowhere with a knife and they had to survive for days? He could probably rub two sticks and make fire. She needed nitrate and sulfur for that. And flint. She needed tap water and a microwave to feed herself, she thought honestly. That and the local Chinese take-out restaurant.

Katherine knew her limits. With men, well, she'd never been able to just talk to them without mentioning her current hypothesis. Or irritating them. That part she never really understood. She'd spent years in school, then in research labs creating everything from the latest wrinkle cream to this antidote. All she knew now was that she had little to contribute to their survival.

So . . . just don't be a bother.

Like coming to get you wasn't? Like getting blown out of the water was a good thing? And he was probably worried about his men. If they weren't here, were they lost at sea? The thought made her stomach twist, and guilt set in.

This was all her fault. She shoved at the notes. She should have let them go up in flames. But then last time she'd looked, Kali wasn't dead.

But he also had no way off that island, either.

However, the reality was that if he had her notes, he could have made the chemical weapons. How could she live with herself if she'd let it get into the hands of a terrorist? She was right to take them.

Even if Jacob Mackenzie—Marine Force Recon commando—didn't think so.

She wrapped her arms around her knees and sighed. The warm breeze stirred her wet hair and she let it down, fluffing it.

The view was spectacular, clear and crisp blue for miles. Peaceful.

If it wasn't for the armed Marine with a bad attitude.

* * *

Jake made several trips back, dumping wood into a pile. The doc didn't say much of anything, watching him. During one return trip, he caught her shimmying out of her torn panty hose and got a good look at a great pair of legs hidden beneath the skirt that hung almost past her knees. She looked dorky with the satin lining hanging below the hem. And her hair in a bun. And the damn shirt tucked in. Jake had the urge to strip her down to her skin and see what was really under those old-fart clothes.

He turned the ragged Zodiak over in the sun to dry it out, then stripped off the nylon ropes and stored them. He still hadn't found water, and didn't have anything in the pack to purify it, either. He'd have to scout the island in a grid to be certain they weren't sharing this patch with anything more dangerous than a couple of lizards and snakes. Birds, he was sure of already.

"You have to give me something to do—I can't let you do it all."

"Yes, you can."

Katherine sighed. He wouldn't even look at her. And she was too occupied with looking at him. There was just so much of him there. Tall, dark and, oh yeah, handsome. There was some of that blackface paint still on his jaw, or was it just his perpetual dark scowl?

The black tee shirt was skintight, stained with saltwater. But that didn't hide the flat stomach and defined muscles in his arms. Big shoulders, a definite hot-bod. Her gaze moved upward. He caught her staring and she looked away and dug in her satchel. After a second, she dumped it on the ground, going through everything.

"Anything useful?"

His voice startled her. He was squatting beside her. "No, not really. My notes, paper, a couple pens, some breath mints. A comb, compact, and a lipstick. And a tiny bottle of perfume."

He smirked, standing. "At least you'll smell nice."

"My purse was left in the cab." She took off her watch, shaking it, then tossing it aside.

"That's how they knew who was kidnapped."

"The driver?"

"Shot."

She paled. "Oh God, no."

"He's alive. Witnesses said he tried to help you."

"I don't remember. I guess worrying that someone was spending my credit limit is sort of petty, then."

"I'd bet the embassy has your suitcases." She looked a little upset, so he didn't mention that the Chinese ministry had gone through her things as if she were a criminal.

Jake strapped on the machete, then flipped up his watch face, checking the compass. He headed off. "I'm going to look for water."

Katherine stood, brushing off her clothes and picking up her shoes.

He looked at her, pointing. "No. Stay."

"I'm not a dog, Gunnery Sergeant."

"I didn't say that, did I?" Nor did he let her comment. "You are, however, an untrained, inexperienced female who's caused me enough trouble. I need to know this island well, and I'm not going to do it while worrying if *you* are getting injured, or bit by a snake, or passing out from the heat while I'm trying to secure the area. So stay here."

It was the truth, she thought, and made perfect sense. She dropped to the ground. "Next time I'm going," she threw at him but he was already out of earshot.

Jogging down the beach, Jake didn't look back. If he did, he'd start noticing how expressive her face was or how that drab blouse and skirt didn't do a damn thing to hide her spectacular body. Or remember that one moment when he'd caught her staring at him and had seen more than just speculation. He wanted to stay mad at her. At least it would help him keep his distance. Looks weren't everything, he told himself. How many women had sought him out but were put off by his attitude? He played it close to the vest—no reason to spread his thoughts around unless they were for a mission.

Women couldn't handle his need for privacy. They clung, choked him. And Dr. Katherine Collier might be a scientist, but she'd already proven that when it came to life, she hadn't a clue.

An hour later, when Jake felt guilty and decided to check on Miss Too Educated for Her Own Good, he expected her to be where he'd left her.

She wasn't.

Three

Jake's gaze shot around the area, latching on to her small footprints and following them around the outcropping of trees that hid their position from the shoreline.

He stopped short. She was ankle-deep in a small lagoon formed with weathered rocks.

Without her skirt.

She was examining the seams closely, turning it inside out, then right side back as if considering how to wear it. Jake didn't care. As long as she didn't put it back on and stop him from looking his fill of her bare behind visible through the tails of her thin blouse. The sunlight offered her silhouette in three-D display.

Perfect. Aside for the hair in a tight bun and scraped across her ears like a sixty-year-old librarian, the rest was, well, illuminating. He had the sudden urge to drop to his knees and beg.

He walked close, enjoying the view, wishing to hell he hadn't seen it—not her long, slim legs or the sweet curve of her breasts that made him drool.

"Problem?"

She yelped, spun around, then put the skirt over her bare legs.

"Something I can help with?" he couldn't help teasing.

Her mouth went into a perfect "O" and she gaped at him. From the looks of her, you'd think the woman had never been half-dressed near a man before.

"Doc?"

"My, ah, my lining was coming out and I was trying to tear it loose."

"And you went to the shore to do that?"

"I was looking for a sharp shell or something."

In a heartbeat, he whipped out a knife and offered it, handle out. She took it, still trying to keep herself covered and cut it. Impatient, Jake stepped close, held the lining, and sliced through the satin.

He handed the lining back. "You can get dressed now."

"Turn your back."

He blinked. "You're kidding, right?" Her prissy look said otherwise. "Christ." He turned. Just his luck. A prude.

Katherine slipped on her skirt, mortified.

When Jake turned back, her blouse was neatly tucked in the skirt. Both were stained. And too damn thin. Without the lining, he could see straight through the fabric, and her blouse, well, that was whisper-thin and shifting over her enough to embellish her curves and show him the outline of her bra. Which was lacy and pushing her breasts out like a museum display.

"I didn't expect you back so soon." She fidgeted with the width of pink silk.

"Obviously."

"Did you find water?"

"No."

"Then why are you back?"

"Checking to see if you're still alive."

"Why wouldn't I be?" When he just stared, Katherine grew annoyed. "I'm not totally helpless, Jake, and I didn't touch your precious gear."

"I knew you wouldn't. You're too scared."

"I am not."

He stepped close, quick and abrupt.

She jolted back, splashing in the water.

All he did was arch a brow as if to say, *Really?* "I'm not going to hurt you. It's my duty to protect you, Doc."

A duty. How very official. She wasn't afraid of him, only intimidated by his stripped-down sentences and those penetrating stares. As if he were trying to figure her out all the time. He turned away, smirking to himself, and she really hated that. It was so, "I am man, you are mere woman" that she ground her teeth before she said something that really agitated him.

"Can we use this for something?"

Jake didn't even glance back, knowing she waved the pink silk. "Not that I can think of right now."

She sighed and marched after him. He was really impossibly macho and she didn't know why it annoyed her. She was on an island with the one man in all of humanity who could keep her alive, and she was irritated? She rolled her eyes, thinking she shouldn't complain, even to herself. All she had to do was imagine being alone to know she had an advantage in the commando walking ahead of her.

He stopped and surveyed the gear, as if countermanding her earlier statement that she hadn't touched anything. She wouldn't dare. There were far too many dangerous things in that pile of equipment. In that, she was definitely out of her element.

He checked his watch, looked at the sky, then the area. "I'll scout for the next two hours, then build a shelter."

She wasn't speaking to her, just speaking, she decided. He headed toward the forest.

"I'm coming with you."

"No, stay—"

"Don't order me around like a Marine. I am not one." His look said she wasn't even close. "And I will not just sit here like an obedient child." She picked up her shoes and was about to put them on when he took them, snapping off the heels without so much as a strain.

She gaped at them for a moment, shrugged and slipped them on, then gestured. "Lead the way."

Jake stared at her for a second as she secured strands of hair in the bun, then gave in. It was probably best if he kept her close. "Stay in step, and do as I say this time."

"Follow orders, I know. God forbid I disobey you again. We might find ourselves captured by cannibals."

"That's not too far off. Southeast Indonesia still has cannibalistic tribes."

Her eyes flew wide and Jake thought, she couldn't lie her way out of a damn thing—her expression gave her away too much. He faced forward, hiding his amusement as they trekked through the jungle.

He really shouldn't tease her, but it was just too damn tempting. Like the woman herself. It was just his luck to get stuck on a deserted island with Playmate of the Year.

Only she didn't know it.

Jake glanced back. She froze, a strained "I didn't do anything wrong, did I?" look on her amazing face. Nope, she had no idea how tantalizing she was. If she knew, he'd be toast.

With the machete, he chopped through the underbrush as if he were taking his anger out on the island's vegetation. Katherine suspected he was imagining all that green foliage to be her head. He hadn't said a word in the last half-hour, just moved though the jungle.

"If you have a compass," she said, "then you know where we are."

"No, I don't. I know where north, south, east, and west is, and what *should* be there, but how far we are from any other land, its impossible to tell."

"Oh."

He paused to look back at her. "You don't get out much, do you?"

Katherine didn't have to think about that. "No, I'm rather solitary." Alone, lonely, an outcast? Pick one, she thought.

"Well, you should be pleased about being here, then, because this is as solitary as it gets." He continued walking.

"I said solitary, not marooned, *and* isolated from all the wonderful things technology has to offer."

Great, he thought, not the outdoorsy type. He expected a lot of complaints in the next few days. He hacked at a big leaf, the razor-sharp machete slicing through as if it were water.

"I'm glad you're here, Jacob."

Calling him by his given name made their odd partnership seem formal. "Jake, or Mac, if you like."

"Your men call you Mac."

"Yeah."

"I'm hoping they're all right."

"So am I."

"It's my fault."

He stopped and looked at her. She met his gaze. Jake felt punched in the gut by the tears in her eyes. So quick and tormented. "It's not all your fault. It's Kali's for kidnapping you."

"But I put us in this situation."

He groaned. She looked on the verge of crying. Jake felt helpless. Give him an enemy he could fight, not a woman in tears.

"Actually, if you hadn't alerted me to the RPGs, we'd probably be dead."

"Really?"

It was the truth, he admitted. "Yeah, really."

She seemed to deflate right in front of him. "Well, that's a little better, I guess."

"You okay now?"

"Of course."

Now she looked affronted? "You're not going to cry again?"

"I wasn't crying. I was a little emotional about thinking of your men. Since they aren't here, they have to be somewhere, and I'm truly hoping it's someplace safe."

"There was a ship to pick us up."

Her perfectly arched brows knit. "I didn't see a ship."

"That's because it was three miles out, dark and storming. We were to rendezvous with it by coordinates." He didn't mention that had they left with a little less notice, and not been forced to set off charges before being miles away, they'd have made it to the ship easily and wouldn't be stuck here. "Does it make a difference now?"

She blinked. "I suppose not. Shall we continue our foraging?"

Jake started walking again, his gaze moving around the dense, moist land. They'd gone a few more yards when she inhaled a sharp breath. He whirled, his gaze shooting over the ground and trees, his body tensed for danger.

"What?"

"It's a yucca, or something like it, since I don't think yucca could grow out here—too moist."

"And?"

"It's a plant—look."

"There are lots of plants—for crissake, there's nothing *but* plants."

She sent him an exasperated look as she knelt and broke off a piece of the plant, then squeezed it between her fingers. A silvery white liquid slicked her finger and when she rubbed it, it foamed. "Not like this. Oh, there's aloe. Thank God."

"And why are you thanking Him?"

"For cosmetics," she said, looking up at him.

"Excuse me?"

"It's a form of soap—this is for burns." She twisted, looking around, and Jake was suddenly struck by how delicate she was. She had curves out the ying-yang, but her shoulder width had to be half of his. Her slender fingers nimbly plucked at plants, and she gathered them into the tail of her blouse.

"Are you sure you know what you're doing?"

"I have a degree in biology, a minor in botany."

"I thought you were a chemist."

"That, too."

Christ. How many degrees did she have? And for God's sake, *why?*

"Besides, I worked for a cosmetic company once."

Did she use them? Even know how to make herself more attractive? That ugly, matronly bun had to go, he thought. "From lipstick to weapons?"

"Oh, that was almost an accident."

"Say again?"

She gathered some flowers and pieces of the plants, tying them off like a bundle in her shirttails. "I had a friend, a research physician, who was working for a military contract company and he couldn't get the antidote right, so he asked me to give it a try." She shrugged. "And I made it work."

"Bet that pissed him off."

She stood, meeting his gaze. "I don't know, he never said."

"It did, trust me." No man wanted to be shown up by a woman.

"I was hired to work for his company to complete the project."

"Why didn't you just give it to him and go back to making lipstick?"

She stood. "He had a hard time explaining how I came to the conclusions I did. You really want to hear this?" He seemed bored, listening for the sake of noise.

"I wouldn't have asked." He walked, chopping a path.

"I couldn't have done it without Rodney's help."

Rodney? People named their kids *Rodney?*

"He was a physician and knew which chemical combination would make the symptoms subside, but he didn't know which ones caused the symptoms, or in what combination. Well, that's not right. He knew that, too. He just couldn't get it to work without killing the lab rats."

"And you did?"

"Obviously."

"And I'm betting you gave him credit for it, didn't you?"

"Why not? It was his formula."

She was more charitable than most people. "Then why were *you* giving the lecture?"

"Because I created the right combination and understood it better."

"You still friends with this Dr. Rodney?"

She stopped for a second. "Actually . . ." She frowned at the ground, then lifted her gaze to his. "He was very testy last time we spoke before Hong Kong."

Jesus, she couldn't be that dense about human nature, could she? "You think he set you up? With Kali?"

"Heavens, no. Rodney? Oh no, no, no. It served no purpose."

"Governments would pay billions for what you made, Katherine."

She thought it was sweet the way he said her name, as if it were tender on his lips. "I don't care."

He arched a dark brow. "About money?"

He looked so formidable when he did that. "No. I have enough to be comfortable, and don't need more."

Okay, this was a first. "Not for shoes?"

She nudged him. "I'm not that vain. The expensive ones are more often the most comfortable."

"So women tell me."

A thought suddenly occurred to her. "Are you married?"

"You don't beat around the bush, do you?"

Katherine reddened. She didn't mean to be blunt, it just

came out that way. "It's a waste of time. So, are you?" She didn't like that she was holding her breath. Then again, when had she last done that much waiting for a man to speak?

"No, I'm not. You?"

"No."

That one word, said on a tired sigh, spoke more than she wanted, he thought, staring above her head and not at how forlorn she looked. "Ah-ha," Jake said, suddenly moving to a tree.

"Ah-ha what?"

"Food." He slipped the machete into its sheath and leapt at a tree. Katherine stepped back as he climbed to the top. Awfully agile for a big man, she thought. He cut a bundle of green bananas. They dropped at her feet. He didn't stop there and swung like a monkey to another tree. Two coconuts fell. Seconds later, he dropped to the ground in a crouch, then straightened to his full height.

She was grinning. Jake felt punched again by her smile.

"You're so . . . Tarzan."

He chuckled lightly, and beat his chest with one fist. "Let's head back." He slung the bananas on his shoulder and Katherine rushed to take the huge coconuts.

"We can't eat these till they ripen some." He inclined his head to the bananas. "They make you sick, trust me."

"I do."

He looked down at her. She didn't have anyone else to trust, he thought, shelving the feeling that gave him just the same. He gestured for her to precede him. "It's safe enough."

"But we haven't found water."

"I will. If not, I'll figure out some way to collect it if it rains."

Rain. Katherine hadn't thought of that happening again. It was so clear and cloudless now. They headed back to the camp area.

He gave her some water from his canteen, making her sip and spit first. It was disgusting. To spit in front of a man. He found it vastly amusing. Katherine didn't care as long as he smiled instead of scowled.

Untying her blouse and laying aside the herbs and plants carefully, she watched him work. One couldn't help but do that. His features were angular, almost mean-looking, yet somehow dashing. When those dark eyes landed on her she felt like confessing her secrets in one blubbering diatribe. She'd bet enemies of America didn't stand a chance when he stared them down.

Did women?

Katherine hadn't noticed too many of those things with the men she worked with; they were always wearing lab coats and more interested in work than talking to her about anything except chemical reactions and baseline testing. Never about dates. Not even gossiping.

In fact she hadn't had a date in . . . she couldn't recall, which was pitiful, she thought. No, pathetic. She tried remembering the last time she had sex and a vague memory drifted over her: of Dr. Alan Partridge's clumsy fondling, then sweating on her and pumping like an engine on its way to Chicago. After a few moments, she'd lost any interest and blessed the moment he was done and off her. Likely why she never went out with him or any man since. Work seemed to give her a comfort, though certainly not the satisfaction she wanted, she needed.

And just why was she thinking about this *now?*

Her gaze moved over Jake. Kneeling by a large, sharp rock, he was working the green hull off the coconut. Oh Katherine, if you have to ask that, you really are a recycled virgin. The man was so far removed from any she'd ever met. Physical, smart—well, she knew lots of smart men, just not survival smart, in-the-face-of-death-and-peril smart. He seemed undaunted by their circumstances. Or perhaps he was keeping busy so he wouldn't be daunted?

He cut through the coconut hull and ripped at the fibrous skin. When he had it off, something she couldn't have done, he took out a small knife strapped to his calf and cut a hole in one end.

"Want a taste of the milk before I crack it open?" Jake handed it to her, and she tipped it over her open mouth. About half of it made it past her lips, the rest spilling down her chin. Jake's gaze followed the milky liquid dribbling down her throat and disappearing beneath her blouse.

"That's not as good as I expected," she said sourly.

"I know."

She pitched the nut at him. He caught it, chopping it open, then gave her a piece.

"Oh, this is better." She chewed, reaching for more.

He stopped her. "You haven't eaten in a while—wait a bit."

It was going to make her sick if she ate too much, a mistake he'd made a long time ago, and he had a feeling that Doc Collier hadn't had fresh coconut before. He stowed the pieces, then started digging a hole in the ground. Katherine decided not to ask for an explanation, and just watched.

He gathered rocks, surrounding the hole, then dumped in dried fronds and old wood. Then he went to his pack, pulling out packaged meals ready to eat, and found waterproof matches.

"You had food?"

He glanced. "Yes, a day, maybe two days' worth. Every Marine has at least that at all times in a pack."

"Then why didn't you say so?"

"Don't get all testy, Doc. We could be here for a while, and we needed to find other sources." He gestured to the bananas, then eyed her forlorn look. "You're scared."

"No, not really."

That was a brave lie, he thought. "It's okay if you are."

"I should think so—I mean, it does look pretty dire, doesn't it?"

Jake looked out over the ocean, hoping to see a chopper, a boat, but there was nothing but sea. "Yeah." He stood, pocketing the waterproof matches, then pulled the rubber Zodiak under the trees. With the machete, he walked a few feet away and started cutting dead trees and some not so dead.

"Tell me what you're doing."

"Chopping."

"Please spare me the minimalist talk, Jake." She stood, brushing herself off. "What can I do?" He opened his mouth to speak and she cut him off. "If you tell me to sit or stay I'll . . ."

He gave her his full attention. "You'll what?"

She tipped her nose up. "I'll think of something vile to do to you in the middle of the night."

He smiled and her heart pitched so hard she thought she'd fall over. A beat later, she thought of the coming night, of lying in the darkness next to this man. Her insides pulled, the spot below her stomach going tight with a need she almost didn't recognize.

Then his eyes changed, smoldering a little, lowering over her body, pausing here and there, and Katherine thought, any second she'd strip to her skin and yell "Take me, Marine!" Then the sexy look was gone, the scowl back in place, and he turned his back on her. Katherine realized he was actually attracted, but wouldn't do anything about it. The thought made her blood warm, since she didn't see anything sexy about herself in her present state. But the question was, given the chance . . . would *she* do anything about it?

She smiled at his broad, muscled back and thought, *Oh most definitely!*

Four

Jake was all business with making the shelter, and he ignored her so well, Katherine decided that special look had been just her imagination. A weak fantasy.

Most men didn't see anything but the brain in her head anyway. Why should Jake Mackenzie be any different?

"You really want to help?"

Startled, she looked up. "I say what I mean, Jake."

Jake eyeballed her for a second.

Just to have him stare at her so intently left her feeling twisted and stretched thin. It was unfair that he had so much power in a single glance.

"Okay, see this?" Jake held up a type of banyan tree with peeling bark. "It has a skin you can strip off." He showed her how to peel back the thin, pliable bark. "When I cut it, you strip off as many layers as you can." She was so eager to help, it made Jake grin.

She blinked, looking shell-shocked.

"What?"

"You're very handsome when you smile, Jacob Mackenzie."

His ears burned.

"You should do it more often."

"I suppose." He avoided looking at her, not wanting to

feel more than he should, not wanting to actually *like* her. She was his duty. Dammit.

"Are you always a grump or is it just our circumstances?"

"Always."

She made a face at his back and plopped to the ground near him, taking the poles of wood and stripping off the bark. "What are we doing with this later?"

"Making rope."

Skeptical eyes stared at him. "This I have to see."

They worked in silence, Jake moving around her; then, when he had a sufficient number of trees cut, he sat on the sand. He put four lengths between the toes of his boots and started weaving.

"That's a French braid."

He looked at her. "Can you do it?"

It shocked her that *he* could. "Yes, I do it to my hair." She took four strips and wove.

A hell of a lot faster than he had.

She finished one and grabbed another. "I can take care of this—you do whatever else you need."

Jake stood to dig holes, then positioned the tree saplings he was using for poles, tying them together with the rope Katherine was making. He draped the torn Zodiak over the poles, making a tent that was big enough for five Marines.

"Have any brothers and sisters?" she said, her fingers flying over the braid.

She asked too many questions, he decided right then. "No. I was an orphan."

She looked up, still. "Oh Jake, that's awful."

"Not really." He should be used to that pitying look. But he sure as hell didn't want to see it on her.

"Yes, it is. What happened?"

"My parents were killed in a car crash when I was four. I survived. No relatives. I was raised in a Catholic orphanage. When I was eighteen I went into the Marines." He shrugged as if that was enough explanation. "You?"

She knew he was changing the subject and she let him. She could nag, but that wasn't polite when he was her only company. "I have a sister. She's married with three children, one on his way to college, and I have a brother. Both are twenty years older than I. My mom was nearly fifty when I was born."

"Whoa. Surprise."

"Oh, yes. My brother and sister were already out of the house and while I had a delightful childhood, the older I got, the more I felt like the grandchild than the child." She kept working on the braids. "Their attention seemed to be on their teaching positions and each other." *So I was pushed off on nannies or boarding schools,* she added silently.

"Is that why you have so many degrees?"

She ducked her head lower, intent on the braids, but in a soft voice said, "I didn't have much choice. I graduated from high school at fourteen."

"Jesus."

"I skipped two grades, and in college I skipped a year and a half. I was too young for the workforce, so I just kept going to school till I was old enough." Not that it made much difference, she thought. Companies loved her resumé till they discovered how old she was. One employer said she wouldn't give the company the respect he needed till she grew up. It was humiliating and unfair. So she started dressing to look older.

"Didn't you mess around at college, have fun? Get drunk and dance on the tables."

She looked up, her eyes so sad just then. "Would you have taken a fourteen-year-old freshman into your fold?"

"I guess not, considering all the illegal stuff that goes on. Christ, you were jailbait to any guy over eighteen."

"I'd like to think men ignored me for just that reason."

Well, that said a lot, Jake thought. That brain put people off and no one bothered to go deeper. He watched her braid, as if really seeing her for the first time. Not the pretty woman who could be prettier, but the woman with so much smarts it kept her from enjoying her college years. Must have been hard to be smarter than anyone her age, and far more advanced than those a couple years older. *Way out of your league,* he thought, surprised by his sympathy—especially when he was ready to feel nothing for her.

"I guess it's why I like being alone."

"No, you don't."

Her head snapped around, eyes narrowed. "I beg your pardon?"

"You don't like being alone any more than the next person."

"And what gave you this great piece of insight?"

"You're just used to being alone and accept it. When I was a kid I was never alone. Never. When I first came into the Marines it was pretty much the same as the orphanage—a line of racks, open showers. Mess hall meals. Now when I get the chance to be alone, I take it. I have a choice—so do you."

"Yes, *now.*" But not the way he thought. She didn't choose to be alone all the time, but her lack of friends was her own fault. She had a tendency to speak first, and question everything. People liked to talk about themselves; they just didn't want anyone to examine what they were saying too closely. Katherine thought it was all a smoke screen for what really lay beneath, and most times, in her experience, it wasn't very nice below the surface.

"Are you saying you like being marooned?"

"No, that's not a choice, but I'll enjoy it while I can."

He was actually in his element out here, she thought. "What made you choose such a dangerous career?"

He scowled. "You're changing the subject."

She stared back, unblinking. "How deft of you to recognize that."

"I like the excitement. It's never the same. Besides, no one depends on me except my fellow Marines." Like his youth, he thought, depending only on himself for everything.

"I find it hard to believe you don't have a girl waiting somewhere." Panting after him. Lying spread-eagled, naked and begging for him.

"No time. It's not an easy life, and I'm stationed on Okinawa. Anyway, single American females aren't in great number. Most of the women I know are either Marines or married to one. This is my last mission before going back to the States."

"Another reason to be thrilled about being marooned, hmm?"

"I suppose," he said distractedly as he moved around her, testing the poles' strength; then he spread a stack of fronds on the floor of the shelter. From the pack, he pulled out a thin, quilted blanket that was camouflaged, like the rest of his gear. Though it was wet, he laid it on top of the fronds.

"The shelter's under the trees, so we should stay pretty dry if it rains."

"It's impressive."

He was still studying his handiwork.

"So now what? Water?" He nodded. "I think I'll stay here this time." She rubbed her feet and he noticed they were blistered from her shoes.

"Dammit, Doc, why didn't you say anything?"

"I was enjoying the walk in the forest and hadn't really noticed it."

"Rinse them in the sea. It will clean it out and heal it faster, but it will sting."

"I think I can manage that without fainting," she bit out.

He stared for a second, his eyes emotionless, then knelt by his gear and took out a small tube of cream. "Put this on it. And for God's sake, don't wear those shoes."

She snatched it. "Don't treat me as if I don't have a functioning brain, Jacob. I assure you, I do."

"Then use it!"

She blinked, hurt in her eyes. It caught him in the gut.

"You have to be extra careful out here. I have a small emergency medical kit and know how to use it, but disease runs rampant in this part of the world. You could die from infection before help arrived."

He was really ticked at her. "I understand. I wasn't thinking . . ."

Jake let out a long-suffering breath. "Sorry, I didn't mean to yell."

"I'll take it as a gesture of caring."

His gaze moved over her for a long moment; she waited for him to say something, but he simply stood and walked off. He really needed to open up more, she thought, watching him go. Who wouldn't watch? The man was a feast for the eyes.

"And quit staring at my ass, Doc."

Katherine inhaled. "Oh! You're insufferable!"

He didn't turn around. "Yeah, sure. But you're not denying it, either, are you?"

He kept walking, and though she wasn't sure, she suspected he was laughing at her.

And that made her smile.

When Jake returned, Katherine was on the ground, folded over, rocking back and forth, holding her stomach. He just stared for a second, his hands on his hips.

"You ate the coconut, didn't you?"

"I was hungry."

He shook his head, kneeling to check her eyes, feel her forehead. "It will pass."

"God, I hope so."

He chuckled.

"It's not funny!"

"I've been where you are. I'm going to make you a bathroom."

"I beg your pardon?"

"Some privacy, because when that runs through you, you'll need it."

She groaned. "I don't think I've been more embarrassed than at this very moment."

"It's life, darlin'. I warned you."

"Yes, you did. I feel thoroughly chastised and regretful, thank you very much."

Jake left her, taking a flat, wide piece of wood with him, and was back in a few minutes. Katherine was still in agony.

"Come on." He helped her up.

Her stomach pitched. "Oh God." She clamped her hand over her mouth.

"Hold on."

"I'm humiliated, in case you didn't know."

"Imagine suffering like this on a submarine."

She thought about that for a second, then met his gaze. "Okay, that has to beat this."

He helped her to the area he'd prepared. "Cover it when you're done."

"This moment just bottomed out," she said, deadpan.

Jake walked away, chuckling to himself as he started a fire, keeping it small with plenty of dead wood to feed it. She wasn't going to be hungry now, and he searched the med kit for something to calm her stomach.

When she returned, her face was flaming red and she wouldn't look at him.

"Do *not* say a word."

"I wasn't going to. Here." He handed her the canteen. "Take a sip, then chew this." He gave her a white disc the size of a nickel.

"And this is?"

"Kaopectate."

"You Marines are prepared for anything."

"It helps when you aren't sure what will happen on a mission." He glanced at the pack. "That's Spooner's, and he can jam fifty pounds of gear in a twenty-pound pack. Mine was weighing me down when we went overboard, so I cut it loose. We weren't supposed to be gone more than a few hours, so there's no bedroll or clothes. There's a little food, a day's worth of water. Which I found, by the way."

She looked up, her face gaunt.

"I have to figure out a way to get it back here. It's just a basin of rock where water collected from the storm."

Katherine looked around. "How about the curves of the boat?" She pointed. "See there, where it's molded and still intact? Cut a bowl shape out and we can poke holes in the edges, then thread the bark rope to carry it."

Immediately he did what she said, cutting away the inner liner of the rubber boat. He punctured holes and she laced it with the rope. It looked like a ball with a handle.

"Outstanding," he said, and her cheeks pinkened with pride. "I'll be back in a half-hour."

"I'll just wallow in embarrassment." She burped and reddened.

"Well, I'd say we're past the polite stage, at least."

"And well into the personal habits." She moaned, holding her head.

"Wash your feet again," he said, moving off.

"Aye, aye, Marine." She stood, staggering to the water's edge. The sun was starting to set and they had food, water, and shelter. It could be worse.

Oh yes, she thought, you could be retching up the coconut on his boots.

Jake returned, hanging the water bucket on a pole, then moving around her, doing something in the woods, and she suspected it was the call of nature. She honestly didn't care. Right now she could sleep for a week. If her stomach would just stop gurgling.

Her back against a palm tree, she closed her eyes. She didn't know how long she'd dozed when a sharp click startled her. Jake was by the fire, some sort of kit spread out beside him. He was cleaning his weapons.

"I suppose that's an essential, too."

"Oh yes. Marine isn't ready for duty without his weapon."

"I could debate that." Only his gaze shifted and she felt pinned to the tree. "You've done amazing things without a gun, Jake."

He flicked her a quick smile. Then she yawned, covering her mouth.

"Why don't you go to sleep." He twisted and reached for his shirt, rolled it up, and handed it to her. "A pillow."

"Thank you. Are you going to . . . ?" She gestured to the tent.

"I've got this to do first before it's beyond hope."

She nodded and crawled under the tent, then dropped like a stone.

Jake listened to her soft breathing. He was beat, but this had to be done. The problem was, he wanted to join her in the tent. He wanted a hell of a lot more than just sleep, too. He kept chanting, "duty, protect, defend" like a mantra as he cleaned the pistol barrel, oiled the mechanisms.

It was pitch-black out when Jake finished and crawled in beside her. She hadn't moved a muscle since she dropped there. He lay down on his side, but couldn't help staring at her, brushing a stray lock of hair off her cheek. He wanted to see that hair down, he thought, then decided he shouldn't want anything from Dr. Katherine Collier.

But he dreamed of it.

* * *

The sun had just started its rise in the tropical sky when a bloodcurdling scream jolted him awake. Jake was out of the tent and following the sound in seconds.

"Damn you, Jacob Mackenzie!" Katherine shouted. She dangled upside down from one ankle caught in his snare.

"I told you not to go anywhere without telling me!"

"I had to pee!" She struggled to get her shirt out of her face and keep her skirt from falling any farther. It was hopeless.

"Your bathroom, as it were, is over there on the other side of the camp." He pointed, but it didn't make any difference. Her shirttails were in her face.

"Well, you could have told me you set booby traps, for heaven's sake!" She swung at him, which only served to spin her around like a party favor. "Jake," she pleaded. "My head hurts."

He walked over to the tree and lifted a bundle of rocks. "It's counterweighted."

"Well whoop-dee-doo." When her butt was on the ground, she yanked off the snare. She looked at him. Her world tilted, and she fell back onto the sand. "Oh, I thought last night was the worst."

"Sorry. You have no sense of direction." He reset the snare.

"Obviously."

He loomed over her, his hands on his knees. "You okay?"

She waved drunkenly. "In a moment. I'm waiting for the earth's axis to right itself."

He scooped her up, carrying her back to the camp. She looped her arms around his neck, her face close to his, tempting him. He had no idea her eyes were green. "Want me to mark the trail for you?"

"Don't be facetious. Or an ass."

He grinned, depositing her by the shelter.

"Go ahead, say it."

"Okay . . . for a smart woman, you sure are dense as a post."

She was oddly touched by that. "Yes, well. Give me chemical equations and I can read it backwards in two seconds, tell you the reaction and what element will make it explode, fizz, or burn." She moaned, her head still pounding from all the blood rushing to her amazing brain. "But I can't find the bathroom in the middle of the night."

He knelt, starting the fire. "It's kind of nice to know." It made her seem more normal and not such an egghead.

"You're enjoying my humiliation."

"Hell no, you're just . . . amusing."

"Glad I could entertain you," she muttered.

"Katherine."

She looked up.

"I'm sorry, but you have to admit, it's funny."

She smiled tentatively, then wider. "Clearly my skill in perimeter defense is weak." He chuckled. "I really need to get out more, I guess."

"There you are." He gestured to the beach. "No one can see you. You can do anything you want. I sure as hell won't judge."

"People say that and don't really mean it. Everyone has an opinion and expresses it when you want it the least."

He frowned at her. She'd been ridiculed a lot, he realized. "Well, *I* mean it."

"So I could run naked down the beach and you'll do nothing?"

"No." His gaze locked on hers, pitch-dark and burning. "I'll watch."

She blushed softly, her mouth gone dry.

"You need to do what makes you happy."

She wished she knew what that was, she thought, squirming. "Well, since I have sand in places it shouldn't be, a bath would make me very happy right now."

He glanced up, giving her a "where, exactly, is the sand?" look before he said, "Go in the lagoon. Then, when you come back, you can rinse the salt off with the water." He nodded to the black rubber bowl of water dangling from a sapling pole.

"Is there enough for that?"

"Enough to swim in. And it rains in this region a lot." He stood. "I'm going to the west side of the island." He pointed. "Stay on the beach, okay?"

It was a request this time, not an order. That was progress.

She nodded and when he was out of sight, she grabbed her plants and headed to the lagoon. Katherine stripped and waded into the cool water, floating, trying not to stir up the sandy bottom. She washed her hair, the silvery liquid from the plant foaming in light suds and sliding down her body. Bare and wet to the sun, she felt decadent, erotic, some unseen weight lifting off her soul. She'd never done anything like this, and Jake's image flashed in her mind as she slid her hands over her slick hips, her breasts. She could almost smell his heat, his scent, wondering how it would feel to be touched by such a strong man. Between her thighs thrummed with a deep ache, thick and aggressive. She'd missed it. Wanted more. From him.

Jake sees you as an egghead pain in the ass and nothing more, she thought dejectedly, and dipped to rinse. She reached for her clothes, rinsing them out, not thinking that she'd have to put them on wet till it was too late. Stupid. Scanning the beach for Jake, she hurried out of the water, and hung them on nearby branches to dry, then walked to the camp.

Using the fresh water sparingly, she rinsed the salt from her hair and body; then, in a moment of defiance, she stood on the beach in the hot sun, naked, combing and fluffing her hair dry. She kept glancing behind herself, not ready to be caught like this, but alone, she felt an incredible freedom she'd never experienced.

Just me and the sun, she thought happily. There was no one to judge, to ridicule.

Here she could ignore the voices of her older sister and brother, both constantly treating her as if she were their child, telling her that her mind was a gift, and it could make her wealthy instead of doing research. There were no colleagues giving her that resentful glare; no men waltzing right past her, only to learn that her assistant wasn't the one in charge. No voice in her head telling her to act older, look older, so other people wouldn't feel uncomfortable.

All her education was a curse, a burden, she thought. She wanted things to be simpler. And on the island, they were stripped away, less complicated. It was survival, and nothing else mattered. Smiling to herself, she stretched her arms out wide, bare to the world, and spun around so fast she almost fell over. A tune played in her head, slow and sexy: Nora Jones, about a lap dancer. And without a thought, Katherine started dancing, imagining the pole dancers, strippers, her mind and heart taking off and finding a long-awaited freedom. She ground against an imaginary man, and she broke open the aloe plant, smoothed on the gel to the tune in her head. It aroused her, the power she felt, and she suddenly understood why women stripped for a living.

To drive men wild.

She slipped into her pink mesh-and-lace bra and panties with a sexy hip gyration she didn't know she was capable of doing, imagining herself with the courage to prance in front of a room full of men. It was a good thing she was alone. She was a lousy dancer, and laughed to herself when she stumbled and nearly landed on her butt. She reached for her skirt and blouse, still dancing. They were damp and she didn't want to put them on—the linen would itch, but she didn't have much choice. Jake would be—

"Jesus Christ."

She spun, eyes wide. *Oh no.*

Jake stood at the treeline, staring.

Katherine snatched her shirt off the branches and struggled to put it on. "I, ah, I washed my clothes . . . they're still damp, and I—" She frowned softly. "Why are you looking at me like that?" His expression was nothing short of stunned. No—shocked.

His dark gaze moved roughly over her, stinging her skin. She felt suddenly torn into little pieces, examined and studied.

"Jake?"

"I already knew you were beautiful when I first saw you, Katherine. What I don't understand is why you hide it."

Beautiful. No one had ever said that to her before, and for the first time in a while, she really *felt* beautiful. "Because I've learned that people are somewhat intimidated by me. They tend to judge me by accomplishments and don't bother to see beyond them."

He frowned for a second. "Men did that, didn't they?"

She nodded, old hurt springing in her chest. She crushed it, not wanting to remember the men who had seduced her into believing she meant something, only to backstab her in the light of day. Jake was the only person who'd ever treated her as if her big brain didn't matter.

"Is that why you always wear your hair up in the god-awful bun?"

"To look older, yes."

"Don't." He advanced, stopping inches from her. "Just because you're smart doesn't mean you have to hide everything else about yourself. Took me ten seconds to see beneath it."

Her lips curved, her gaze searching his for the truth. "Don't tease me, Jake."

"I'm not." Unable to resist it, he plowed his fingers into her hair, watching his moves. "It's like a fire is trapped in there. I had no idea it was that long."

He'd never touched her like this and her breasts felt suddenly too big for her bra, and everything below her waist went warm and liquid soft. "It's just hair."

"But it's part of who you really are."

Katherine was so deeply touched, her throat tightened; slowly, she lifted her gaze to his. His every nuance battered her with a sudden heat and awareness; his scent, the carved muscles of his chest, her need to touch him. She tipped her face up a little more, and he gravitated toward her. For a blessed moment she thought he'd kiss her, and she realized how badly she wanted him.

Then his fingers slipped from her hair, the backs of his knuckles grazing her breast. One finger slid lazily down over the swell at the edge of her bra, and Katherine swore her bones melted. "The dancing was . . . interesting."

"You spied?"

"You betcha." He lowered his hand, but didn't step back, his dark gaze scorching over her face. "Now that I know what's beneath that plain-Jane scientist, its going to be hell keeping my hands off you."

"Why would it?"

He groaned, moving back and scraping his hand over his head. "Because no matter what I want, this island isn't the real world, Doc."

Doc. Katherine's heart sank so hard her throat ached. "I see. Because in the real world, you wouldn't come near me, right?"

"No, you wouldn't come near me."

Her eyes narrowed dangerously, anger piercing her tone. "You're assuming a lot about me, Jacob." She leaned in to add, "Don't."

She turned her back on him to slip on the skirt, then marched off down the beach to lick her wounds in private.

five

She was pissed at him, and as much as he wanted something to crush his attraction for her, Jake didn't like it.

He kept whittling the spear to a razor point, planning on taking his frustration out on some unsuspecting fish. But temptation won out and he glanced up, spotting Katherine a half-mile down the beach heading back this way. He wished she'd stay there, wished he'd never seen her in her underwear—dancing and looking like a fucking centerfold.

The image was burned into his brain. Taunted him. Tight behind, breast spilling over the edge of pink lace. Her dark, lush nipples pushing against the mesh fabric, begging to be trapped in his mouth. He slammed his eyes shut for a second, willing his breathing to slow down, his erection to melt.

Not happening.

It wasn't that she was beautiful and didn't know it. Nor that she was the only woman around and he was suddenly extremely horny.

It was her innocence. She had no idea how unbelievably provocative she was. How appealing her lack of common sense was to him, which was kind of weird. The woman could make chemical weapons, antidotes, and had a damn doctorate, for crissake, but she didn't have enough sense to take off her shoes when her feet were blistering? Or know west from east and avoid getting snagged in a snare?

He shook his head, thinking he was a man grounded in reality, the defense of his country, the risks, the Corps. But with *that* woman, he was pretty much clueless. In the space of twenty-four hours, she'd gone from dignified brainiac Dr. Collier to sexy, provocative Katherine. It was like watching a caterpillar change.

He almost wished she'd put her hair back up in that butt-ugly bun, but he knew that wouldn't make a difference. He'd know what was really there, and he'd still be going nuts, little by little. Sorta like water torture.

A half-hour after she'd stomped off down the beach, she'd come back and asked for his knife. For a second he'd thought she'd use it on him, but she simply cut a slit in the long skirt to above her knee. Now, every time she moved, he got a flash of thigh. Temptation he didn't need, because he wanted to slide his hands up her legs and dip into the heat between. The thought of her panting and wet made him sweat worse than he already was. His dick was rising for the occasion again, too.

The rapid thump of footsteps made him look up. She was running toward him, and if he hadn't noticed her boobs before, he did now. The woman should be outlawed.

He dragged his attention back to the spear.

"Look what I found," she said, breathless.

He chiseled the point. "Buried treasure?"

"No, evidence that we aren't alone."

He looked up, shielding his eyes. She held up a long piece of pale rubber.

"It's a . . . a—"

"Condom. I'm sure you're familiar with them."

Her cheeks brightened. "But how would this get here? Intact?"

"It's mine."

She blinked. "Yours?"

"We use them to keep moisture and dirt out of the machine gun and pistol barrels."

She looked from the limp condom, to him, then back again. "Interesting." She paused for a heartbeat, then said, "Do you have . . . more?"

He choked on his breath. "Jesus, Katherine, don't go there."

"What? I was thinking of your big guns. It *is* sandy and wet here, after all," she said blithely, dropped it, then walked away.

Jake ground his teeth, knowing he had handfuls in his LBV, and didn't want to think of putting them to use. With her. He glanced over his shoulder. She sat by the gear, peeling a ripe banana.

She bit into it, then looked up. "Want some?"

He shook his head, throwing the knife into the sand.

"So where do you plan to fish?"

"Beyond the lagoon."

"In your clothes?"

"It won't make a difference."

"I've a really good theory on weight and drag under water that would contradict that."

"Spare me." He met her gaze just as she wrapped her lips around the banana. She drew on the fruit, her lips sliding slowly up the length. Jake's heart beat a little heavier. Christ, in a second there would be no room in his pants.

"Stop that."

"What?"

"You're teasing me on purpose."

"Who's teasing?" Her look was sly as she bit hard into the banana.

Jake flinched. Yup, still pissed, he thought, and removed the boot bands that bloused his trousers above his ankle, then shucked his boot and socks. He rolled his pants up and stood.

Then he stripped off his shirt and reached for the spear. Katherine choked on the banana. *Oh my God.* He practically rippled with muscle. It wasn't bulky, but long and sinewy, oozing with strength. There wasn't a single hair on his chest, except for the dusting that dipped below his waistband like an arrow to his groin. He had a Marine Corps emblem tattooed on his upper deltoid. Some tribal Celtic-looking band on the other arm above his bicep. She'd always thought tattoos were vulgar, but now they looked incredibly sexy on him. As if the man needed help?

He looked at her, spear in hand, and opened his mouth.

"You don't need to give me instructions, Jake."

His brows rose. Now she was reading his thoughts?

"I think I've survived the trial by fire." She finished off the banana, then stood to bury the peel. "I'll go for fresh water."

He scowled. "I don't think so."

"Too bad." She marched off, swinging their water bucket.

"Katherine!"

She paused, turned, her expression bland.

"Since you're going to be stubborn about this . . ." He handed her his knife, calf sheath and all. "Just in case."

She strapped it on. "Bring home big fish, Tarzan," she said, then jogged away.

Jake frowned at her back, confused. If she wasn't mad, she had a real sadistic streak he was just beginning to recognize.

The rock basin of water was almost as tall as she was, and Katherine climbed the stones, kneeling to wash her face and throat. Then she pulled a few strings from her fraying skirt and tied her hair into a ponytail, sitting on the rocks to braid it. It was too heavy and hot to wear it down. She twisted to fill the rubber bucket and heard her skirt rip. At this rate she'd have nothing to wear by morning. Without missing a beat, she took it off and cut a few inches off the bottom. That was certainly cooler, she thought, dressed again and heading back to the camp.

She could see Jake in the distance, a sliver of dark against the white sand and blue water. She was still fuming over his comments. As if she were a snot and wouldn't want anything to do with him if they weren't stuck here. Though she knew she'd have been too intimidated to even start a conversation with him had they met otherwise. That was before she knew him. Before she understood that although he might not claim to judge, he did. Even if it was more of a judgement on himself.

As if he wasn't good enough for her.

A crock.

She didn't have any plans to make him admit it, and though she kept telling herself she didn't care what Jake Mackenzie thought, it was a bald-faced lie. Unexpectedly, water rushed over her feet and she realized she hadn't paid attention to where she was going.

She looked up, spying the camp to her right, then looked left.

"Well, that's a lovely sight," she muttered to herself.

Apparently her drag theory had made a dent in his thick skull. Jake was hip-deep in water, naked except for a pair of olive green boxers.

She walked closer. "Wash day?"

He didn't glance her way, but smirked. "Yeah."

"Good, they stunk."

"Is that so?" He jammed the spear into the water, lifting out a flat fish, then threw it on the shore near two more. Only then did he look up. His eyes flared, scraping over her from toes to head. "What the hell happened to your skirt?"

"Isn't it obvious?"

He waded out. "Christ, don't take anything else off."

"Did you have something in particular in mind?"

Jake frowned. It seemed like each passing hour she was getting bolder, tougher. "What are you trying to do, drive me crazy?" Up a fucking tree?

"Just enjoying my freedom, Jacob." She deposited the water bucket on the post, then went back for the fish.

Jake tested the dryness of his clothing hanging from a branch, praying his body didn't betray him. But it did. He pulled on the pants.

His clothes molded to him so well that Katherine knew what he looked like naked. It was a good look on him.

On the shore, she scraped the scales off the fish, cut the head off, then gutted them. Jake peered. "Don't tell me . . . you have a degree from the Culinary Institute?"

She rolled her eyes, looking too adorable, he thought. "No, I like fresh fish, and I'm an exceptional cook."

"Oh, yeah?"

She nudged him. "Don't look so skeptical, it's like mixing elements after all—milk, flour, sugar."

"You bake?"

Bless his heart, he had a sweet tooth. "When we get back, I'll make you whatever you want, I promise."

"I'd almost swim to Vietnam for brownies." He looked at her, sort of bashful. "My weakness."

And he was hers, she thought. She rinsed off the knife, her hands, then collected the fish. Jake was kneeling by the fire, adding wood, and she looked around for something to spear them. He hopped up to set two Y-shaped sticks in the ground near the fire, then she skewered each fish on a piece of dead branch, laying it over the low flames.

Katherine grinned at it like it was a masterpiece, then lifted her gaze to his. For a long moment he just looked at her.

"You still mad at me?"

She took off the calf knife, tossing it near him. "Yes."

His shoulders slumped a little. "Thought so."

"You insulted me, Jake."

"The truth often hurts."

"Go to hell."

His brows shot up.

"I might have been wary of you—"

"Scared silly."

"*Wary* . . . but I wouldn't have let that stop me."

"Yeah, sure."

She put her hands on her hips. "If you think I'm such a sap, then how did I manage to get my doctorate? How did I weather the insults and condescension from everyone in my field? Hmm?"

"Nothing better to do." The hurt in her eyes made him regret his words.

"You're different from any man I've ever known—"

"So what," he cut in. "Curious how the other half lives?"

Her expression sharpened, her gaze thin with contempt. "You know, you're right, I wouldn't have sought you out. Not because you're a Marine and a little intimidating, and very uptight, but because you're a *moron!*"

She spun around, storming away.

Great, he thought, now he was stuck with a woman who hated his guts.

Talk about the shoe on the other foot. Isn't that what you want, for her not to tempt you, for her not to like you so this won't go further? Jake rubbed his face, wanting on one hand, yet knowing the reality on the other.

Katherine Collier was out of his league.

She walked fast, her round behind rocking inside the now much shorter skirt, and all Jake could think about was dragging her back and going primeval on her. Bringing her to a climax. Tasting it. Feeling it wrap around him.

He was depraved, he decided. Because furious at him or not, he *craved* her.

But Jake had taught himself never to want anything too much, because as a kid he'd had his world shattered by maybes. He wasn't ready to risk his soul for that. And Katherine was the kind of woman who'd trap him in limbo for the rest of his life if she vanished. And he knew she would.

The sun was setting when Jake came out of his brooding long enough to notice the calf knife was on the ground and Katherine hadn't returned. The sudden need to find her right this second spurred him down the shore where he'd last seen her. He called her name, fear slipping over his spine. The island was riddled with dips and holes from past storms, and the sharp black rock told him it was once a live volcano.

He trotted down the beach, trying to see her footprints in the sand, but the tide moved up, erasing them after a few yards.

"Katherine!" Was she sitting somewhere, waiting for him to notice her absence?

He moved closer to the forest, pausing to decipher wind-and-brush movement from human. Then he saw a print in the dirt near trees and tracked it farther into the woods, bending once in a while to touch the shape and make sure it was hers and not an old one of his.

"Katherine! Answer me!"

"Jake?" Her voice was barely a whisper.

"Speak up."

"I don't think that's wise right now."

Frowning, he moved slowly, the fear in her tone seizing him in the chest. There weren't any dangerous animals on this island.

"Keep talking."

She didn't, and he heard a soft whimper. Oh Jesus.

"By the big rock."

Jake pushed aside fronds and giant leaves, checking for prints, wishing he'd brought his NVGs. He stopped short when he saw her legs, his gaze traveling up them to her face. She was on her side, still as glass. Then he saw the lizard the size of a small dog just inches from her face.

"We're having a staring contest. I think I'm winning."

"Stay right there."

"Please tell me you have better advice than that."

Jake drew his knife and threw. The nine-inch black Marine K-bar sank into the lizard and pierced the ground, barely drawing blood.

"Oh God, that was disgusting."

"You can move now."

"No, I can't. My legs are asleep."

"Christ, Kat, how long have you been like that?"

"Practically since I left."

Hours. Good God. He came to her, scooping her off the ground, and walked to the beach. He set her gently on the sand, then started rubbing her feet, her ankles.

She giggled. "It tingles."

"Why didn't you yell for me?"

"I didn't know what it would do, lunge for me? Bite? It was so close to my neck and I remembered what you said about injuries and infection, so I didn't dare move or aggravate it, and then it just—"

Suddenly he cupped her face in his broad hands. "You're safe now."

She stared into his dark eyes. "I'm sorry." Her own eyes watered and the sight cut him in half.

"It's okay, baby." He sat, drawing her onto his lap, and she clung to him.

"I feel incredibly stupid."

He snickered. "Bet that's a first."

She nudged him, smiling to herself.

"You did fine, considering you weren't armed." He

tightened his arms around her. "I should have noticed you were gone too long."

"Yes, you should have." She tipped her face up. "Why didn't you?"

He shrugged. "I figured I'd let you cool off."

"You're still a moron."

He smiled. "So you said."

"And you don't talk enough."

"Now you sound like my buddies' wives."

"Most people are telling me to shut up."

"Want me to beat the shit out of them for that?"

"You would, wouldn't you?"

"Yeah, so I'm still a moron?"

"I'll think about it. *Jerk* is clearly your current level."

Jake laughed, squeezing her. No one talked to him like that. Most were scared to—most were his enlisted men and would be written up for it. But women, they all behaved like perfect angels till he wouldn't spill his guts to them.

He kept rubbing her legs; she curled more tightly against him.

"A little higher, please."

He stopped. "We can't."

"But my butt's asleep, too."

He smiled softly. "You're *trying* to torture me."

"Me? The egghead?" She twisted on his lap, feeling triumphant at the erection against her hip. "The dumb-as-a-fence-post geek? The woman who couldn't possibly want a man like you?" She straddled his lap, pushing her crotch against his hardness, and he groaned. "Who's the one lacking smarts now?"

"You are, because I can torture you right back."

"Really?"

In a heartbeat, his hand was under her skirt, a straight dive for the line of her panties. Deftly, he hooked the edge and sank a finger inside her. Her breath trapped in her lungs, her eyes wide.

"And I can prove it." He plunged deeply and slid back out, his thumb circling the bead of her sex. She squirmed and moaned, but Jake kept her prisoner against him, wanting to open his trousers and slide inside her, feel her pulse around his erection and not his fingers. Instead he slicked over her heated flesh, and felt the flood of moisture, the quiver of her muscles. He wanted to see her face, watch everything about her as she climaxed, but it was already too dark.

"Want me to stop?" He stilled for a second, and she whimpered, hips rocking.

"You're stupid if you have to ask that!" Her body shivered, her breathing skipped.

She was coming apart already, and he insinuated another finger, thrusting slow and deep, and she pushed in tempo, digging her fingers into his shoulders.

"Jake! Oh God."

She came in seconds, stiffening, grinding down on him, her hips slamming, throwing her head back, and Jake flicked his fingers till the last of her pleasure was spent on him. Till she begged him to stop.

Then she collapsed, her lungs laboring.

"Been a while?" That was the wildest thing he'd ever seen.

"Years."

Since a man touched her? "That's surprising."

"Me and a vibrator ever since."

He tipped her head to look at her, then shrugged. "Whatever works."

"It never worked like *that,*" she choked.

He slid his hand free, wrapping his arms around her. Moonlight spilled, the water rushed up the shore, slipping over his legs.

Leaning back, Katherine touched the side of his face. "Do you realize you did that and never kissed me?"

"Yes."

"Why not?"

"Because I'd eat you alive."

That made her body tingle with anticipation. "And this is a bad thing?"

He couldn't help it—he cupped her behind. "Yeah." He'd never stop, never come up for air.

She pushed him hard, taking him off guard. He fell on the sand and Katherine loomed over him, a dark shadow in the twilight. "You're back to being a moron, Jake."

She shoved off him, and walked down the beach on unstable legs.

Jake just lay there, letting the sea water wash over him. She was right—he was a moron. What man wouldn't take what she offered and damn the consequences?

But Jake saw the distant future, that they might not get off this island, that if they did, the real world, his and hers, would crash and burn.

Six

Katherine nibbled on toasted fish while Jake gutted and skinned the lizard. It was gross, his hands bloody. But he seemed to know what he was doing. "Is this what they mean by eating your own kills?"

It was the first words she'd said to him since leaving him on the beach. The tension between them raged like smoke, and Jake was aware of her more now than before. Her scent still clung to him, the memory of her slick climax riddling his thoughts. He had a perpetual hard-on that wasn't going away without some serious help.

"Can't let it go to waste."

"Are we ever getting off this island, Jake?"

"Yeah, sure, but it will take some time for them to scout the area."

"But I haven't seen a single aircraft or boat."

"I know, but it's only been a day or so."

"Look at me, Jake, and tell me the truth. I can handle it."

He lifted his gaze. "The U.S. will use satellite surveillance and thermo pictographs to locate us. Then send out a chopper off a ship from West Pac. But as to when, I don't know. We drifted, and I doubt they've widened the search yet."

She sighed, pitching the fish bones in a pit he'd dug. She washed her hands and mouth as he spitted the lizard over the fire, and added twigs to the flames.

"This will be done by breakfast."

"Bet it tastes like chicken, right?"

"Hell if I know." He rubbed his jaw, fingers rasping over the beard shadowing his face.

Katherine yawned and stretched, then, without a word, crawled into the shelter, loosening her skirt. A little sizzle skipped over her skin as Jake slipped inside and lay down beside her. They didn't touch, each staring at the black rubber ceiling.

"Why are you pushing me away, Jake?"

He wasn't startled by the question; she asked a lot of them. "We've been over this."

"I'm trying to understand, because right now, I'm feeling very unattractive."

He looked at her, brows up. "You've got to be kidding."

"I practically invite you to have your way with me, and you run for the hills. What would you think?"

"That one of us is being smart."

She laughed to herself. "Or just noble?" She rolled to her side onto her elbow, propping her head in her hand.

Jake mimicked her, his gaze moving smoothly over her body.

"See, when you look at me like that I know what you're thinking."

"You couldn't possibly." Because he wanted to bury his face between her thighs and lick her till she screamed.

"You want me."

He didn't respond. That was pretty obvious.

"But you won't touch me. Not even kiss me."

"Well, considering you haven't brushed your teeth in two days . . ."

She threw a pebble at him. "At least I have breath mints."

His expression grew serious. "I have a job to do, even if we're on this island alone. I still have to make certain we survive."

"I'm still the duty, huh?"

"Yes." *No.*

"You're trying to keep yourself from feeling anything. I think it's because you grew up without enough love."

"What would you know about my past?"

She ignored his sharp tone and said softly, "Only what you tell me."

"It's not pretty. And why do you want details?" *Why did anyone?*

"So I can understand you better."

"I was alone in a crowd, Katherine."

"Me, too."

He gave her a "yeah, sure" look.

"In different ways, I guess, but you had no one touching you, holding you when you were hurt."

"No pain, no gain. I'm over it."

She made a face at him. "Ha, you're afraid to even risk getting hurt."

"Like hell."

Her lips curved. "I didn't insult your manhood. But you don't talk enough."

"Christ, you want me to spill my guts, too?"

"Ahh, so women have pestered you about it."

He gave her a sour glance. "I'm in touch with my *feelings.*"

"You mean you have them?"

"Smart-ass."

"Macho man."

"I like my life just as it is."

Liar, she thought, but knew she wasn't making any

headway. "Well, I don't like mine, and I plan to change it."

"How?"

Her shoulders moved in a halfhearted shrug. "I don't know. But I've had nothing to do out here but examine my life, and I've realized that what I've been doing with it isn't what I wanted, but what was expected of me."

"You don't like brewing chemicals anymore?"

"I'd rather simplify things."

"Nothing is ever simple."

"God, you're such a cynic." She yawned.

He put his hand over her face and pushed. "Yeah, yeah, go to sleep."

She smiled and lay back down, closing her eyes. Jake propped his head on his crossed arms and for a long time, just listened to her even breathing, knowing she was right, but never wanting to admit it aloud. Reality kept creeping in. The right thing was not always the best thing.

"So, Dr. Katherine Collier, what is it that you really want?" he whispered into the dark, knowing she was asleep.

"To belong," she mumbled sleepily.

His heart took a dip just then, stinging him, and without a thought, he scooted close and drew her into his arms. She sighed, patting his hand on her stomach, then sank back into her dreams.

"Yeah—me, too," he said, and kissed her temple.

Jake was on his one-hundredth push-up when he admitted it was just avoidance therapy. It didn't stop him from circumventing the island twice, gathering her special plants, then leaving them outside the shelter before taking off again in a dead run. After fifty pull-ups, he was gasping for breath, and on impulse, dove into the water.

I'm a masochist, he decided, swimming hard up the

shoreline. For two days he'd been avoiding contact with her. For two days they'd spoken only when necessary, and he missed the sound of her voice. Missed her questions, her ability to peel away layers in a conversation and take it in a new direction. He'd lie next to her, listening to her fidget, to her breathing, and want her so badly he could taste it.

He found a couple of disposable toothbrushes in Spooner's gear and gave one to her. All she did was grin and use it. He'd shaved, more because it was routine—and whiskers itched.

Jake stopped swimming and waded out of the water, looking at the sky—hoping for a plane. He wasn't going to last much longer, and when he approached the camp, she was in the water—diving, then doing handstands—playing. In her underwear.

He was used to it. She'd pranced around in what was left of her blouse, then ripped off the torn sleeves. The armholes were so big, he didn't have to imagine any further. Every damn inch of her was branded into his brain.

She swam for a few feet, then left the water, walking to something on the beach. Jake watched as she went back in, and with what looked like a screen stretched over twigs, she plunged it into the water.

"Yes!" she shouted. A crab clung to the screen thing.

She marched to the beach, frowning, twisting it upside down to keep the crab on it, then paused and he knew what she was thinking: what was she going to do with it now?

"We have nothing to cook it in," he said.

She looked up, startled. "I was trying for a more balanced diet." She eyed the crab. "He likes my stockings. But I guess I'll have to set him free."

"Just put it in the water, don't try to—" She shrieked suddenly, trying to shake off the crab latched onto her finger. He hurried to her, snapping off the claw and hurling the creature into the ocean.

She sucked her finger. "You took its claw?"

"It'll grow another."

"Oh." She shrugged and turned back into the water, splashing like it was the best thing in the world. She floated, her breasts breaking the surface.

Jake stared. She splashed him.

"Brat."

She splashed him again.

His eyes narrowed. It was a menacing look. Katherine smiled in the face of it, then dove backwards, and Jake thought she looked like a mermaid speeding through the water. When she came up he was closer to the water, and she swept her hair off her face. Jake's gaze was drawn to her hips, the sleek glide of her thighs. She cupped her hands and shot water at him.

"What do you think you are, a kid?"

"Recapturing my childhood playfulness. I think you, Jacob Mackenzie, forgot how to have fun."

His eyes went liquid dark, scraping over her with answering heat. "Depends on your idea of fun."

"Come show me, then."

"You just want me to sleep with you."

"You've *been* sleeping with me, Jake. I want more than that."

"You've got sex on the mind."

"I've got *you* on the mind. I have a lot of men in my field, but not one of them made me feel . . . *inspired.*"

He arched a brow. She loved it when he did that. He reminded her of a pirate daring her to cross swords with him. Daring her to break him.

And she had just the weapon. She reached behind for the bra clasp, popping it. She let the top slide as she sank underwater. Then she threw it at him.

"Kat."

He could see the outline under the clear water . . . and God help him, it was magnificent.

She fidgeted underwater, then threw the scrap of panties at his feet. She twisted away, diving deeper, the pale flash of her bare behind making Jake grind his teeth.

"This isn't fair."

"All is in love and war."

Jake cursed foully, then splashed into the water, diving toward her and not waiting for her to come up for air. He grasped her arms and dragged her above the surface.

"You're a deadly adversary."

"Never underestimate a woman with a strong mind."

"But when this is over—"

She put her fingers to his lips. "Cross that bridge later, Marine."

"You make me insane, Kat."

"Mutual."

"No, I don't think you realize."

"Are you saying it could get a little . . . raw?"

"Oh, yeah." He didn't know if it would be enough, get him close enough to her, deep enough inside her. She was like a virus eating him from the inside out. He wanted this woman so bad he could taste nothing else but his untamed need.

"Yippee," she said softly, and inched closer till the cool tips of her breasts touched his chest. "Kiss me first."

His expression went hard with desire, his gaze ripping over her face so intently she felt the sting. He bent a little, pulling her flush against him, moaning darkly as his mouth brushed hers, once, twice, lightly.

Kat thought she'd split apart. "Jake." His name said *now, more, please.*

"Give me a second." He licked the line of her lower lip. "I feel like I've waited a century for this."

Katherine's heart jolted.

Then he pressed his mouth more firmly to hers and kissed her.

Really kissed.

An eating kiss.

Uncapped. Ravishing. Yeah, that was it, she thought, her head going light, her feet leaving the soft, sandy bottom as he pulled her more tightly against him. Her hands swept up around his neck, her contours meshing with his, soft against the hard steel of his body.

And oh, it was hard, she thought, plunging her tongue between his lips and battling with his. He left nothing untouched, no corner of her mouth untasted, and still she wanted more. Wanted to feel him sliding into her, the hot pressure of him.

As if sensing her, Jake drew back, staring into her soft, dreamy eyes. "No turning back, Kat."

He seemed to be waiting, offering a chance to back out. She smiled into his troubled gaze, sweeping her fingers down the side of his jaw, loving that he turned his face into her touch.

"I never thought there was."

He swept her into his arms, carrying her out of the water to the camp. He lowered her slowly, his gaze taking in every inch of her as he pulled the string from her hair and let it flow damply over her shoulders. She looked down, shyly, and Jake was moved that the past days hadn't stolen that from her.

He cupped her face, forcing her to meet his gaze. "No reservations."

She had a feeling that sex wasn't a casual thing with him. "If I had any, I wouldn't have stripped for you."

He smiled devilishly. "Just checking."

She wasn't going to ask why he was so apprehensive. She already knew. Big, tough Jake Mackenzie was afraid, just as she was, that this would turn the tables in a whole new direction and neither of them was sure if they wanted to follow.

Kate stepped closer, grasping the band of his boxers. His eyes flared. She slid her fingers round the edge, then beneath, pushing them down, baring him.

"Get these off."

They were gone, kicked aside, and she lowered her gaze. His erection was thick and dominant, a hard spear between them. She did something she never had and wrapped her fingers around him.

Jake was on her in a heartbeat, his kiss devouring, his hands cupping her behind and pulling her to him. He pried her fingers free, his mouth traveling over her throat, and lower, till the rosy tip of her breast slipped easily into his mouth, where it belonged. She cried out, tipping her head back, and Jake laved at the salty taste of her skin, wanting to draw her in deeply. The sun shone on her body, still glistening with water droplets, and he cupped her breasts, sucking, pulling, and she told him how good he made her feel.

How hot she was for him.

He backed her against a palm tree, the wind-bent curve laying her out like a pagan offering. Jake struggled to savor the moment, but his body was screaming at him. He slid his tongue over her breasts, massaging them, then moved lower.

She held his head, feeling his mouth on her body, as if wanting as much of the sensation as they could give and get. "Jake, please."

"Not yet." His mouth mapped her flat belly, the slide of her hip, the concave juncture as he slipped his hand between her thighs, nudging them apart. "I'll come in a heartbeat."

"But Jake, I want that with you."

"Believe me, you will." He dropped to his knees, peeling her open, and when his mouth covered her softness, she let out a little startled shriek.

He licked and dove, stroking her intimately, then slid a finger inside, moving in and out at a leisurely pace. A flood of rich moisture answered him, slick and hot, and when Jake's touch sluiced over the bead of her sex, she bowed, and lifted her knee to get closer. He pulled it over his shoulder, devouring her soft, velvety folds and thrusting his fingers deeper. Each touch was a knife to her control, sensations clawing at her skin, narrowing to the cleft between her thighs. She felt her climax roar through her, cupped his head as she thrust against him. She cried out his name.

Jake kept teasing, kept tasting, wanted her spent for the next round. He was hard enough to do damage to himself if he didn't find release, but something in him told him that Katherine had never been properly loved. It angered him, and made him patient when he wanted to be pushing into her and pounding till his own agony was gone.

Her breath came in short, quick gasps, and she pushed his head back. "No one's ever done that to me."

"Glad it was me, then."

She smiled, utterly content, and Jake rose, giving her a full look at what she did to him.

"Can I do that to you?"

The thought of it nearly undid him. "You can do anything you want, Kat. Just not that, not now."

"Oh, come on." She reached for him.

Like a striking snake, he caught her wrist.

Katherine smiled softly, cat-like, moving in, making Jake feel as if he'd just lost control. "I want to taste you," she said with an unfamiliar boldness. "I want to lick you all over."

Jake gritted his teeth. Just hearing that turned him inside out. He reached for the LBV and pulled out a handful of condoms. "I have about thirty of these." He tossed them to her.

She caught one, tearing it open, moving toward him as if stalking a prey. "Come on, Marine." She ducked into the shelter.

Jake's gaze latched on to her round behind and followed her, sliding down beside her. Instantly she reached for him, cupping his erection and rolling on top of him. She spread her thighs, rising up, her hands on his erection, working him into madness.

"Kate, Jesus, put it on."

"Not yet." She shifted, sliding wetly along his length. He gripped her hips, grinding her to him, and Kate slipped on the condom, rolling it down to the base and squeezing.

"Baby, you're making me so nuts I'll hurt you."

She held him in her hands, rising up just a bit and guiding him inside her. The tip of him met white-hot heat. She leaned forward, her hands braced beside his head.

"Look at me," he said. She did, and he grasped her hips, pushing her down. The slick, hot slide of her nearly did him in.

The pressure of him ached with fullness and she knew this is where she fit—not just sex, but with Jake. She stared at him, his features strained yet tender, and she rocked, biting her lower lip.

Jake whispered, "Talk, scream, anything—no one will hear you but me."

She let out a long, pleasure-racked sigh. "You feel so good, Jacob. So big."

He smiled. "Thank you, ma'am."

She met him, urging him. "More Jake, more."

He rolled her to her back, leaving her completely then plunging in long, hard thrusts.

"Yes, like that. Oh, Jake." She wrapped her legs around his hips, drawing him back. "I can feel you pulsing inside me. You're rubbing all the right spots."

He shouldn't have told her to talk. Braced over her, staring into her eyes, he thrust harder, his hips pistoning.

Her delicate muscles squeezed him in a wet, velvety glove, locking him in a vise of pleasure. "Kat, oh God." The roar of passion pawed, threatened.

She touched his face. "Show me how it can be." He reached between, but she stopped him, lacing her hands with his. "Just you."

Braced over her, he pumped into her, his gaze never leaving hers, loving that she didn't shy away, that she was bold and jungle-raw for him. She spread wider, bracing her feet, pushing as he did. She strained, called out his name.

He felt the rapid grasp of her body around his and he thrust, and thrust, the pulse of her pleasure dragging him into a dark chasm of desire. He growled low and shoved. She grabbed him to her, digging her heels into his hips and riding against him like a wild colt. It seemed to go on forever, a hard, unceasing rage of passion. Then they strained, suspended. She felt fused to him, her skin raw, her blood savaging wildly through her veins.

The crest broke like a wave, washing over them, and they clung, shattering together in a mindless tumble of passion.

"Oh Jake," she breathed. Nothing in her life compared to that final moment.

He lifted his head, breathing hard as he smoothed her hair back and stared into green eyes. "Yeah." He swallowed, more than physically drained. "I know."

Seven

Jake kissed her awake, smoothing his hands up her hip to her breasts. He wanted her again. And again.

She smiled sleepily. "I'm hungry."

He chuckled to himself. "Same here."

She opened her eyes, and knew he didn't mean food as she ran her finger over his jaw, across his lip. She kissed him, flinging her leg over his hip. "I really *am* hungry."

"Coconut?"

"God, no."

He laughed and shifted out of the shelter, pulling her with him. He took off into the woods, she in the other direction. But when he returned, wearing boxers, she was pouring water over her body. The sun had set, moonlight coating her as water slid down her skin. Jake's mouth went dry and he wondered if he was salivating. She pulled on her tattered blouse, then sat on a hunk of fallen palm tree and tore off a piece of the lizard, tasting it.

"It really does taste like chicken," she said, holding out a piece. He took it, chewing, staring. She tilted her head to the side, smiling. "I think my bra and panties went out to sea."

"Oh Christ." He jogged down to the beach. She heard

him splashing in the water; then he returned, holding the items on one finger.

"My hero." She tossed them aside.

He arched a brow.

"Why bother?" She shrugged.

"Because if you prance around like that, I won't be held accountable for my actions."

"And this is a bad thing?"

Chuckling, he sat on the fallen tree, then straddled it, sharing lizard and what was left of his MREs. "That was your first orgasm with a man, wasn't it?"

She flushed, embarrassed, especially at her age. "Yes. Sad, isn't it?"

"You just had men who didn't care enough."

"Do you care, Jake?"

"I wouldn't have made love to you if I didn't, Kat."

"Are you saying you care about all the women you sleep with?"

"No, yes, well. Why are we discussing this?"

"You brought it up." His past conquests made him uncomfortable and she couldn't resist teasing him. "I want to know." She faced him more fully. "Are you a slut with women or not?"

"No. They throw themselves at me."

She understood that. "So did I."

He shook his head. "You were shaking in your boots when you first got here."

"True, you can be a bit terrifying when you want to be." She laid her hand on his tanned thigh. "But then, I know the softer side."

"Do you?"

He looked insulted. She grinned. Her hand slid higher, molding his erection. It was amazing to feel him grow harder in her hand. He slammed his eyes shut, going incredibly still.

"Katherine."

She inched closer, sliding her hand inside the boxers and closing over him. "Yes." She squeezed, stroking him, watching his face contort with strain. Then she bent and took him into her mouth.

He cursed, his breath staggering. "Kat, jeez. Katherine!"

She didn't stop, making it impossible for him, tasting him till he trembled, till he gripped her shoulders and pushed her back. "You trying to kill me?"

She rose up, a condom in her hand. "Well, we do have thirty of these."

Straddling his thighs, she rolled it down. He grabbed her to him, probing her, and in a heartbeat, he was inside her, his broad hands on her hips, grinding her to him.

She leaned back, forcing him deeper. Jake smoothed his hand over her face, down her lush body. He toyed with her, loving the little tucks of her hips, the way she arched when pleasure struck her hard.

He rocked her on him, and she rose up, her arms around his neck.

The fire glowed a few feet away, coating them in yellow light.

Jake mapped her contours, the luxurious shape of her breasts, her waist. She was so frail in his hands, soft, and made him feel stronger. God, he loved being a man.

Katherine slid wetly on his thick heat. She needed to love this man like he'd never been loved. He'd had so little in his life, then chose a career of total uniformity. She wanted to be possessed and possess in return.

"Oh God, Kat."

She was incredibly tight. Jake gripped her hips and plunged, the heat of her trapping him, pushing him to the brink quickly. She spoke softly, erotically, telling him things that his ego didn't need, but he loved it just the same.

"Jacob," she said on a breathy sound. He plowed his fingers into her hair. Holding her gaze, holding her heart in his palms.

"I need to see your face."

She pressed her forehead to his, their soft motions like a living pulse between them. Her limbs seemed liquid, fluid, his body in command of hers. He thrust and she captured, stole everything from him when she touched him. He didn't want to think of the moment when she wouldn't be in his life, in his world. He clutched her, wrapping her legs around him. Her arms threaded around his neck as they rocked and danced.

Hard strength meshed with feminine softness.

Steel muscle rippled to capture her with a fierceness that defied reason.

He'd never been greedy, never hungered for what he had no right to, but Katherine, he claimed. Katherine, he adored.

He gazed into green eyes, so luminous, and felt the sheer power of their loving. Her eyes teared, her heart in them, and Jake kissed her, feeling her climax tear through him, wrap him. Trap his soul.

He sank willingly.

He groaned as he spilled his pleasure and gripped her to him. Sweat glistened and still they clung. Like hope grasping for anything before dying.

Jake knew, without her, he would.

They were quiet, each deep in faraway thoughts. Then, as if a thick, hard shell cracked, he started talking, and Katherine listened as the words spilled, laced with old memory. He remembered his parents, what they looked like, but the picture had faded over the years. He knew his mother's scent, the tone of her voice. How he'd played in his backyard, and laughed; then he told her of the orphanage, the cold, imperialistic routine, the punishments and prayers.

Her heart broke for him; she could hear the loneliness in his tone. Though he was surrounded by people, he, too, had felt alone. Then he spoke of his friends, their families, the Marine Corps and his tours of duty. He'd been in a war zone at least four times, and yes, he had nightmares sometimes, but not for long. On the thermal liner, Katherine snuggled against his chest, listening as his tone changed, when it ached as he spoke of losing some of his men, of moments he dismissed when she thought they were heroic.

His arms wrapped her more tightly, and she shifted so his head was on her chest, and she cradled the strong man, wanting so badly to love him if he'd let her. When he asked her about herself, Katherine spoke, telling him things she'd never mentioned to another soul—that she loved her sister and brother, but they thought of her as a gifted geek who had to be sheltered, and for a while she'd let them. She told him of lovers, of the hurt they inflicted without realizing it. And Jake suddenly understood that her intelligence had made her such an outcast that she never sought to change it. Didn't think she deserved it. Till now.

He rolled over, taking her with him, laying her across his body like a warm, supple blanket. His hand smoothed her naked spine in gentle motions. Then he knew, without a doubt, he'd lost what he'd guarded most of his life.

And for the first time in years, he ached.

They played like children. Jake hadn't laughed so hard in his life, hadn't smiled so much. He felt silly and stupid as he chased her down the shore, snatched her around the waist, and dragged her into his embrace.

"Jesus, Kat."

"Well, it's true, right?"

"I wouldn't know."

"But you're a man—men know if they want a three-some."

He scowled. "This one does not."

"Ooh, you're looking very territorial."

"Right now, I am."

She grinned. "Me, too, but there is the 'more boobs' thing you guys seem to be fascinated with."

"Two are plenty." He cupped hers through the thin shirt.

She moved into him, tipping her head back. "Kiss me."

"You don't have to ask."

"Hey, I had to ask you to make love to me, so I'm thinking you're slow."

"Slow? You're the one who keeps falling in the garbage pit."

"Then mark it."

"Look where you're going."

"I have no sense of direction, you know that." They walked, not touching but wanting to. "Teach me about the Marines."

"Big order."

She looked around. "And do we have somewhere to go right now?"

"Okay, then you can teach me how to concoct, say . . ."

"Explosives?"

"Already know that."

Figures. "How about from household stuff anyone has in their kitchen?"

He shivered. "Remind me never to piss you off." Since she seemed truly interested, he told her about the Marines, boot camp, his training, and they walked on the beach, sometimes holding onto each other, sometimes far apart and perfectly content.

Contentment. That was something Jake had never felt.

Kate was thinking the same thing. She didn't want to be

found, not yet at least. She watched him scoop up a shell, pitch it into the water. This was simplifying things, she thought. His life wasn't simple. Hers wasn't either, but she was going to change that. She'd made the choice days ago, and out here, it just grew stronger.

Some of that was up to Jake. She wouldn't ask anything of him, not now. But when he caught her gaze, flashed her that sexy smile that made her see the man he truly was, she knew—she was falling in love with him.

A storm came—not like the night of the rescue, but with enough wind and lightning to force Jake and Katherine into the shelter at night. They made good use of the darkness, loving each other till they were exhausted.

Jake was sleeping in her arms when he heard a faint sound. He sat up, listening, and Katherine woke. "What?"

"Listen."

Her eyes widened. "Is that a—"

"—a chopper."

He rushed out of the shelter, grabbing up the flash grenade, pulling the pin, and throwing. It exploded in midair, and he hurried to the pile of wood and tried to light it. "Dammit, it won't light."

Katherine ran for her bag, pulling out the bottle of perfume, then returned to him, kneeling as he struck the match, igniting the coconut fiber. She poured the perfume on the flames and it blazed fast and hot. Smoke curled. The chopper turned toward them, and they stood on the beach, watching it draw closer.

"I almost don't want them to come."

He grasped her hand, kissing her knuckles. He understood that. This island was a private haven, and he didn't really want to head back into the real world, either.

Rain poured down, turning the bonfire to white smoke; Jake was afraid they wouldn't be seen. But thermal imaging would pick it up. The chopper rocked, signaling they'd spotted them. The wind roared across the island, kicking up huge waves and sand. A bundled package on a small parachute dropped on the beach. Jake opened it, turning on the radio.

"Delta One, this is Rescue Angel. Glad to see you're alive, Gunny."

"Glad to see you guys." He asked about his men and smiled when he learned they'd all survived without injury.

"We're a flying gas can, Gunny," came over the radio with static. "We have just enough fuel to get back to the carrier. Dropping clothes and food, and will pick you up in the morning when the ship is closer."

"Roger that, Angel."

Jake had suspected that the instant he'd seen the chopper and no ship in sight. A package fell to the beach, and Katherine went to it, dragging it toward the camp.

Jake waved the chopper off, then went to her, lifting the package into the shelter. She didn't ask why they weren't taking them back now. She'd heard.

"So we have one day?"

His gaze snapped to hers. One day alone. One day before they had to face the world and be torn apart.

As if sensing his thoughts, she smiled. Prying open the pack, she said, "Then I guess we should make the most of it. Hmm, pudding—wonder what we could do with that?"

"Eat it."

"I was thinking of something a little more creative."

Jake blinked, a little shocked as she unbuttoned her blouse, slipping the rag off, then her bra. She was getting tanned, he noticed, as she spread chocolate pudding on her body. She leaned back in the sexiest pose and said, "Dessert?"

Jake grinned, strode close, dropped to his knees, and started licking the chocolate. "I always loved dessert before dinner."

She moaned as his lips wrapped around her nipple. He

feasted on her, making her climax twice before he slipped into her body. They were raw and savage, outrageously erotic. Both capturing what would be gone in the morning.

At dawn, Jake stood on the beach as the rescue chopper landed on the shore, then helped Katherine into the jump seat. He threw in their gear, then climbed in beside her.

Men smiled at him, the rescue pilot grinning. "We took you two for dead."

"Maybe if I was with a sailor," Katherine said, smiling at Jake. "But not a Marine."

The Marines in the chopper muttered an ooh-rah, and Jake squeezed her hand as the chopper rose and headed to the ship. Their arrival caused an uproar, nearly the entire crew cheering as they stepped off the chopper.

Katherine smiled and waved, greeting the captain, making jokes, but wanting Jake by her side. It was almost overwhelming, the attention making her light-headed, but when Jake's hand pressed to the small of her back, she felt a wave of comfort and the tension eased.

Katherine was ushered by an embassy official and a CIA agent. Jake was ordered to report in two hours to his commanding officer. He looked over his shoulder as they dragged her in the other direction. She looked scared, and he stopped, moving toward her. The CIA agent had ahold of her and Jake pried him off.

He glared. "Listen, Marine—"

"No, you listen. She's not used to this—you're scaring her. Give us a minute."

Jake pulled her aside, away from the onlookers, and there were plenty. Few women were on board the carrier, none looking like Katherine, wearing a short, tattered skirt and his camouflage shirt.

She met his gaze, so much hope and uncertainty there that Jake felt stabbed by it.

"Will I see you later?"

"No."

"What?"

"This is it, Katherine. We part here."

She frowned, confused. "Why are you being like this?"

Jake had thought about this, planned his words, but when they came, he felt almost ashamed of them. "Look, I was a little excitement for you, Doc. We're too different for this to go further."

"Further than practically devouring each other?"

"Yeah. My life isn't nine to five. Yours is. Beyond sex, what do we have in common?"

She couldn't say. Did they have to have anything in common to love? Didn't opposites attract? "So I was convenient and willing."

He hated how that sounded. "It was mutual."

"That was with the Jake I knew on the island. Not the one I'm seeing now."

"This is me."

"No, it's not. It's the man who is too ready to face death for his country, but scared out of his mind to risk his heart for me." Her voice broke, and it slayed him.

"Kat, my heart was never in this."

"Liar."

His brows shot up. "My life is like this. I won't give it up."

"I didn't ask you to."

"And I won't ask you to give up all you've worked for."

"Isn't that my choice?" When he said nothing, she snapped, "You are the most pigheaded, asinine man I have ever met."

"I imagine so."

"And a moron! You don't get it, do you, Jacob? I lo—"

"Ma'am, we need to go," the officer interrupted.

"Wait a minute!" she snapped, then looked back at Jake. His expression, so stoic and void of emotion, warned

Katherine that there was no use talking to him now. But that didn't stop her heart from shattering, each piece falling away to melt into the emptiness she'd lived in for years. Her eyes burned with tears, and she looked up at him and in a dead voice said, "Thanks for keeping me alive, Gunny, and making me *feel* alive." The CIA officer grasped her elbow, guiding her toward the hatch.

Jake stood there as the officer led her away, almost dragging her. From him, from his life. He couldn't ask her to be a part of it. But as the hatch closed behind her, Jake knew he'd just let the best thing to ever happen to him walk out of his life.

Sergeant Cook walked up beside him. "And here I thought you were the smartest man I knew, Gunny."

Jake snapped a look at Cook, scowling.

"Apparently not," the sergeant said, shrugging as he walked away.

Eight

Marine Corps Air Station
Cherry Point, NC

The aircraft touched down, and inside, the cheer was deafening.

A couple of hundred Marines were eager to disembark, but Jake dreaded this part. The end of the deployment, the trip home, and landing on the Cherry Point Airfield to the trumpets of the Marine Band. And the scores of family, wives, girlfriends, and children littering the flight deck, impatient for a first glimpse of their Marine.

All Jake saw was the drive home to an empty house and probably some dead plants.

The image of Katherine had plagued him through the mission, threatening his concentration. All he could see was the hurt so vivid in her eyes, hear the venomous words she'd thrown at him. She'd been right. He was scared. He had so little in his life outside the Corps, but it was moments like this that he felt like the kid in the orphanage, wishing for more and knowing he'd never get it.

Though Jake had always been greeted by his fellow Marines' families like he was a part of theirs, he never was. He was an outsider, alone, and as he stepped off the hydraulic tongue of the C-130, he never felt more isolated than at this moment.

Man, you royally screwed up a good thing this time, Mackenzie.

The noise on the flight deck pumped with energy in true Marine fashion: music, joyful screams, and cheers. He walked alongside his teams, each spying their wives or girlfriends.

"Anna's lost weight," Spooner said.

"Well, my wife gained some."

Jake spotted Cook's wife. She was three months pregnant when they left; now she looked ready to deliver their firstborn on the flight deck. Grinning, Cook hurried toward his wife, the two other single men following alongside him. The young Marines searched the crowds for familiar faces. Jake didn't bother. The one he wanted to see wouldn't be there. And it was his fault. All his.

"Who's that?"

Jake didn't pay attention; some young Marine always had a new babe waiting for him, ready to welcome the warrior home properly.

"Man, would you look at that hair."

"Forget that, check out the body in pink."

Jake looked up, his gaze slipping over the crowd. He stopped dead in his tracks and just stared.

Surrounded by Marine wives and families, Katherine stood out in the flowery pink dress, her hair blowing wildly under the straw hat that made her look more delicate, more lovely. She took his breath away.

The instant her gaze met his, Jake knew without a doubt that his world had just tilted right.

"If she's here," a Marine said, "then she belongs to someone."

Something locked up inside him as Jake said, "Yeah. To me," and without taking his eyes off her, he started walking faster.

* * *

Katherine stood beside a very pregnant Linda Cook, watching Jake come near, her heart pounding. He looked tired and wary. *I'm risking everything for him, everything.* She almost turned to run, to go back to her well-ordered, very boring life. But she couldn't. She knew the instant that Jake touched her that her future was right here.

She hoped he was going to smarten up and see that.

Nearby, Cook grabbed up his wife, kissed her passionately, then looked at her. His eyes went wide. "Doctor Collier?"

She smiled. "Hello, David."

"You're the Katherine Linda's been writing me about?"

She nodded, winking at Linda. They'd met a couple of months ago, and Linda had been gracious enough to introduce her into the Marine life. Katherine considered it her greatest challenge and admired the women who stood by these men. "Welcome home, Marine."

"Thanks for watching out for her, but does the Gunny know—?"

Katherine followed Cook's gaze and turned. Jake was inches from her, his gear on his shoulder.

"What are you doing here?" he asked. He realized that he hadn't drawn a decent breath till this moment.

"Isn't it obvious?"

"No, it's not." Jake's heart skipped a beat as she stepped near, her hand slipping behind his neck to pull him down for a kiss. Passion flowed, wrapped them warmly, and Jake dropped his gear, pulling her into his arms.

Katherine knew she'd just arrived exactly where she belonged. Jake needed her as much as she needed him. This man fought for freedom, yet no one had fought for him. No one had ventured beyond the rough exterior to understand how alone he was in the crowd. He wouldn't let them. Protecting himself, but isolating his heart. Trapped on the island with him, she'd seen it, the gentler side, the part of him aching to be a part of something that was bigger than the Marine Corps.

She wanted the chance to love him, and she'd follow him anywhere to do it.

"I missed you, Jacob." Tears caught in her throat, her voice cracking.

"Katherine, honey—" Jake started.

"Welcome home, Gunny," Fletcher's wife said. "Katherine, I'll catch you later at next week's meeting."

She nodded, still holding onto Jake.

"Hey, Miss Collier."

Jake gaped as a teenage boy raced past them, waving and smiling. *"Miss* Collier?" He looked around for someone to explain.

"Katherine's the new high school chemistry teacher," Linda Cook said.

He looked down at Kat. "You've been busy."

"Well, you know I'm an overachiever."

He smiled for the first time.

"I've been waiting for you to come home. To me."

Home. God help him, it was the brass ring he wanted to catch, to grasp and never let go. He swallowed hard, taking a step into the unknown. "Katherine, this is not an easy life. You're alone a lot."

"I was completely alone before, Jake. I think I can handle it."

As people spoke to her, saying hello, wishing them well, Jake stared down at her. "What did you do?" He didn't really have to ask. She'd already given up her life to be here, a part of his life.

She touched the side of his face, her expression so tender and loving that the world around them tumbled away. "I fell in love with you, Jacob."

"Oh Jesus, Kat." He swallowed hard, his throat raw and tight.

She rubbed his lower lip. "I love you, Jacob Mackenzie."

"I love you, too. It took me a while—"

"That's because you're a moron."

He grinned, crushing her to him, burying his face in her throat. "Yeah, I know. I lied to you. My heart was in this from the start."

"I know, Jake, I know *you*." Most women would wait for the man to come after her. Katherine wasn't that patient and she understood Jake. After all he'd achieved, he still felt he was undeserving—silly man—but all she had to do was prove to him that he was.

"Yeah, you do." Jake felt a heavy weight lifting off him just then. "God, I missed you." He ground kisses up her throat to her mouth.

"Me, too," she said against his lips, then drew back enough to look him in the eye. "This is where *we* belong."

Jake choked, staring into her soft eyes, his love for her so shining and strong that people stood back and smiled. "Marry me."

She blinked.

"Marry me, Kat, let me love you forever."

"Ar—are you sure?"

"I might be a moron, but I'm smart enough to recognize a gift when I see it."

Her smile sent tears tumbling down her cheeks. "Yes. I will." She tightened her arms around his neck, rising up on her toes to kiss him. "*Forever* sounds good to me."

She heard a soft ooh-rah from him, unaware of the audience witnessing their love blooming before their eyes. But Jake didn't care. His world was in his arms, and a new life awaited both of them.

For once in his career, he was glad the mission had gone bad.

Hot Target

One

0600 hours
South America

Cradling his MP5 assault rifle, Gunnery Sergeant Rick Cahill dangled one foot out the open door of the attack chopper. Warm wind buffeted his face as the lush green terrain of the Venezuelan border passed swiftly beneath him. Farther inside, his teammates littered the chopper, a couple catching an extra five minutes of sleep despite the noise.

"Command on the wire, Gunny." The copilot handed Rick the headset.

Probably going to scrap the training operation, Rick groused as he slipped on the set and adjusted the mike at his mouth. "Bravo One to base."

"Base to Bravo One. Operation Drop Cloth aborted. New orders."

"Roger that, sir." His team was instantly awake and watching him.

"Call sign 'White Knight.' This is not a drill. I repeat, not a drill. Live extraction."

A package?

The officer gave the coordinates for the pickup. "Bravo

One, LZ three miles north of Delta 10, and retrieve American Sam Previn, Peace Corps."

Rick didn't question what the hell a Peace Corps volunteer was doing in the middle of the Amazon regions and why they were snatching the man out. Orders were orders. Delta 10 was the intelligence name for a village, nothing more than a cleared plot of land with a handful of huts.

Rick punched the coordinates into the GPS computer. The terrain displayed the village where Sam Previn was located and the route they'd take in. "Sir, that's Burn Out territory."

The Colombian government and DEA knew the drug cartels were cooking heroin and cocaine underground. Instead of ferreting out each lab, Operation Burn Out would sweep the area like a plague.

If it breathed, it would die.

If it was illegal, it would be blown to hell.

In four hours. Not much time. And that was hotfooting it double time. Going to be tight, and a combat zone.

"Affirmative, Bravo One. Essential that you get package out before the sweep. Package is unaware."

"Roger that, sir. Rules of engagement, come back?" No one wanted to drop into a hot zone and be forced into politically correct fighting.

"Do what you have to, Gunny. It's your game. Base out."

Handing back the headset, Rick relayed the plan to the pilot. The Attack Huey chopper, armed with M-240 Gulf machine guns, would come back for them in under four hours, but couldn't risk hanging around. Drug cookers had armed sentries who'd opened fire on anything that moved. Especially a U.S. Marine helicopter.

He looked at his team. "Ready to jump out of a perfectly good chopper and hump through the jungle?"

Four men smiled behind the green-and-black camo paint as the chopper tipped, heading away from the border and deep into the Colombian jungle.

* * *

Locked and loaded, each man positioned himself on the edge of the chopper door frame, a nylon rope wrapped around his fist and left leg.

With a machine-gunner manning the 240 Gulf, the chopper lowered, and when it reached a reasonable distance, the Bravo One Recon team pushed off like spiders down a web. They hit the ground running, MP5 assault rifles poised for anything that moved. They headed to the treeline, melting into the forest as the chopper tipped and flew off toward the horizon.

Cahill's team dropped low and scanned for the enemy. Drug cookers had enough illegal firepower to outfit a battalion. And this was their playground.

Nothing like running through hostile territory to get the blood rushing in the morning, he thought. Rick led the way, fast and silent, heading west without radio contact, using only the earpiece and the throat mike on a Velcro strap pressed against their voice box.

The sun barely reached the jungle floor, yet the heat was oppressive, the shriek of birds and slither of reptiles the only sound. Moisture misted the air, a liquid curtain suspended and dripping. They'd covered the three miles at a hard run before Rick put up his fist and the team stopped. He made a circular motion and pointed. They spread out, heading up a slight hill. Positioned behind the rise, Rick dug out his binoculars and sighted in on the small village.

"Christ, it's the fucking dark ages."

Grass huts and wandering goats and chickens. Children were carrying buckets from a low-slung well. Dark-skinned women moved around with baskets on their heads or stood around talking. The only thing remotely modern was a metal box outside the door of a hut. No sign of Sam Previn. Few men. No weapons.

"Donahue and Kane, circle west, check for booby traps, unfriendlies. Parks, Kramer, east and north. Clear the west huts first. This village was reported as noncombative. Don't take chances." Marines moved slowly. Rick took point, slipping over the rise, then onto the dirt road. Hugging the treeline, he rotated in a half-circle, his gaze flicking over the jungle beyond the village. He caught a glimpse of his buddies before they melted into the dark again.

"Anything?"

"Negative, nothing but dung and garbage piles. Christ, this makes me love American garbage men."

From his position, Rick saw his men emerge from the jungle and inch along the side of the four huts, peer in, then move to the next. "Bravo Three, clear. Bravo Two, clear," came through the tiny earpiece. He waited for the last man to report, then walked into the village.

A woman saw him, screamed, and dropped a clay pot. It shattered, water instantly absorbed into the ground. Children scattered, women ran. The few men that were there shielded children. Then a shapely figure in khaki shorts rushed out of the forest to his right, pausing to keep a villager from running into the trees. Rick swung his rifle in her direction. She wasn't the least bit intimidated and walked right toward him.

Rifle aimed, Rick moved forward, his men coming in from all sides, half the weapons aimed on the treeline.

"Sweet," Kramer muttered.

"Haven't seen a body that hot since Caracas," Donahue added.

"Pipe down!" Rick snapped, then looked at the woman. "U.S. Marines, ma'am."

"I can see that. What the hell are you doing here?" she demanded. "You're scaring these people." She paused to shout at the villagers in rapid Spanish. They stilled, staying where they were.

"We're here for Sam Previn."

From under an olive green baseball cap, her brown eyes narrowed. "Why? What for?"

"That's not your concern, ma'am."

"It is in this village. And put those guns down!"

The Marines didn't move, rifles sighted from the shoulder.

"Who sent you?"

Cahill ignored her and inclined his head to the men. They fanned out to search the remaining huts. She tried to stop them, rushing after Donahue, but Rick caught her arm, yanking her back.

"I'd advise you to stay right here, ma'am."

Pretty eyes turned lethal. "Let go of me."

"Then don't piss me off."

She glanced around at the frightened villagers, then said, "Fine." He let her go. A second later, she rounded on him.

Cahill didn't give her a chance to open up—he was in her face. "*You're* Sam Previn."

"Yes, I am."

"Shit." Rick immediately informed his team. They didn't stop, but he heard the groans. Getting a man out was one thing; a woman, especially one who was untrained, would be like baby-sitting a time bomb complete with a panic button.

"Get your passport." He'd no description to verify her identity.

She looked him over like he was a bug she wanted to squash, then headed to the hut with the metal box. Cahill was right on her heels. She glanced back briefly, then brushed a curtain aside and stepped into the darkness. She went to a neat pile of clothing, slipped out the blue booklet, then handed it to him. He stood in what served as the doorway and inspected the passport.

Then he pocketed it.

"Hey! Give that back!"

"Miss Samantha Previn, I'm Gunnery Sergeant Richard Cahill, Marine Force Recon. I have orders to bring you home." He kept his attention on the land outside the door, moving only enough to grab a backpack and toss it at her. "Grab some gear—we leave in five."

"I can't leave these people now."

Only his gaze shifted. "What are you, a missionary, a doctor?"

"I'm a nurse. I'm inoculating everyone in this region."

"Have you inoculated this village?"

"Yes, of course."

"Then you're done." Rick pressed his throat mike. "Bravo Two, recon our path out and report back." He looked at her. "Move it or I take you as you are."

"I'm not leaving, Marine. Just tell them you didn't find me."

His glare was deadly. "*Oh hell, no.*"

"You can't force me."

"Yes, ma'am, I can." He checked his watch. "I have under two hours to get you to the RP."

"RP?"

"Rendezvous point. If we don't get on that chopper, we're going to be caught in a joint government sweep of the jungle."

"For drug factories."

He arched a brow.

"I've been here for months—I know what goes on around me."

"Then you know we'll be in deep shit if we don't get moving." He inclined his head to the doorway. "*Now.*"

Grousing to herself, she grabbed her backpack, stuffed in clothes, a small medical bag, and a couple of personal items.

"That's enough—you won't need it." He grasped her arm firmly, pulling her out of the hut.

She twisted. "You know, Gunny, I've understood English since I was one. Try speaking, or perhaps you could manage a grunt?"

He looked her dead in the eyes. "Two hours, fire sweep, combat zone. One chance. That clear enough?"

"Perfectly. But what about the villagers? I don't want to leave them."

"They'll head into the hills, and you don't have a choice." His team was already in the forest.

Outside, the villagers rushed her, the air peppered with Spanish. They were worried about her—he understood that. But he had orders and no time left. In a loud, clear voice, he told the people to head east till it was safe. Some just stared, some grabbed baskets and chickens and children, fleeing.

"Bravo One, we've got activity."

Rick scowled, pressing the earpiece, and took a couple of steps away. "Say again."

"Movement, five hundred yards west. Looks like Colombian regulars."

Shit. Time was up. "Roger that. Recon for their ETA, but do not engage."

He looked at the woman, gesturing for her to come to him. Previn gave him a rebellious "make me" look. Any other time it might be intriguing, but she was really pissing him off. He muscled his way between her and the villagers. "I'm not putting my men in danger because you're having a do-gooder tantrum!" Without missing a beat, he bent and wrapped an arm around her legs, then hefted her up onto his left shoulder.

She choked, "Barbarian!"

"Close. U.S. Marine."

She squeaked when he shoved his hand between her thighs, gripped his camouflage uniform shirt for security, and, with the machine gun braced under his right arm, went from a walk to double time into the forest. He didn't stop till she begged for mercy.

"Okay, okay! I give up. Put me down. I can't breathe!"

"My pleasure." He dumped her on her ass.

She glared at him from the ground, stuffing deep red hair back into the ball cap. It didn't all fit.

"Are you always this much of an asshole?" she snapped.

"If the occasion warrants." He yanked her to her feet. They were nose to nose. For a split second he noticed how pretty she was, and that she wasn't wearing a bit of makeup. "You going to quit being a pain in my ass and co-operate?"

"Yes."

"Outstanding." He forced her around and pushed.

She stumbled, glared back at him, then started running.

His gaze lingered over her. Nice, he thought, then focused on the terrain, his finger on the trigger of his MP5 assault rifle.

Samantha was breathless by the time they stopped for a water break—for her benefit. After two miles at a hard run, the Marines didn't look the least bit winded despite the heat.

Samantha felt like melting into the ground and becoming compost.

Gunny Cahill handed her a water bottle, and when she sat on a log, he pulled her down to the ground.

"Stay low, be on the lookout for snakes," he said, then squatted a few feet away and took out a map.

She glanced around at the ground. Cahill nudged her, then pointed upward to the tree limbs hanging over her head. She inched closer to him. After all, he had the weapons. Hell, he was armed to the teeth, and beneath the black-and-green face paint there was no mistaking he was a good-looking man. And big. You could land an aircraft on those shoulders.

She glanced at the others. They were on one knee, intent on the dense jungle, and she wondered what they were thinking about all this. But she knew.

Who the hell ordered her retrieval? Who was she that the Marine Corps would risk the lives of five Marines to get one Peace Corps volunteer out of the Amazon jungle—which is exactly where she wanted to be.

But she knew it the instant she saw the Marines.

Daddy really flexed his muscle this time.

She was guessing that the team had no idea who she was, or why she was getting special treatment, especially since she was using her mother's maiden name. *Suits me fine.* Everyone treated her differently anyway, except out here.

Cahill must have an internal clock, she thought, because exactly two minutes later, he signaled his men to move out, then pulled her tired butt off the ground. She handed back the water bottle. He stowed it, his face expressionless as he motioned for her to follow the team.

They'd gone a half-mile when the first explosion shook the jungle to its roots.

Two

Fire and debris shot up through the trees as Rick threw himself at her, pushing her to the ground, shielding her body with his. After a moment, he moved off her enough to sight through binoculars.

Smoke and flames were faint in the distance. "Shit, someone jumped the gun." She started to get up, and he lunged at her. "Jesus, lady, stay down!" Hurling rocks plunked on the ground. What the fuck did they use, a missile? "Report!" When he got confirmation that everyone was alive, he said, "Move out, double time!" He rolled away, stowing the binoculars.

"You said two hours."

"Blame it on Intel." He pulled her up as he stood.

Black smoke billowed through the trees, scattering birds.

One of his men lagged back to position himself directly in front of her. It hit Samantha right then that he was willing to die to protect her. It was scary to think she'd be unworthy of the sacrifice. They moved fast, leaping over fallen logs, rocks, splashing through knee-deep creeks. She tripped, and from behind Cahill steadied her, then pulled her along.

Sweat rivered down her spine, soaked her legs. It felt

like hours, the Marines moving as if they weren't carrying sixty pounds of packs and gear. And here she was, with a measly ten-pound pack and trying to keep up.

Gunfire erupted in the distance, the cries of pain echoing through the thick rain forest. The air went rancid with the odor of burning flesh and trees.

"Oh God."

"Focus ahead, Miss Previn." His calm tone was a balm to her fear.

But the noise was moving closer, ahead of them.

Rick sacrificed radio silence to contact the chopper. At least the drug cookers didn't know the Marines were in the jungle. "Two hundred yards—we have to hurry."

Hurry? More than she was?

She put her attention on the man at the lead hacking a path into the jungle with a machete. She could barely hear the chopper over the double pull of explosions and her out-of-control heartbeat. Then she saw it.

It was a beautiful sight. U.S. MARINES emblazoned on the side. Made her want to put her hand over her heart and sing the national anthem.

Cahill pulled her down and made her focus on his face. The earth shuddered. Samantha didn't think she'd been this scared in her life.

"The Huey's going to touch down for thirty seconds. My men will get in and lay cover fire, then we run out into the open. You'll have to dive in—can you handle it?"

"To get out of this? You betcha."

"Whatever you do, do *not* leave my side. Got it?"

"Yes, Gunny."

He nodded curtly, giving her hand a squeeze that was ridiculously reassuring. The chopper, a big sucker, started its descent. Marines ran toward it, two moving backwards, watching the jungle. They jumped in, gunners ready to lay down cover fire, the chopper blades beating the smoky, pea-soup air.

Hunching, Cahill pulled her with him out into the open. They were less than twenty yards from the chopper when Cahill froze. Then she heard it, the high-pitched whine. A white streak shot out of the forest.

"Down! Down!" he shouted. She obeyed and Cahill covered her a split second before the rocket hit the chopper.

The blast punched the air. Smoke billowed, filling the cabin. The aircraft tipped hard.

All Samantha saw was these men dying because of her.

"RPG hit! It's not gonna hold at this altitude!" the pilot radioed.

Cahill shouted into his radio, "Lift off, go! Go! Go!"

The chopper rocked and shimmied as the pilot struggled to get the giant Huey in the air. It rose like a screaming dinosaur. And from beneath the protection of Gunnery Sergeant Cahill, Samantha saw their rescue fly away in a curl of black smoke.

Then a second blast plowed into the ground, shooting rocks and dirt clumps into the air and down on them.

Rick rolled off her. "Crawl to the treeline, keep your butt down!"

Samantha obeyed. On his elbows, Cahill slithered to the treeline with amazing speed, and dove behind some rocks. Then he reached for her.

His hand closing over her wrist won her eternal gratitude.

He pulled her to his side. Samantha sagged against the rocks, trying to keep from puking up her heart.

"You okay?"

Head down, arms on her knees, she waved. "Oh yeah, sure, just peachy. Do it all the time."

"Breathe slowly, it'll pass." Hidden behind boulders, he radioed the chopper. All Samantha heard was abbreviations and numbers.

"They're flying low—the shot went in and right through

the other door. The pilot thinks the hydraulics took the hit," he said. "They'll have trouble setting it down in a safe zone."

She looked up. "What's that mean to us?"

"Nothing. We head to the alternate RP."

"Jeez, I'm glad you guys plan ahead."

He flashed her a smile as he pulled out a map. How could he be this calm when all hell was breaking loose?

"How far is it?"

"About ten miles, if we went through that." He gestured toward the sound of explosions, studying the map.

Ten miles. The last time she walked more than two miles, it was shopping in New York. *Don't kid yourself, Sam. You took a cab!* "And if we don't?"

He shrugged, flipped up the compass under his watch face, and checked their location. "About four-five days travel."

"Oh, no."

His gaze flicked to hers. She was suddenly very pale. And breathing fast. Rick dropped his gear and cupped her face. "Look at me." He waited till she did. "I *will* get you out of here alive, Miss Previn. I swear it."

She nodded slightly, touching his hands. "I believe you, Gunny, but now they know we're here."

She looked so frail right now, all Rick wanted to do was hold her. Instead, he let her go. "They know the chopper was here, not us." He stowed his map.

"And that makes a difference?"

"Oh, yeah. At least we aren't hunted." Yet, he thought. "We won't have any radio contact till we're in a safe zone. Drug dealers will be listening." He gave her a water bottle. "Keep it and make it last. I don't know when we'll find fresh water." She stored it in her pack and when he stood, she did. "Stay close to me, Miss Previn."

"Samantha," she corrected. "Hardly seems right to

stand on formality now, especially after you had your hand between my legs."

He flashed her a sexy smile, his blue eyes bright against the dark camo paint. "Rick."

She nodded. "Thank you, Rick."

He arched a brow.

"That's just in case I forget to say it later, when the bugs are crawling over me, and I get all bitchy."

"So you're saying you were showing your best side in the village?"

She made a face, hiding a smile. He started walking fast, and Samantha followed, very aware that they wouldn't be in this situation if it wasn't for her father.

But that was the last thing she'd ever tell Cahill.

The man didn't need to know he was rescuing the daughter of a two-star general.

He might use her for target practice.

God knows she would.

Rick quit wishing they'd made it to the chopper the instant he'd pulled her to the boulders. If they had, they'd be dead: the hit took out the jump seats. Exactly where she'd have been sitting.

He kept glancing back to make sure she was okay.

Samantha was right with him, her feet stepping in his footprints. Her face was flushed, sweat soaking her clothes. She hadn't complained once. They'd been moving for hours and the sun was quickly setting. The dropping temperature was little relief this deep in the forest, but he'd have to find some shelter or make it. His biggest concern was getting her far enough away from the DCs and the explosions. They could still hear the rumble echoing through the valley. No telling how wide the sweep was going to get.

The drug factories were on the plateau, nearly in the

Andes. When the coffee growers couldn't get a good price for their crops, they turned to more lucrative assets. So they were scattered everywhere. They had to skirt them. Which meant heading into the valley, then up the opposite side of the mountain before coming down to cross the river. They were in uncharted territory, and when rain came, it would be hard. There was no question of *if* it would come. There was a good reason they called it the rain forest. Rivers overflowed, land would wash out, and the chance of a mud slide was too damn good for his liking.

He stopped. She blinked at him, glancing around for trouble. "Take a break."

"Oh, thank God." She dropped where she stood and drank some water. "How do you do it with that pack?"

"I trained wearing it." That reminded him that she was unaccustomed to this and to take it easy. His gaze slid over her. Her clothing was filthy now but it was the cuts on her legs that concerned him. They'd attract all sorts of creatures and disease.

"Do you have pants in that pack?"

"Yeah."

"Put them on, but let's clean up those scratches first."

She looked down. "I didn't even feel them." She pulled out her medical kit, then after searching it, sighed. "Well, if you need a shot, I'm your gal. No antiseptic except teeny alcohol swabs."

He opened his small med kit and cleaned her wounds. He stroked the cloth over her legs, moving to her thighs.

"I can manage," she said smartly.

He met her gaze, smiling. "But I'm trying to cop a feel," he teased, then handed over the cloth.

Samantha finished, then found her cargo pants. She removed her boots, then stood and opened her shorts. Cahill was watching her. "Do you mind?"

"Shit, can the modesty, Samantha, I'm not letting you out of my sight."

"Turn your back, at least."

He simply shifted his rifle, his gaze slipping past her to the jungle beyond.

Samantha conceded, since he was ready to shoot anything that approached them. Good thing she actually put *on* panties this morning, she thought, then turned her back and peeled the damp shorts down, bending a little.

Rick's gaze snapped to her rear. She had legs up the yahzoo and an ass that was round and tight.

And fuck me, she was wearing a thong. Bright pink. His groin went hard as a gun barrel, and when she bent for the pants, he thought he'd accidentally pull the trigger. When she faced him, zipping up, he'd managed to wipe the drool off his chin and look unaffected. Okay, so he did notice her when he first saw her. Who wouldn't? All that dark red hair and those whiskey-colored eyes. And a body like a porn star. He was cataloging her assets and getting an eyeful of that sweet behind when a voice in his head reminded him they weren't in some bar in Caracas.

She was his duty, his job. And she was counting on him for her survival. Christ, this was going to be a long five days—and nights.

"Get a thrill?" Sam noticed his slightly pained expression beneath that hard-core silence.

He gave her a deadpan look. "Yes, ma'am, I did." Yet his eyes sparkled.

She stuffed the shorts in the pack. "Savor it, Marine. It's your last."

He leaned down, in her face. "I don't know about that—you're going to be sleeping right beside me for the next few days."

She sputtered and, grinning, he pulled a machete from his pack, then started walking and chopping.

Samantha stared at his back, then hurried to catch up. With the exception of her girlfriends, no one ever dared talk to her with any kind of frankness. Most times the men she'd dated were all worried about impressing her to make points with her father. Which is the big reason she stayed far away from Marines. If she didn't, she was inviting trouble.

And here you are, girl, stuck in the middle of nowhere with the crème of the Corps.

She followed, the walking mindless, and while Rick would stop occasionally to get his bearings, he didn't say much. He didn't have to.

The man had "do or die trying" written all over him. Big, strong, skilled, and handsome. What more could a girl ask for in a rescuer? What woman wouldn't want to just melt for a man like that? He'd removed the throat mike and earpiece a while ago, and clipped his helmet on his pack, occasionally scraping a hand over his short, dark hair. What there was of it. She's always thought that if a man with practically no hair was good-looking, imagine what he'd be like with more? Oh yeah, Cahill'd be down-right dangerous.

"Hey, you on this planet?"

She nearly collided with him. "Huh?" Good thing at least one of them was paying attention.

"We're stopping for the night."

She looked around, seeing nothing but green. "Oh, honey, you got reservations at the Hyatt."

"Yeah, right here." He pushed back giant fern fronds to show where the fallen branches and plants had formed a small dome against the base of a tree with big, curling roots.

"A suite, how lovely."

His smile was faint and diabolically sexy. "Get in and rest. The temperature's going to drop some at night."

She started to duck in, then met his gaze. "Where are you going?"

"For food." He took off his pack, shoving it inside, then offered his sidearm. "Don't shoot me, okay?"

"Of course not. You have the map."

He snickered a laugh, then pushed her head under the fronds before walking away.

Sam found a spot near the tree. It was small inside—the pack took up half of it, the rest would be by six feet of Gunny Cahill. Not that she'd be able to see him. She couldn't see the pistol, yet felt for the safety, keeping it on. Then she checked the load. Full. He didn't need to know she could shoot. Her father had put a gun like this in her hands when she was twelve and made her learn.

Rick wasn't gone long, calling her name, then crawling inside. He dumped fruit on the ground.

"What? No gourmet MREs?"

He frowned at her for a second. "I'll save those for when I can't find anything."

She eyed the selection as if she were dining at the Four Seasons. "Nice. You had to climb trees for this." She picked up a banana and started peeling it.

"Yeah. Got a chance to check the location, too."

"And your findings were?"

"We're a helluva long way from the RP."

"Still four days?"

"Yeah." If it didn't rain, if they didn't encounter the DCs or anyone else. Like rebel guerillas. A pretty American woman would make a nice hostage. Rick wasn't going to let that happen and he sure as hell wasn't going to scare her by mentioning it. Because rebel guerillas wouldn't keep him hostage. They'd kill him and display his body for the eleven o'clock news.

He whipped out a knife and cut into a guava, offering her a slice. She slipped the drippy fruit into her mouth.

Rick couldn't take his eyes off her. Great mouth. He wanted to taste it. Hell, he wouldn't mind having more than a taste of the rest of her, too. When she put her lips around the banana his imagination went wild and nasty. He'd thought of little else since she dropped trou a few hours ago. How'd she kiss? What she'd feel like with those long legs wrapped around him? He didn't have trouble finding women; they loved a man in uniform, but finding one who was pleasant to be around after sex was a different story.

He rummaged in his pack, and Sam heard a snap before the area glowed green. "Chem light," he said, hanging it from a branch. He rolled out a mat. "It's waterproof, sit on it," he told her, then offered his poncho liner. "Cover up with this—it's warmer than it looks."

There was one of these in her toy box when she was a kid, she remembered. She pulled off her boots and her shirt.

Under it she wore a stretchy, skintight tank top that left nothing to the imagination. "Jesus."

She paused, meeting his stare and when she'd thought it was almost too dark to see his eyes, the hot sting of his gaze slipped over her like stroking fingers. It made her nipples tighten. "I know you've seen breasts before, Rick."

"Sure, just not yours."

Smiling, she folded the shirt for a pillow, ignoring the tingling racing over her skin. He was looking at her like he wanted to eat her alive. And all she wanted to do was keep stripping and give him the chance. Okay, that was slutty. She was alone in the jungle with a stranger, and though she didn't think Rick would attack her, she didn't want to get that close to a Marine. They'd crowded her life since she was born and she had to go to the Amazon to get away from them. Apparently, that wasn't far enough.

"Could it be that I'm the only woman for a hundred miles?"

"Could be." Not. Rick tried to be a gentleman, but when she adjusted the thin straps, bouncing a little, her nipples clearly outlined, it was pretty much hopeless with Playmate of the Year sitting next to him and a hard-on filling his trousers.

She's my duty, he kept repeating as he removed his kevlar vest, then pulled off his camouflage uniform shirt.

Samantha hoped he didn't take anything else off because the tee shirt stretched tight over his skin, showing her a work of art in muscles and shoulders. She wanted to touch him. Lick him. She blinked, looking for something else to keep her attention on. Down, girl. Down.

"Doesn't that paint on your face itch?" The line of the camo paint stopped at his collarbone.

"Nah. Hell to get off though. Done?" He gestured to the food.

She nodded, popping the last of the banana in her mouth, all too aware he was watching her every move. And she was making it worth it. *Six months in the jungle and I've turned into a sex-starved tramp.*

Every muscle in his body locked as her lips wrapped around the section, slowly pulling the piece into her mouth. He met her gaze, and for a split second every erotic, X-rated fantasy he had materialized. He smothered a groan, hurriedly gathering the leavings, slipping out to bury them.

Samantha covered her face. *What are you thinking?* She rubbed her face, then unpinned her hair, hoping to get a handle on this sudden inexplainable lust before he came back. Then he was there, filling up the tiny space. And Samantha felt her heartbeat pick up a little.

He laid his rifle and pistol within reach, then propped his back on the pack. She settled down, shifting to get comfortable.

His eyes drifted close. "Are you going to do that all night?"

"Heck if I know. I slept on a floor with a sleeping bag for six months—this should be easy."

"Come here." Over her shoulder, she sent him a skeptical look as he inched down, curling on his side. He took away the choice when he drew her into the curve of his body. "Sleep—we're safe for the night."

Samantha sank into him, her head on his bicep.

"God. You're hard as a rock." She stuffed the shirt under her head.

In a low voice he said, "If you keep wiggling that sweet behind against me, I will be."

She went still, then laughed uneasily. She felt his erection against her rear. *Oh Lord. Don't think about it.*

"Relax, Samantha, I'm not going to try to jump your bones."

"As *if*."

"When I want you," he whispered in her ear, his hand sliding around her waist and under her breasts, "you'll know it."

Her breath stopped somewhere between her mouth and her lungs, his warm hand sending a hot shot right to her center. Her thighs practically quivered. When? Not if? She shouldn't ask. She wouldn't. She did. "And just for the sake of clarity . . . how would I?"

His voice was close to her ear, deep and mind-bogglingly sexy. "Because I won't leave any doubt."

She made a sound, something between denial and moan.

Rick smiled in the dark and tightened his arms around her lush, soft body. Even if they weren't in a jungle with their lives in danger, he'd want her, any way he could.

Duty or no duty.

Three

Samantha woke with a tingling curling over her skin like a brush of warm water. It took her a second to realize her breast was firmly cupped in Rick's warm hand, his thumb making slow, lazy circles over her nipple. She bit down on her tongue to keep from moaning and shifted.

Over her shoulder, she met his gaze.

Rick smiled, his hand sliding to her stomach. "Sorry, it was just, well . . . there."

"I suppose it just leapt into your hand?" She peeled it off.

"No, slipped in there right nicely." He wiggled his brows. It was dastardly, he thought, but her breast was in his hand when he woke and he wasn't a guy to miss such a delicious opportunity. "You must have liked it—you were moaning and twisting."

"I was not!"

"Then you were having yourself a really sexy dream." He patted her hip, then sat up, scooted out of their cave, then pulled the pack out.

Samantha flopped on her back and stared up at the roof of greenery. Dew dripped on her face. It was a good thing, because she was hot, between her thighs screaming for attention. His.

Oh, this is not happening. She'd come out here to get away from the Corps and the bad odds of men to women. And now she let a Marine feel her up? And worse, she liked it. Really liked it.

Disgusted with herself, she decided she was just horny. It *had* been a while, and he was handsome—and here. *Oh, get a grip. You're in the jungle, depending on each other.* Well, that wasn't true. She was depending on him. She didn't think Rick had a problem adapting to any situation.

She pulled out clean clothes, changing, thinking she should have skipped the toiletries and packed more essential things—like more panties. Dressed, she grabbed her pack, the mat, and poncho liner and crawled out.

A mist hovered over the ground, cloaking Rick where he squatted near a log using his helmet as a basin to shave. She rolled the mat, folded the liner, watching his quick, efficient moves. When he finished and looked at her, Samantha thought her chin must be on the ground somewhere.

He swiped a small green towel across his chin. "Something wrong?"

"You just look different without the camouflage paint."

"At the risk of getting my ego bruised, better, I hope."

Better? How about oh-my-God good. Shall I strip now? Would that be good for you? "Well, Hulk green does suit you."

"Smart-ass."

"Jarhead." Remember that. Marine. That alone should keep her alert. But it wasn't. Because images of his big hands on her just wouldn't go away. She could almost feel them on her skin still, hard and a little callused, leaving an impression of heat behind. Stop, stop, stop! *Marine*, she reminded. Trying to rein in her sex-starved thoughts, she set the mat and poncho liner near his backpack, found her brush.

Rick tossed the water, glancing her way. She looked like an elfin queen sitting cross-legged on a log. Long red hair spilled to one side as she dragged her brush through a ton of curls, her tanned face tipped toward the sun struggling to make it down to the forest floor.

He didn't know what it was about her that attracted him beyond her looks, which were exotic enough to give him dreams of slick bodies on cool sheets for the next month, but Samantha was different. She was tough on the outside—it was what made her tick that he wanted to understand.

There's a first. And dangerous. He had a job to do, and that duty was sitting ten feet away looking good enough to eat.

"We leave in five."

"You don't do anything in *more* than five minutes?" she said, and he scowled at her sour tone. "I'm sorry. I'm not real good without some coffee, and the prospect of going without makes me cranky." Not to mention that he was watching her, and making her tense in all the right places. Denial is such an annoying thing. She gestured to the woods and stood. "I have to, ah, answer the call." When he stood, she put up her hand, glaring. "You are *not* coming with me."

"As wondrous as that prospect might be, I've checked the area already. Here." He handed her a folding shovel. An E-tool, she remembered.

She didn't have to ask. His message was clear. Bury it. "Ick." He was laughing as she stomped into the forest. When she came back, all embarrassment fled as he walked up to her with a kidney-shaped tin cup. She could smell the coffee already.

"Oh my God. Really?"

"Didn't want you going all bitchy on me so soon."

She met his gaze. He winked, and her stomach chirped.

"Thank you." She took a sip. "Oh God, I love you for this." She sat down to drink and didn't see the startled look on his face.

Rick repacked his gear, and found the mat and poncho liner rolled and tied precisely to stow. He couldn't have done a better job. He glanced at her, frowning, then said, "You can't wear that shirt." She looked down at the pale pink cotton shirt. "It's too light—they'll see you coming."

"They?"

"Anyone who's not *us* is a *they*." He handed her a camouflage shirt. "Wear this."

She shook it out. The pattern was green and black, almost like wide tiger stripes, identical to the one he wore. This was special operation gear, she realized. She finished off the last sip of coffee, handed him the tin mug.

"Thanks." Removing her blouse, she put the camo shirt on over her tank. The sleeves covered her hands.

Rick made a face. "That looks incredibly wrong on you."

She rolled back the sleeves. "That's because it needs to be properly accessorized." She modeled it.

He shook his head, thinking she'd be the last person he'd expect to give up a couple of years to help Amazon tribes. "What made you come all the way out here to work?"

"Need for bugs, heat, and disease. Oh yeah, and good coffee."

"Can't you give me a straight answer?"

She met his gaze. "I wanted to get away from the life I had."

He frowned. "Was it bad?"

"No. It was pretty great, in fact. Most people would enjoy it, but it was a little confining."

He faced her fully. "Okay, that needs an explanation."

She'd only fess up so much. "Dad's a . . . popular man,

and while everyone watched him, they also watched me. It was like living in a fishbowl. I couldn't do anything without it coming to his attention." That wasn't the whole of it, but enough.

"What about your mother?"

Her expression turned sad and faraway. "She died about eight years ago. My dad's practically smothered me ever since."

"Sounds like he loves you."

"Oh, I know he does, and I adore him."

"You didn't have to come halfway around the world to get away, Samantha."

She met his gaze. "Yes, I did. I haven't lived in his house for years, and it didn't matter. See, the men he works with, and most that didn't,"—she thought of the junior congressmen who wanted to get into her panties like it was some Medal of Honor—"didn't see me as *me*. They saw me as his daughter, a trophy, and a beeline up the corporate ladder." So to speak. An analogy, true, but she didn't want Rick to know about her father and begin treating her like the others. Like she was fragile, brainless, and a way to suck up to the big boss. Or just scared of her.

She had to hand it to her father. When she had dated an officer, he quizzed him. If she dated an enlisted man, he'd question him on improvements. He had his priorities in order, but he still wanted her home, near him, and though she suspected he was a little lonely in that big house alone, it was too much in the public eye. At her age, she wanted something more for herself than *his* military life.

"How about you? Why'd you join?"

"I wanted to make a difference in the world, instead of wondering if I was."

She smiled widely. "Well, you've made a difference in my insignificant life."

"No life is insignificant."

His expression looked pained for a moment, and she didn't have to ask if he'd had to pull that trigger on a human. She didn't want to know for sure.

"I love my job. I won't stop till I'm dead or they pry me out in thirty years."

That sounded like her dad and most of the Marines she knew. "You're good at it, Rick."

He glanced back. "How would you know?"

She tipped her chin. "I watch Discovery Channel—I know." *And I've lived it.* She remembered her dad packing up his gear to leave for a year-long duty without her and Mom, her shining her father's combat boots in front of the TV when she was ten. The memories were endless—mostly good, she admitted, till her mother had died.

Something hit her in the head, and she flinched. Lightning fast, he spun around, his rifle aimed to the trees. They saw the monkey just as it shrieked.

He adjusted the rifle, sighting through the scope. "Monkey meat is good eating."

"Oh yuck, no. Don't shoot it. It's just playing."

He lowered the rifle and gave her a sour look. "Tree hugger."

"Have a heart."

"Those things are mean." To punctuate that, the monkey threw something at them. It pinged her in the shoulder.

"Good shot." She threw it back.

"Okay, kids, enough. Let's move out." Packed up, they started walking. The monkey swooped through the trees, high above, getting ahead of them, shrieking a high-pitched cry. A couple more joined them, the noise like fingernails on a chalkboard.

She winced as the animals shrieked louder. "Oh, *focaccia!* I give up, it's my fault."

"*Focaccia?* As in Italian seasoned bread?" He was grinning.

She blushed. "It's better than swearing. My mom used to tell me almost daily that ladies do not repeat vulgar language." She didn't mention that being around Marines all her life, she'd heard it all, and far too often, her mouth had gotten her into trouble.

"Sometimes the right cussword fits."

"I know," she said with feeling. It had been a hard habit to break.

Suddenly the jungle went quiet. No birds, no monkeys.

Rick looked out over her head, then grabbed her hand. "Go, move."

She did, right behind him. "What is it?"

"Quiet!"

Rick pulled her behind an outcropping of rocks and huge trees, sighting in on the movement coming closer. Samantha huddled behind him, nearly cupped by giant tree roots. He motioned her to be quiet, then she heard it. The tromp of footsteps. And Spanish. At this distance she couldn't understand the words. It didn't matter. The Colombians didn't want anyone in their jungle, especially Americans, and considering the drug labs were blown to hell last night, they'd be perfect targets for retribution.

Rick's heart thumped with "if they find us, we die." She'd be raped and her picture sent to the media. He leaned back against the tree, making hand motions she could understand. They had to go into the valley, away from whoever it was. He was outnumbered and couldn't risk engaging them for no reason. He gestured to the river, to stay close to the treeline, and they started moving. Avoiding the rebels who came down to the river to use boats to ship their wares was going to be chancy. They had canoes hidden on the shores.

Out of earshot, Rick hurriedly motioned her into the forest. On the ground with their heads together, he said, "You did great."

"I aim to please. Who is it?"

"Rebels, I think."

She swallowed. "As in guerillas?"

"Yeah. And the drug cookers. One finances the other and we're near their territory, though they change locations a lot. Makes them hard to catch."

"What do we do?"

"I'm going to see where they're headed. You going to be okay?"

"Yes." She wouldn't tell him she was more afraid for him than herself. He gave her his side arm and bullets. She checked the load, and pocketed the ammo.

"Something tells me you're familiar with a weapon."

Oops. "Yeah, a little. We had one in the village—it was old, but worked."

He eyed her for a second, then shrugged off his pack and pulled out a throat mike and earpiece, putting it on her.

"Cool. I get to play commando?"

He put a second one on. "That's so you know I'm coming and don't shoot me." He started to move away.

She touched his arm. "Rick." He twisted, meeting her gaze. "Please be careful."

He smiled, the idiot! "Yeah, I have the map."

She punched him. "Don't be reckless. I'd hate to have to carry your two-hundred-pound butt back to civilization. Especially when I don't know the way."

He saw it in her eyes; she was really scared for him. He cupped the back of her head, his gaze locked with hers. "This is what I do." He pressed a kiss to her forehead. "No movement. Keep watching for me. Call sign is 'White Knight.' "

She rolled her eyes. That had to be her father's doing.

He moved out. For a big man he was very quiet as he slipped over the ground, almost graceful, pushing aside branches, holding them till he passed, then releasing them slowly so they didn't snap or brush. Samantha looked

down at the weapon in her hand, the pack he'd left behind. She pushed the pack closer to the buttress tree roots
that flared from the trunk nearly to her shoulder; then she
quietly pulled dead fronds around herself.

She peered into the jungle. It was incredibly noisy—
macaw birds squawked, animals she couldn't see played
high in the trees. Sweat pearled on her skin, trickling down
her spine and between her breasts. The morning mist still
hovered. She couldn't see Rick anymore.

Her heartbeat thumped so hard she felt her own pulse
in her ears. She took a deep breath, praying it would pass,
then admitted her adrenaline was running hot. If she wasn't
so scared she'd wet her pants, this might have been fun.
But all she could think was, please don't let him get hurt.
She heard a noise nearby and glanced around. Seeing nothing, she focused where he'd disappeared.

"White Knight to—"

She flinched, looked around frantically. It sounded like
he was right beside her.

". . . ah . . . Fairy Princess."

She smiled and pressed the earpiece. "I prefer Goddess."

"I stand corrected. They're headed to the chopper site."

"Dang, they'll see our trail!"

"Calm down, darlin', I'm covering it up."

"Oh." Man, she was glad he was smarter than she was,
but that meant he was doing a lot of zigzagging.

"It'll give us some time, but not much."

"Does this mean I have to run again?"

"With legs like those, it shouldn't be a problem."

She smiled, calmer now that she heard his voice. Then
the noise came again. "Rick," she said carefully. "There's
something here."

"Hold tight, I'm coming."

Samantha turned her head slowly, her gaze flicking over
the area. It was dark where she was, though the sun shone
bright and steamy hot only about thirty yards away. Water

sloshed softly at the riverbanks, shifting the marsh grasses. Okay, it was just the fronds, she decided, then watched for him.

She could hear him breathing as he ran to her. "It's nothing."

"What do you see?"

"Nothing," she repeated.

"Look above you."

She did. Her eyes went wide. "Snake. Oh God. Rick!"

"Don't fire, be still. I'm close."

The snake, purplish and gold-orange, moved closer, suspended in the air from the tree limb.

"Rick, it's coming toward me." Samantha swallowed heavily, imagining the thick-bodied snake wrapping around her and crushing her. She'd be blue and dead by the time Rick got here. Its body, as big around as her arm, serpentined toward her. It was less than three feet away. And moving closer. Then it opened its jaws, hissing.

She aimed the pistol, her finger trembling on the trigger.

"Don't shoot, Sam."

The air whistled. Something silver swiped in front of her. The head of the snake dropped to the ground. Samantha smothered a cry and backed up like a crab. Blood dripped from the limp carcass and she looked up.

Rick stood over her with a bloody machete. "Bushmaster." He studied the snake head, then flung it and the carcass away.

Eyes wide as coins followed him as he knelt. With exceptional care, she laid the pistol down.

"That was poisonous, wasn't it?"

He nodded. "Deadly."

She wet her lips, her breathing raspy.

"It's okay, it's dead."

"But if you hadn't—if it had—"

She was shaking. Rick reached for her. She threw herself into his arms, clinging tightly, and Rick whispered in her ear, "Slow breaths, slow, in and out, in . . . out. Come on, sweetheart, *do it.*"

She obeyed, and gradually she calmed, her body going boneless against him. He kept rubbing her back, knowing how scared she was, and how helpless.

Still, he held her.

"I don't get it. You've been in this jungle for a while— you had to have come across snakes before."

Her face was buried in his chest, her voice muffled as she said, "The truth is out, okay. I'm a wuss. I've seen plenty and run in the other direction. The villagers checked the hut for me every night. We burned the circumference of the village to keep them back."

She sounded so disappointed in herself. "You're not a wuss. You were calm and took action."

She lifted her head, meeting his gaze. "Don't patronize me."

"You didn't shoot because I told you not to. So as far as I can see, you'd have gotten the job done without me."

Her lips curved. "Now you're trying to be gallant." She would have never made the shot, even at that close range.

His look went boyish, almost shy. "And here I thought I already was, rescuing you and all."

Her laugh sputtered on a shaky breath.

His gaze swept her features, boring into her. The race back here had been an exercise in sheer terror, the knowledge that he might not reach her in time eating him alive. He brushed strands of hair off her face. The gesture felt far more intimate than he'd ever imagined. It made him notice the dust of freckles across her flawless skin, the fiery red streaks in her hair.

"I'm grateful you did."

His features tightened a little. "You already said thanks and I don't want your gratitude." His gaze flicked to her ripe mouth. Her tongue slid over her lips, wetting them.

The air between them went heavy and thick, sizzling

with an undercurrent. His fingers moved on her back. Samantha wished they were on her bare skin.

His head tipped, his mouth nearing. For a second, he went still and just breathed her in. Her senses clarified with a tingling sharpness, her body tensing with anticipation. *We shouldn't open this door any wider* passed aimlessly through her mind, dragging with it images of them sliding against each other, eager and naked and as hot as the jungle. Oh God.

His breath dusted her lips, his damp mouth a fraction from hers.

Then his mouth was on hers, and everything between them went hot and savage.

He never expected the steamy slap of electricity, the heated charge shooting through his blood straight to his groin. He wanted her naked, wanted to plunge inside her right now. So much that he couldn't catch his breath. He devoured her mouth, hungering for more as his arms closed around her, hands diving under the too-big shirt and palming her breasts. She pushed into his touch, and like a sleek cat she crawled onto his lap, thrusting her hot little center to his groin.

Oh man.

Rick felt unhinged, unglued, pulsing with need.

Then abruptly he jerked back. She blinked, her eyes slow to open.

"No. We can't do this." He eased her back as if setting aside a package, then stood, shouldering on his pack. He pulled her off the ground.

Samantha tried to catch her breath, almost choking on the sensations pelting her from the inside out. "You can just shut that off?"

He covered his mouth with his hand. "Shh. No, dammit," he whispered. "I *have* to. We're in enemy territory, for crissake."

"You're mad?"

"You're my duty, Samantha. It's my job to get you home, not get you on your back."

Her expression withered. "Duty. I see."

Without a shred of emotion, Rick motioned for her to move ahead of him and focused on the terrain and not her. He couldn't afford to have his blood *not* be in his brain right now. Because Samantha Previn had just gotten the best of him. Hell, more than that.

One kiss turned him inside out and lit him on fire. If they'd gone any further, they'd be sending up smoke damn signals. And right now, that could get them killed.

Four

"Pick up your feet—you're stomping."

"Yes, Gunny."

Rick's shoulders drooped. She'd been answering him like that for the last three hours.

"You're being a nag."

"Actually, this is my bitch-on-wheels stage. Nagging comes later. It isn't pretty."

He had to smile at that. "Does that mean it'll pass?"

"You live to learn, Gunnery Sergeant."

He winced. After what they'd been through, calling him by his rank was damned impersonal. Especially when he had to walk nearly a mile with an aching groin *she* gave him. Without much effort, either. He knew he was right to stop himself. Stop them. They were alone out here with only each other, like Adam and Eve, but he wasn't going to snatch the fruit. Even if she was more temptation than apples, more than he had a right to taste.

He supposed he should be flattered she was so pissed off. He wasn't. He didn't think he'd be any less if the tables had been turned. He'd teased her. He wasn't ashamed of it, but he knew his place. And that was to be her protector.

Not her lover.

"Gunny?"

He stopped and turned. "Would you quit calling me that?"

"I'm the duty, remember, just a job."

So that was it. "I didn't mean it *exactly* like that, but you gotta see my point."

"I do—honestly, I do. The last person I want to be involved with on any level is a *Marine.*"

He wasn't sure he liked the way she said Marine. As if it left a bad taste in her mouth. "What do you have against Marines?"

"Nothing—our country's finest, ooh-rah and Semper Fi and all that."

His scowl darkened. "So what's the problem?"

"I'm trying to keep the lines between you and me defined, just so you don't go off half-cocked, as it were." She gave him a sour, prissy look that was cute and annoying as hell.

"You wanted to kiss me, too."

"Yes, I did. Didn't it feel like I was enjoying it?" His lips quirked, but she went on. "Though it was probably a normal reaction after nearly being swallowed by a viperous snake." His look said, *yeah, right.* "But what I don't like is how you turn it on and off at my expense in the name of *duty.* I've been used before, Gunnery Sergeant, and I will not allow it again."

Her eyes flashed with a temper he hadn't seen before. Idiot that he was, it attracted him.

"Listen up, cookie, I don't know your father, nor would it matter." He towered over her, menacing and dark. "I got where I am on my own merit. And if you think I'd stoop to using a woman for professional gain, then you don't know me at all." Why were they having this conversation? Their lives were no way connected. And what would he gain from sleeping with her?

"You're right, I don't. You don't know me, either."

"I say again, what's your problem?" he barked.

"Do you always kiss perfect strangers."

"Honey, I have *fantasies* about perfect strangers." Just not the kind he was having for her.

Her brows shot up. "And they'd be—?"

"My first one is to see you dumped in Daddy's lap."

"And second?"

"You don't want to know."

"I asked, didn't I?"

He advanced, making her back up. "To strip you naked and kiss every inch of that delectable body till you're screaming for me to eat you alive."

Samantha's nerve endings went suddenly raw and aching. "That clear enough?"

She blinked, swallowing. "Y-yes." Was that her breathing so heavy? "See, now we're getting somewhere."

He stared. Her smile was mischievous and feline, pulling him in places she didn't have to touch. Rick didn't need more enticement. Or more confusion.

He scraped his hand over his head. "Woman, you're driving me nuts!"

"I know. The real me. How'd you like it?"

He chuckled, shaking his head, then took a step closer. "Do you always run this hot and cold?"

"Yes. Annoying, huh?"

He spared her a comment.

"Don't hide behind that badge of honor and duty, Gunny. Last time I looked I wasn't a country that needed a peacekeeping force."

He gave her a long, thorough look from head to toe that made her nipples stand up and salute. Good thing she was wearing his shirt.

"Honor and duty aren't something I could hide behind—it's just *there*." He shrugged, then eyed her again. "You still pissed about that kiss?"

"I never was."

He scraped his hand across his skull as if it would come off his shoulders.

"I was annoyed that you stopped for all the wrong reasons."

"Jesus. I did not need to hear that."

"Because I'm your duty?"

"No, I've already got sex on the brain, woman."

"And?"

God, he wished she'd just shut up. "That's a level I don't think we should go to. And before you ask, since I know you're not going to let this rest, sex is not something I take that lightly. It's as intimate as it gets. I mean, my body is *inside* yours."

That just made her quiver all over and grow wet. Yet for the sake of womanhood everywhere, and men who thought they could have them on their backs because they were hot bods and handsome, she gave him a "you wish" look.

"Well—any woman's. There's nothing to hide. You can't hide emotion unless you're a player, hide need—or—"

"Fake a climax?" she put in.

His look went sour. "That's just mean. You either both get satisfaction or its unfair and selfish." He drank water, swiping the back of his hand across his mouth. "I've had women do that—they weren't honest about it when I confronted them. Like I'm too stupid to know."

An intuitive man—how novel. "So what did you do?"

He flashed her a devilish smile. "Made them find it."

"It?"

"Satisfaction, a climax."

"Like a job unfinished, huh?"

"No, like the reason we're between the sheets. To find mutual pleasure. Without that, it's never as good as it could be, and I sure as hell don't want to be thought of as a lousy lay."

"Your reputation would be toast, then."

"You act like I have one." He winked and started walking.

Samantha let that go and followed. "So you're a romantic, huh?

"Is that bad?"

"Unexpected. Especially from a bad-ass Marine."

"Just because I fire weapons doesn't mean I'm not very aware of what I hit."

She didn't have to ask if he'd been in combat a lot. He was Recon. That said it all.

"I can't stand dishonesty in any form—it serves no one."

Oh, shi-shoelaces, she thought. "What if it's to protect yourself?"

He thought about that for a second, thinking instantly of covert and CIA operations. "Depends on what the reason is."

Overhead, the sky darkened with rain clouds.

"Heartbreak? Disillusionment, anger."

He stopped, scowling. "Whoa—what are you saying?"

"The absence of truth spares some people hurt."

"As in?"

Great, he was making her *think*. "Like with my father. I don't tell people he's my dad, and it spares me from being used and people liking me for *his* achievements."

"It can't be that bad."

"Lied to about why men want to date me? Lied to by people who I thought were friends? The brunt of gossip?"

"Yeah, I see your point." He turned back onto their path.

"It made me suspicious, and I hated it. So I stopped telling anyone anything, then went as far away as I could get."

"Did it help?"

"No, just made me lonely."

"Even around those villagers?"

"Oh no, they're great. I left some good friends behind. But they made me see that my problems were infinitesimal, and I felt ashamed." Rick held back branches as she stepped over a log. "But that's out here—home is another story. They needed simple things, and I needed to feel worthy of helping them."

"Man, those guys did a number on you."

She was ashamed to admit it, so she didn't.

"They were morons. But you don't give yourself enough credit, Samantha."

He looked down at her with such an endearingly tender smile, Samantha felt as if she'd melt into a puddle. Damn him. How was she supposed to keep her heart out of this when he was just so much fun to spar with. Clearly, being a bitch wasn't fazing him.

He eyed her. "You don't trust what people say, though, huh?"

"Not till I know them, and even then it's failed me."

"Well, I say exactly what I mean, and I think I know where you're coming from."

"Do you?"

She had that "make me" look again. "Yeah. I have three brothers. All of them work in the family business and I did, too, because it was expected. Till it just wasn't enough."

"So you chose danger and excitement."

"I went into the Corps because it felt right for me. Did coming out here feel right?"

"Yeah."

"Then don't blame it on Daddy or other people's opinions. This is what you needed to do. And the only opinion that matters is your own."

"Hard to say that when your heart gets involved."

"If the heart's not involved, then it's not worth doing."

Oh my God, was he for real? She smiled brightly, and leaned up to kiss his cheek.

He blinked, his eyes intense. "What was that for?"

"For being one of the good guys, Rick."

His expression went dark, his eyes smoldering as they roamed her from boots to hair. "I can be very good."

"The prospect tortures the mind."

"It's not your mind I want to torture."

She licked her lips.

"You're making me hard."

"You have sex on the brain," she reminded. "It wouldn't take much to put you over the edge."

"Oh, yeah."

"Too bad we're running for our lives."

"Yeah, too bad."

"So now what?"

There was that hot-and-cold thing again, he thought. He was going to be a twisted mess before this was over. And probably happy about it. "We keep moving toward the objective."

"Then maybe we should check that out first." She pointed to the right where the land sloped upward toward the mountain.

Now he saw it, a definite trail leading into a drape of vines.

Quickly, Rick scanned the terrain. If there was a trail, then it was a well-used area. And possibly watched by unfriendlies. He pushed her low, then moved in slowly, looking for booby traps. "Stay here." He nudged the vines apart with the rifle barrel, then ducked under the fabric of the jungle.

Samantha closed her fingers around his side arm tucked in the pocket of the camo shirt. They still wore the throat mikes, just in case they got separated. She'd no intention of being less than five feet from him.

"Anything?"

"It's clear. Get in here." She looked around, then ducked inside. Crouched, he flicked on a flashlight, then motioned to his left.

"Holy Hanna."

"That about says it."

Weapons. The walls of a wood hut were lined with rifles. On the floor were boxes of ammo, a reel of some sort of wire, and cartons. And there were very distinct packages of white stuff stacked in the corner.

"Those are Russian rifles."

He glanced at her. "How do you know?"

Think fast. "The drug cartel carries them all the time. It's the easiest to acquire, I'm told."

"Yeah, they are, and a couple of assault rifles that look like ours."

She picked one up, tipping it toward the flashlight. "These are old and not oiled. This one is U.S. military issue."

"Discovery Channel teach you that, too?"

"No, it's an older M16. Not like that thing you have." She nodded to the MP5 assault rifle, which was state-of-the-art weaponry. "And with the words 'property of U.S. government,' it's a dead giveaway."

He stood, his head touching the tin roof. "There's only one way in or out of here."

"I didn't see any boats on the river, and the ground is overgrown."

"But smashed enough that someone checks on this."

"Oh God," she said, looking at the small entrance.

"We need to get out of here. Now. This is a storage unit. I'm betting someone is skimming the boss." When she looked confused, he added, "It can't be a warehouse—there's not much dope here, not like they're mass producing. It's private stock. But someone's going to come for this stuff to sell it."

He was already at the entrance when she said, "We have to destroy this."

He spun, his brows shooting up. "We? *Oh, hell no.* We can't risk the noise and the notice. I'm outnumbered and underarmed for a major attack."

She flicked a hand at the arsenal. "How many more weapons do you need?" She laid aside the rifle and knelt by a crate, opening it. "Grenades."

Christ. She was serious. "Sam, come out—now."

She met his gaze. "These weapons are in the wrong hands, agreed?"

"Yes."

"They will be used to hurt innocent people."

"Agreed." He felt he was being led up the path of righteousness.

"But they use these to help transport drugs into the U.S., Rick. The Colombian government and DEA were already here, making a sweep, but they aren't this far north. We can't just leave it."

Rick let his head drop forward, his rifle slung low. Samantha shifted from foot to foot.

"We have to be far away."

She grabbed the reel of rope like a kid showing off her best Christmas present. "We can use this for a ripcord to the trigger or detonator or whatever . . ."

"Are you suggesting we make a bomb?"

"Well, yeah." She smiled.

She was actually excited about it. "I'm afraid to ask if you know how."

"No, actually, nursing chemistry didn't go into that area of expertise, but look at all this stuff." She pointed to the drugs. "We can't let this get out of here."

"We can dump it in the water."

"And taint the water or let some nearby village take the blame?"

She was right. He made the decision. "Okay, let's move. I don't want to be here any longer than we have to."

"Me, either." Now that he mentioned it, this was a little too accessible. The structure was wood with a tin corrugated roof and no door. It was meant to keep it dry temporarily. And from the look of the clouds gathering, it wasn't going to be long before the heavens opened up. Someone could come to remove it.

Rick was on the ground, going through the munitions. "I know how we can do this."

She knew he would. "We have to move fast, Rick, the storm is coming." It would dump a lot of rain in a short period of time.

"We can't, not with this stuff. God knows how long it's been sitting here."

She swiped a finger over the kilos of drugs. "Not long, very little dust."

She was a smart cookie, he thought, removing his pack. He told her to arrange the weapons and ammo in a circle, the drugs in between the crates. Samantha was careful not to brush up against him as he removed grenades. She knelt, watching him.

"Get near the door, Samantha."

"They're that volatile?"

"I don't know, it's a precaution."

"Then maybe you shouldn't handle it."

He didn't look up, stripping wires and looping them through the grenade pull rings. "We're in it now."

"Jeez Louise, it sounded so good at the time."

"It is. We should do this, but please go near the door, keep a watch. You have the nine mill?"

"Of course."

"Take the Uzi."

"Huh?"

"Take that one." He inclined his head to the right. "It's the cleanest."

"And scary."

"Come on, darlin', you've been packing for a whole day now. You can handle it. Take the magazines."

Hovering over the ammunition, Rick's gaze flashed up and clashed with hers. He trusted her, she realized, the thought bringing a strange pleasure. She did as he asked, slipping out of the shed. Nothing moved but low-lying clouds. They had yet to cross the river north. If the rain started before they could cross, they'd have to stay on this side of the bank. With the bad guys.

Samantha nestled herself against a nearby tree, the vegetation all but obscuring her view. Crouched, she held the semiautomatic ready to fire. If her father could see her now, he'd be grinning.

She tuned her ears to the jungle noise, to the shrieking birds, the monkeys, and a sloth clinging to a tree, nibbling his way to the top. In the distance she could hear the rush of the river. It sounded like thunder. She glanced back, barely making out the outline of Rick's body as he laid out the grenades.

"Ooh-rah, Rick, very ingenious," she said.

He stilled, glancing her way for a second. "Just trying to be smarter than the last guy," he said, as he set the last carefully on the ground. The grenade pull rings were linked with trigger lines in a web around the weapons and drugs. He moved carefully, sparingly. He'd loosened the release pins on the grenades to hold barely a quarter-inch.

"Rick?"

"Yeah."

"Remember, lowest bidder made those things."

His soft chuckle came through the earpiece. "Believe me, I know."

The instability of the grenades made her nervous and her hands grew clammy on the weapon. But wishing he'd hurry up was just plain dangerous.

"Hear or see anything?"

"No, nothing." *Except my heart beating in my ears.*

He brought the lines of wire and rope together, tying them so when he pulled, they would all yank at the same time.

"Almost there."

Sweat rippled down the side of his face when he lifted his pack over the display. He pushed it out of the hovel.

She breathed a relieved sigh when he was beside her. She glanced briefly, resisting the urge to touch him.

"That was a little hairy."

"I've handled worse."

"You trying to impress me, Gunny?"

"Is it working?"

Her gaze slid to his. She smiled. "Yeah, but don't let it go to your head."

But it was Rick who was impressed. She was watching the land like a trained sniper, her body tucked behind giant leaves and ferns, only the tip of the barrel exposed.

"We ready?"

"I want you to head that way." He nodded up the mountain toward the cliffs.

"Not without you." She moved from behind the disguise of vegetation.

"Samantha, don't fuck with me right now—this is dangerous." He was moving backwards, glancing back, then a step, then unrolling a little more rope.

"I can run, *Gunny,* and I'm not going anywhere without you." She adjusted the Uzi. "Deal with it."

I've created a monster. "I'm going to enjoy wringing your pretty neck later."

"Yeah, you and what battalion?"

Shaking his head, he unwound more detonation line. "Watch my six."

Rick walked backwards, Samantha faced forward.

"The blast will go out and downward," he said. "We have to be above it to avoid the debris."

"I am *so* hoping we are alone out here now."

So was he.

He had to make a fairly straight line from the storage to their next position or the pins wouldn't pull hard enough. If only one went off, it would do little damage beyond throwing the weapons against the walls and maybe igniting a box of ammo. And bring quick attention to their location. Rick was hoping a couple of the grenades would set off the entire arsenal.

"This is as far as we get." No more line.

She glanced, then returned her gaze to the area.

Rain fell softly, misting the air.

Rick fished in his leg pocket, and Sam glanced, then blinked owlishly. "Is that what I think it is?"

He winked, using his teeth to tear open a packet. "Yeah." He rolled a condom down over the rifle barrel. "Keeps the water out and I can shoot through it."

He handed one to her, nodding for her to do the same on the Uzi. As she did, he got the clear image of her putting one on him. Christ, his mind was a porn movie.

"Get going," he said, then looked up the mountainside. It was steep and dense. When she gave him a mutinous look, he added, "For God's sake, don't argue with me!" and leveled her a dark, penetrating stare that gave her chills and said there would be consequences.

Without a word, she turned into the woods.

When she was far enough away, Rick counted backwards from three and pulled.

Nothing. "Shit!"

Samantha froze, horrified. She looked back.

Rick was rewinding the detonation lines and moving south. "Keep going, Sam," he said. "I have to get lower or they won't go off."

"Then leave it!"

"And have some kid find this and pull the charge?"

"Okay, okay. Point made."

"Go, go! Climb higher."

"But—"

"I'll find you, I swear it."

"I'm going, I'm going. Just don't do something macho, okay?"

He looked through the thicket and barely made out her

figure between the movement of underbrush and leaves. The rain grew heavier by the second. Lightning cracked as if to push him along. Rick caught a glimpse of movement south, near the river. For a split second, he differentiated between nature and human.

"Double time it, Sam, we have company."

"This just keeps getting better and better."

He could hear her heavy breathing. He prayed she was far enough away.

He counted off five seconds . . . four . . . three . . . two . . . He pulled.

Explosions ripped off, one after another, like the blast of fifty-caliber machine guns. The ground shook. Debris and rocks shot up high into the air, some plopping into the water below. Before it landed, he was on the move.

Rapid Spanish echoed up the valley, bounding off the mountains and cliffs without distinct direction. They were pissed, and headed this way.

Then the ammo went off, sounding like a battalion executing a ground assault of artillery fire. He hoped whoever was behind them thought more than one Marine had landed.

The rain came with a crushing force, softening the ground. Rick's boots sank to his ankles. His muscles strained as he grabbed vines and bushes to pull himself up the hillside. Christ, it was straight up. He wanted to ditch the pack but if he did, they wouldn't survive the night.

"Sam!"

"I'm okay." She was moving, her breathing so hard it came through the ear mike as if she was right beside him. His lips quirked when she muttered one of her silly curses.

Then the worst happened.

A scream so terrifying Rick's skin crawled. Then it cut off sharply. He called to her, but only a deafening silence answered him.

Five

He never wanted to hear a woman scream his name like that. "Samantha!"

She didn't answer.

"Sam. Talk to me!"

A thousand disasters shot through his mind at once, distracting him. He pulled himself up onto the next rise. The rain made the mountain like a kid's slide. Slick and steep. Up two feet, down one. He jammed the toes of his boots into the mushy ground and pushed. The pack weighed a ton.

"Answer me, dammit!"

Rick heard her choking for air and he climbed like a wild animal, clawing the dirt and rocks and plants. "Sam! Baby, please say something!"

"Rick." Her voice rasped. "I'm down here." She sounded as if she'd run a marathon.

"Down?"

"The cliff."

Jesus. He stood on the rise, looking for her. For a sign. Beyond the storm, the sun shone in the deep north. The rain clouds were tightly packed, dropping water in a black curtain onto the forest. Water rushed around his boots, and disappeared over the edge of the land. There was a fresh break in the ground, roots sticking up.

He'd seen the map; he knew what was there.

Nothing. A sharp drop to the river.

Please God, no.

He moved out toward the edge, looking down onto the river. To his left, he saw men moving up the hillside, deep inside the jungle. His only saving grace was that they were having just as tough a time getting up the mountain as he had. He took a step toward the edge. The ground shifted. He lurched back and, shouldering off the pack, he dropped to his knees, then lay flat. Crawling, he peered over the edge. Muddy water shot round him in a tremendous rush to spill hundreds of feet below.

Through the ear mike, he could hear her, but not see her. He inched forward. Then he saw her. Oh Christ. "Are you hurt?"

"No, but my arms feel like they're coming out of the sockets."

She dangled from a thick root, both hands clutching. She kept swinging her feet out to try to catch on the rock face. Below her was nothing but air, rocks, and water—and a very long drop.

She looked up and met his gaze, offering a brave smile. "Sorry."

"I'll think of something." She had her pack on and the Uzi slung across her. Extra weight. Crap.

"I don't mean to sound ungrateful, but I don't know how long I can hold on."

Rick inched back and tore into his pack for nylon rope. It wasn't thick enough for her to grab, but it would hold his weight. He just wasn't sure it would hold them both.

"I'm coming down."

"No, it's too unstable! Ten feet of land gave way under me."

He ignored that and said, "Can you get your feet on anything stable?" He quickly tied the rope to a tree, checked its strength.

"I've been trying. It's too far."

Removing his helmet and kevlar vest, he looped the rope through his war belt, listening to her grunts as she gave it another try.

Then she caught it. A second later, the earth tore. She screamed.

His heart slammed to a stop. "Sam!"

"I'm still here. Oh jeez, Rick!"

Backwards, he started lowering himself down. "I'm not going to let you fall, baby, believe that." *Please God, don't make me a liar.*

"I trust you."

She didn't sound convincing.

With the rope threaded around the tree and then his waist to his foot and back up, Rick used the line like a rock climber, letting loose enough to inch himself down over the edge of the cliff. Wet earth sprinkled on his shoulders and head, the rain sending watery dirt like liquid chocolate past him.

Terror clawed at Samantha, making her almost mindless, and the only thing keeping her from wailing like a baby was Rick. She tried pulling herself up, but she didn't have any leverage, and she was too chicken to let go of the root to grab at something. The root was the only thing keeping her alive right now. She didn't trust herself to hold her own weight, and that's exactly what she had to do. Or die.

I should have gone on a diet, she thought angrily. Then she saw him.

"Oh, please be careful." The rope threaded around him, he let off inches at a time, lowering down to her.

The hard drum of rain and thunder echoed off the valley. Rick concentrated on reaching her. But the image he saw stuck in his mind.

The tip of her boots barely braced on the rock face, she looked like a diver about to do a backward dive from under the diving board of rocks and dirt. There was nothing for her to grab onto to get around the lip of land.

She was nearly under it.

Water pounded her shoulder in a steady blast like a fire hose. Any second, it was going to unearth her only lifeline.

Rick could tell what had happened. She'd stood on the cliff edge, several feet back, not realizing the previous rains had forced dirt and underbrush to flow and build on the rock ledge like a cake spilling over the pan. It gave out right from under her. She was lucky to have caught the root at all.

He worked the line, the rope biting into his glove, choking off the circulation in his fist. He drove his boots into the wall of rock and mud, searching for purchase. His feet braced apart, knees bent, he made little hops downward in an almost perpendicular squat. It was familiar—he was used to rappelling. Just not pulling himself up with an extra hundred and twenty pounds.

He was within a yard of her when he heard the drug dealers calling to each other. Rain washed over him, and he met her gaze.

"Grab onto me."

"I can't. I'll have to let go!"

"Yes, you will," he said firmly. "I don't have any more line."

She shook her head violently.

"You're strong, Sam—you have to do it or we both die!"

She took a breath, rubbed her face against her upstretched arms, and looked at him.

"I'll catch you." His right fist wrapped in line, he stretched the other out to her. Only a yard separated them.

Sam braced herself, preparing her muscles, her mind for the leap of faith. There was a plea in her eyes not to let her drop. Rick would rather die himself than fail her.

"On three. One, two, three!"

She lunged for his outstretched hand, her arms reaching as she started to fall.

She missed.

Like a snapping whip, Rick arched backward, his hand shooting out. He latched onto the camouflage shirt. His body jerked hard. She dangled from his fist.

The rope cut into the earth like a knife.

"Keep your arms down!" The shirt was so big, if she put her arms up she'd slide right out of it. He curled his arm, his bicep straining to bring her up. "Reach now, now!"

She hyperventilated as she grabbed onto his arm.

"Climb! Use me like a ladder."

Samantha gripped his elbow, her weight pulling on his uniform shirt. Her muscles quivered as she reached his shoulders.

Rick thought his back would snap and forced himself to use his stomach muscles, curling to bring her up so her weight rested against him and she could get some leverage.

When he felt her weight, he said, "Put your arms around my neck, catch your breath."

She obeyed.

Then he worked the line, bringing them upright. It took some of the pressure off his spine. Rick's boots shifted on the wall, and he inched in more line to bring three hundred pounds over the edge. It felt like hours.

Lightning cracked the sky, mud and rock slopped over the cliff.

"Can you reach land yet?"

She tried. "No. Oh God, Rick. I'll take us both down."

"I'm not gonna let that happen." He grunted with the strain, inching his hand up the line, grabbing securely, then doing it again. His fingers were nearly numb. Muscles burned.

Samantha grabbed for a rock, her fingertips going white. Determination multiplied through her. She lifted her hand to grab higher. The simple task threatened her life.

"Climb, Sam, they're coming."

Samantha didn't know which was worse, going over a cliff or being shot in the head and *then* going over the cliff. She braced her knee on his shoulder, and grappled for stable land. She found it, clawing the earth, digging her knees into the mud.

A rock tumbled over the edge and hit his shoulder, knocking him sideways. Rick cursed, and lifted one hand and quickly gripped, pulling the extra length against himself.

She lurched onto solid ground, then faced him, grabbing the rope. She dug her boot heels in and pulled hard. And prayed. Then his head crested the cliff.

The rain splashed mud on his face.

Rick threw his leg over the edge and she was there, gripping his shirt at the shoulders, yanking, her legs braced to keep from going forward. He crawled, and when they were on sure ground, they collapsed.

For a moment they just lay there, breathing hard, water and mud puddling around them. Then he lifted his head, meeting her gaze.

Her lips quivered, her eyes tearing. He rose to his knees, crawling on all fours to reach her. They slammed into each other, his hands charging a wild ride over her spine, then to her hair. He crushed her to him, burying his face in the curve of her throat.

His lungs labored. She slid her hand over his skull and pressed him tighter. *Thank you, God.* Hands groped for assurance, for confirmation. Then his mouth was on hers, rough and demanding, a deep, eating kiss that devoured her soul.

Every cell in her body answered him, begging for more.

It was electrifying. Lightning cracked, torrents of water pounding them, and still he kissed her and kissed her.

"I thought I'd lost you for sure," he said against her lips, then savaged her mouth again.

She matched his kiss, untamed power riddling through her and into him. "I never want to be that scared again—" His mouth slid over hers and she consumed him. "Oh, God."

A gunshot cracked. The report echoed. They tore apart and scrambled for the trees. He had his rifle and was sighting in before Samantha knew what was happening.

"Get behind me." The dealers knocked off a half-dozen shots, a couple thunking into the trees shielding her head. She scrunched down. She knew Rick was waiting to see where the shots were coming from. Three more shots from the dealers, and he returned fire.

The cracks were deafening and quick. The succession of shots echoed in the forest. One, two, three; one, two, three . . . she flinched with each one.

Birds flapped and scattered higher into the trees. Animals skittered. She didn't hear screams of pain, nothing. Just silence.

She didn't look, either. It was a reality of the military, and she'd rather avoid the visual.

"Reel in the rope line and get ready to leave," he said. "Stay here."

She waved him on, her stomach rebelling.

Rick approached slowly, checking the first man. He had a clean hole in his forehead, one in his heart, the other in his jugular. He checked the others, stripping them of cash, weapons. He dumped their personal stashes of drugs on the ground and let the rain do the rest.

When he returned to Samantha, he found her still on the ground, staring at the sky. "Sam?"

She lifted her gaze to his. "They wanted to kill us." Hate was one thing; intent to murder just plain boggled her mind.

"Yes." He knelt. "They would have hunted us till they did." He smoothed his hand over her wet hair.

"But I didn't do anything to help you."

He smiled with tender humor. "You stayed calm, and I never expected you to shoot, babe." Still kneeling, he watched the terrain as he almost blindly tore the tattered condom off the barrel, and replaced it.

She smiled at that, glad to be amused, glad to be alive. And with him.

It was all she could think about down there dangling over the river. Wondering if he'd find her, then knowing in her heart he wouldn't stop till he did. It's amazing what thoughts channel through your brain when you know you are going to die. She'd never been more terrified in her life, but more so, that she'd never see him, never know him. Taste him.

It was an opportunity she wouldn't pass up again. Life didn't throw you too many second chances, and Samantha just got a big one. Defying death was a real eye-opener.

Over the gear, he met her gaze, then suddenly reached out, bringing her close to kiss the top of her head. Although they were soaked, muddy, and exhausted, the gesture slipped right into her heart.

"You were incredibly brave, Sam."

"Only because you were here." She touched his face. "Thank you for saving my life, Rick. Again. And again."

"You're welcome."

It was humbling how easily he shrugged off his gallantry, Samantha thought. Rick wasn't much different from the other Marines she knew. She wasn't sure she wanted to examine what it was that attracted her so strongly. Sexy, brave, courageous—sure. But he had a heart. A big one. He'd shown it to her a few times already. He was mentally strong, too, and suddenly the belief that he could survive the gossip and scrutiny of her twisted life made her want to grab onto him and never let go.

"Let's get outta here."

She stood, her soggy backpack caked with mud like the rest of her.

He eyed her. "At the risk of getting slapped, you look like hell." God, he was so glad just to look at her!

"Yeah, but the mud does wonders for the complexion." She took a step and swayed. "Oh, I am so not good at this."

"Easy." He caught her against him, gazing into her whiskey-colored eyes. "You did just fine, Sam, and I'm really glad you're alive."

"Think this makes up for being a snake wuss?"

He grinned. "Yeah, baby, I think." Then he brushed his mouth over hers.

"Am I still your duty?"

He pressed his forehead to hers, his smile slow and heart-poundingly sexy. "Not since I had my hand between those gorgeous legs."

Samantha laughed shakily, her fingers pawing his face, her thumb gliding over his lips before she tipped her head to kiss him.

Tenderness was left behind. Primal need escalated. Rick gripped fistfuls of clothing, crushing her to him, nearly lifting her off the ground.

A dark moan rumbled in his chest.

Her emotions suddenly choked her, ripping through her till she couldn't separate one from the other and didn't want to, didn't need to. She only wanted more. More. To get closer to him, feel him inside her, and hope her heart matched the feelings he created in her body.

A monkey shrieked close by, and they parted slowly, breathing hard. He tipped her chin up, and slowly, she met his gaze. His vivid blue eyes spoke volumes, nearly knocking her back. She prayed she was reading him right.

Then, without a word, he took her hand, and they headed down the mountain.

Six

Rick wasn't concentrating on paddling.

His attention was riveted to Samantha. She sat at the front of the flat-bottomed boat they'd found tucked near the shore. Its condition was debatable, but they only had a couple of miles to go down the river, and it was better than trekking through the jungle, then trying to find a shallow place to cross. The sun was starting to set, the creatures of the Amazon coming out to play. The rain had stopped, leaving a cool mist hovering over the water.

Samantha was vigilantly watching the terrain.

Rick was busy watching her. Not good recon, but a better view.

The first thing she did when they reached the water was take a dunk to rinse off the mud, then strip off the heavy camouflage shirt. The stretchy tank was molded to her torso, showing him every luscious curve he wanted to possess. She'd lost her ball cap in her tumble off the cliff. He was damn glad that was all she'd lost.

He didn't want to relive those moments; admitting he'd been scared out of his mind was hard enough, yet they'd shown him who Samantha really was. Strong, resilient—a sense of humor in a crisis, and she confused the hell out of him. He liked it.

No, he corrected, *he loved it.* She kept him on his toes, that's for sure.

"You're staring at me and not the direction," she said, then drew her gaze from the land to him.

"I know."

"You want in my panties, don't you?"

He blinked, then gave her a cocky smile. "What man wouldn't?"

"Why?"

"Huh?"

"Why? Big boobs? Because we're out here alone? Because we've survived the odds? Why?"

"You want a confession? Okay. I'm crazy about you. You're sexy and smart and have a mean streak through you that's annoying as hell—and kept you alive out here."

Her expression was filled with emotion when she said, "*You* kept me alive, Rick."

"I'm not going to argue about it. My opinion." She had more backbone that any woman he'd ever met.

"You like mean women?"

"I like strong women. Women who don't go along like sheep and leave everything up to men. Even ones who're scared of snakes."

Samantha chuckled lightly. "Most men are afraid of me, or want to take care of me."

"Or use you?" he added, remembering their conversation about her father's influence.

Her expression went bitter for a second. "Yeah."

"You could have been a Marine, Sam."

She considered that a tremendous compliment, but knew the reality. "I don't follow orders very well. Plus, the uniforms would make my hips look big."

He chuckled. "A crime, I'm sure." He dug the paddle into the water.

And for a second, Samantha watched him as he steered them toward the safe zone. Muscles flexed, sculptured and sinewy. He had six-pack abs to die for. She loved them; those muscles had saved her from becoming a pancake on the rocks.

"And I like the way you feel in my arms."

Clearly he'd been thinking about her question longer than she had. She met his gaze head-on. "Me, too."

He grinned, the smile full of sensual promise. "You make me hot without doing a thing. We fit, Sam, face it."

"I've faced a lot of things in the past forty-eight hours." One was that the men she'd dated before never measured up to some fictitious expectation she'd had in her mind. But Rick did. In spades. She'd avoided Marines, thinking they were just a younger version of her father, overpowering, demanding she walk the thin line. Rick was a strong man, physically and mentally—she got a quick flash of her panic with the rocket hitting the chopper, the snake, then dangling off the cliff—and knew she was right. He'd faced each situation with calm and determination. And he never once lost hope that they'd overcome.

Nothing would faze him, except maybe her lies.

She looked at the water, praying he wouldn't hate her later. She didn't want to lose his respect.

The river rippled harder, and she frowned at it, tensing and grabbing the rim of the boat.

"It's the current from the fall." The boat rocked as he steered it around a small inlet.

Then she saw it.

White water spilled from high in the mountain, broken only by the cut of Mother Nature before it pooled in a small lagoon just long enough to rush into the river and stir the boat. She craned her neck to take it all in: vibrant with a thousand shades of green; the vivid hues of wild orchids tucked into the cliffs. It took her breath away.

"Better than the Hyatt?" he said, and she glanced up long enough to smile. "We're docking here for the night." The bow scraped on the shore.

Rick hopped out, splashing through the water to bring it up onto shore. He secured it, then reached for her. Grasping her waist, he lifted her out, letting her slide down his body. The solid feel of him revived her, pushing away the last of her fear.

He kissed her, a quick slide of lips and tongue, then went for the pack. "Jesus, this is waterlogged."

"That's what I feel like, dirty, waterlogged . . . crabby," she said from the shore.

"That a new stage I should be aware of?"

She tipped her nose in the air. "I'm a multifaceted woman, Rick."

He was chuckling to himself as he led the way.

Rick took her up the right side of the fall where it spilled onto rocks, then flowed again into the lagoon. The setting sun glistered off the rippling water, turning it bright gold.

"You should get out of those clothes." He dropped the pack.

"See, I knew you just wanted in my panties."

He winked at her. "You can stay in that muck if you want." He studied her for a second. "It's not your best look, though."

She nudged him. "Everything I own is soaked and muddy."

"So rinse it out." He went to the lagoon, wading in to inspect the depth. "Looks safe," he declared. "I'm going to scout the area for shelter. You going to be okay?"

"Yup, me and Bertha"—she patted the Uzi—"promise not to shoot you."

He took a step away, then turned back, liking the startled look on her face as he grabbed her against him, the rifle in one hand, the other around her waist.

"Kiss me."

"Demanding macho ooh-rah Gi-reene."

"Kiss me. Like you mean it."

Her arms slid up around his neck, her smile seductively feline. "I've always meant it, Rick."

She laid her mouth over his, giving him a kiss that locked his muscles and gave him the fastest hard-on in recorded history. She was slow and sensual, her tongue outlining his lips, then pushing between to dip and play. Rick's knees softened. Her lips moved with a cat-and-mouse teasing, making him flex and jump to her tune. It was unexpected.

He loved it.

When she drew back, he was breathing hard, his fingers digging into her spine. "Damn, you're dangerous."

"I thought you thrived on danger," she said against his mouth, then sucked on his lower lip, making him quiver.

He groaned and moved in, took possession. His kiss was primal and overpowering, driving need and insatiable hunger down to her bones. She dampened between her thighs, yearning for his touch, her passion rising to meet the steamy temperatures.

Samantha felt at once captured and freed.

"Yeah, sure," he said between thick, hot kisses, "when I know the odds, the enemy, and the terrain."

"Odds are good, no enemy,"—she gasped when his mouth ground against her throat—"and exploring the terrain—"

"Will be a mission of utmost importance," he finished, cupping her behind and pulling her against his erection.

"Don't get cocky."

"Already there. Your fault, too." He was grinning when he abruptly released her, and without looking back, took off into the forest.

Samantha sank to the ground, a little numb. The man was raw sexuality and chained power. Nothing like being alone in the jungle with a bonafide white knight to get the heart pounding and her fantasies headed for Mach one. She licked her lips, needing to calm down some or she'd be all over his gorgeous self the instant he came back. She glanced at the rippling water.

It looked like heaven, wet and cool. And clean.

Digging into her pack, she found shampoo and soap, then stripped and waded into where it rippled hard. Less chance of snakes. She sank under the gloriously cold water, then put the bottles on a rock. She rinsed and floated, then lathered her hair. She felt wildly uninhabited to be outside, naked under a waterfall.

It took three shampoos to get the mud out of her hair and she swam under the fall. She let the hard force of the water pound her sore muscles. She swam back for her soap and grabbed her clothes to wash them, then threw them on the rocks before she paused to scan the area for intruders. Reptile or the two-legged kind. Then she lathered herself.

Rick stepped into the clearing, and his heart slammed against his ribs, then beat hard. Blood rocketed through his body, settling thickly in his groin.

No man on earth had seen anything so beautiful. Samantha, head tipped back, her dark red hair spilling down her naked back. Her skin glossy with wet.

Her hands slicked over her body, cupped her breasts. His erection flexed in his trousers, eager. Almost painful. His gaze flicked around. The Uzi was within her reach.

Good girl.

His attention was on her sweet ass when she turned, giving him a soapy, sleek profile. It beckoned him. Rick moved quietly forward, stripping off his tee shirt, then his boots. He walked into the water; she turned, startled for a second.

Her gaze locked with his. She made no move to cover herself.

"I see you're out of your panties."

Her smile was almost sadistic as she moved toward him, then slapped the soap on his chest. "You're filthy."

"Wash me, woman."

"My pleasure, Gunny." She lathered his chest, so close her breasts pushed against him. He seemed to be restraining himself, his hands resting on her hips. She slid the soap lower, jerking on his belt buckle, then flipped the buttons of his fly. She had trouble, and her rubbing him made him groan a little. "Clearly these aren't meant for rapid disrobing."

His fingertips dug into her hips. "You know where this is leading."

She dipped her hand inside, enfolding him. "I was right—you're smarter than you look," she teased, shaping him, her fingers trailing up and down his length.

Samantha knew well what she was doing. She'd no reservations about having sex with him. It seemed inevitable. She wanted to tell him who she was, why she kept it secret, but she didn't want to spoil this. He'd find out soon enough and despise her for the deception. He wouldn't understand her reasons; no man ever had before. It was her father, not her, who wore the two gold stars. She didn't know if Rick would react the same or not. She'd fallen for a couple of guys who'd been great till they learned who Daddy was. Then everything fell apart. It had happened often enough that she expected it.

And expected nothing. Except now.

"I want you," she said.

"Yeah?"

"Like nobody's business."

"It's the pecs, isn't it? Gets the women every time."

She had a wicked look in her eyes as she dragged her tongue over his pecs, circling his nipple and lapping at the salty taste of him. "Not really; it's this. The goody line."

She ran her finger down the center of his stomach, dipping below his waistband. She brushed her mouth over his stubbled chin. "What are we going to do for two days?"

"Three. And no radio contact till then."

"So we're the only people out here?"

"Nearest village is ten miles, so yeah. That means you can scream with pleasure."

"Boasting?"

His hand slid across her stomach and smoothly between her thighs. At first touch, she inhaled sharply, then sighed. He rubbed, parting her a little with each stroke. Her eyes flared, her breath quickening.

"Oh, that's good boasting."

"I'll make you come right now."

She gave him that "I dare you" look he loved.

He pushed deeper, slid a finger inside her. She moaned for him, warmed for him, and he wanted to taste her liquid heat. He would, till she screamed for him to plunge inside her. He introduced a second finger and Samantha thrust against him.

"Oh Rick."

"Yeah?"

"Faster. Deeper."

"Yes, ma'am." He insinuated his knee between her legs, spreading her, thrusting deeper. His gaze never left her as she fell back over his arm. Water splashed and misted around them. She looked like a glistening sculpture, his for the taking.

He dipped his head, pulling her nipple deep into the hot suck of his mouth and drawing hard. She squirmed, her body riddled with sensations. Then he quickened his pace, thrusting harder. "I'm going to make love to you for three straight days, Samantha."

The promise was enough to hurl her to the pulsing edge of an orgasm.

"I'm going to taste every inch of you, feel you come in

every position possible." He leaned, his lips near her ear. "I'm going to lick your clit and suck it till you're screaming for me."

She couldn't respond, couldn't speak. Her body was in control and he was in control of her body. His fingers slickened, a deep push, then withdrawing and plunging deeply again and again. Then she came, gripping him, devouring his mouth as it throbbed through her, flexing her muscles. He pulled her against him, holding her tight to feel it all.

Her body was like a curving wave, her desire rippling down to her center and thrusting against his hand. Her wet nerve endings pawed his fingers.

Rick tore his mouth from hers and demanded, "Look at me."

She did, and he watched the passion erupt and fuse. She went still and tight and he stroked her, pulling the last of her desire to the surface and letting it spill like hot wine. Then she fell against him, her forehead on his chest.

"Oh my God," she gasped.

"That was beautiful."

"Oh my God."

He laughed over her head. She inhaled rapidly and lifted her gaze. "Two can play this game."

He grabbed her against him, his stare dark and intense. "It's not a game. Not to me."

She understood instantly. And a pure joy ripped through her. She flicked open the last buttons on his fly, then drove her hand inside. He ground her palm to his erection. Her fingertips slickened the wet tip of him. Then she slithered down into the water, peeling open his trousers, and took him into her mouth.

"Oh, fuck."

She swallowed deeper, her lips pulling as she released him.

"Sam, Sam!" He scooped her out the water and strode to the bank, laying her down and then lying over her.

She smiled up at him, fished in his leg pocket, then held up the condom.

"Hurry and get that damn thing open because I want to slam into you"—he ground against her center—"right now." She opened it and took her time rolling it down, caressing him deeply. He kissed her and kissed her, kneeing her thighs apart and kicking off his trousers. Then suddenly Rick scooped her off the ground and sat back on his haunches. She straddled his lap and she lifted herself, positioning him. Eyes locked and he lowered her slowly, his Adam's apple working.

"Oh Christ, you're hot."

She wasn't having any of that and thrust, burying him inside her. Samantha closed her eyes, arching back. Feminine muscles squeezed around the solid thickness of him.

He felt it, groaning in pure ecstasy. "You're killing me, baby." Heat sizzled between them, and he wanted to throw her on her back and pound into her so much that his body trembled.

"Don't hold back."

He arched a brow. The woman could read his mind. "I could hurt you."

She rocked on him. "If you do, believe me, I'll speak up."

She wasn't giving him much choice, and gripped his shoulders, thrusting against him, pulling back so it was a long, smooth ride back into her body. Rick watched her face, fascinated with her smile, her panting.

The rifle lay beside them.

The sun was on the horizon, painting the sky deep purple and orange.

In the misty darkness of the jungle, her hips pistoned

and she threw her head back, her hair spilling black in the setting sun. His lips closed over her nipple, and he rolled it with his tongue as he cupped her ass and quickened their motion.

Oh Jesus. Nothing in his life had ever felt this good, this right. Her body clamped him in a slick, wet fist, crushing him, stroking him. He pushed her to her back, the raw primal power of each plunge sending them across the damp grasses. Overhead birds squawked. Her legs trapped him and he shoved harder, and harder, and she begged for more.

She whispered in his ear what he did to her, how she could feel every thick inch of him, and Rick's ego leapt like a crazed animal, and he focused on her, on hitting the spots that made her squirm.

Then it came. His climax ripped up his spine like a creature cut loose from its cage. She joined him, bowing beneath him, all curved, fevered flesh and sensual power.

For a split second, they were in the same place, the same moment, that vibrant edge teasing them with raw rapture.

Then white heat speared her and his erection flexed and elongated inside her. A groan tore from his lips, echoed into the trees. Her muscles convulsed rapidly, accepting his power, clawing for more of it. She cupped his tight behind, pulling him deeper, wishing herself inside him.

Then they collapsed, breathing hard, kissing any skin they could reach. When his breathing returned to something close to normal, Rick lifted his head and smiled down at her. He pushed her hair off her face, then buried his hands it in.

Then carefully, almost cautiously, he kissed her with such unbelievable delicacy, her heart melted right there on the jungle floor.

She lifted her gaze to his. He sketched her features, his lips curving ever so slightly. But there was something in his eyes she hadn't seen before. It made her feel liquid and adored.

And Samantha Previn Bricker knew she was a goner. He had her heart in his strong fist.

"Three days, huh?" she said, and rubbed her thumb across his lower lip. "You going to make good on all those promises?"

He grinned. "And then some, baby."

Seven

Rick emerged from the water, his gaze on Samantha. Hers was locked on him.

"Now, that's a fantasy," he said. She wore nothing but his camouflage shirt, and held the Uzi.

It made him hard.

"That's just because I'm packing more firepower than you." Her gaze lowered pointedly to his groin. "Well . . . maybe."

He laughed, stopping a few inches from her and bending to kiss her. She sank into his mouth, her free hand sliding up his bare, wet behind and squeezing.

"Be careful, Marine, this gun might go off."

He drew back and bent for his clothes. "It's time to get out of sight—it's getting dark fast and we've risked too much being out in the open."

Samantha gave the fall a longing look. She'd already bathed again, but it was so much cooler in the water. "But there isn't another village for miles."

"That doesn't mean the rebels aren't near." Rick pulled on his trousers and boots, then checked his weapons. "I found a cave." He gestured beyond the falls. "It's only a few yards back. Good cover—it will be drier in there, and I checked it for snakes."

"My hero."

Slinging on the pack, he led her to the cave.

It was small, the ceiling low-slung. Neither of them could stand completely upright inside it. Although it was tucked in the forest enough so they could risk a fire, Rick was cautious. Besides, finding dry wood was another matter. And the last thing he wanted to do was fight off drug dealers or rebels again.

He had other plans.

In a few minutes, Rick had the mat on the cavern floor, the poncho liner over it.

Samantha rested against the pack, her shoulders aching like crazy. She wore clean, slightly damp shorts and one of Rick's tee shirts. And nothing else. Rick thought she looked like a centerfold. Samantha thought she looked like crap.

"Give me a job to do," she said when Rick popped in and out, not saying much.

"Sit tight . . . and save your strength for later." He flashed her a cocky smile and played the he-man, gathering fresh water and discarded clothes, then returning from his last trip into the jungle with an armload of wild fruit.

Gee. Her very own white hunter.

He sat across from her and broke out his MREs and cooking tools. "Teriyaki chicken," he said.

"Benihana, eat your heart out." In minutes the cave smelled like a four-star restaurant. "My mouth is actually watering over that."

He glanced up, his eyes dancing with something she couldn't name. "It's not bad. Not great, but not bad. Have some crackers." They hadn't eaten since last night.

She tore open the pack, breaking them and offering him some. In minutes they were feeding each other, licking teriyaki sauce off their fingers.

"I'm going to need another bath."

"I'll lick you clean," he murmured, sliding down her

body and pushing up the tee shirt. He buried his face between her breasts, massaging them. Braced on the pack, Samantha arched, wanted him again.

"You're like a drug," she said, leaning to kiss him.

"Good, 'cause I'm addicted. God, your skin is so smooth." He enfolded her breasts, sucking her nipples in turn till she was squirming and breathing hard.

"Rick?" She flicked a condom packet.

He shook his head. "Time to make good those promises." He mapped a wet path over her stomach, tugged open her shorts, tasting the skin he revealed in slow, grinding kisses. Her stomach muscles contracted. She lifted her hips.

He pulled her shorts down. "I don't know why you bothered."

"Well, lying here buck naked and saying 'come and get me' seemed a bit pushy."

He grinned. "You *are* pushy."

"A girl needs *some* secrets."

His gaze locked with hers. "Not from me." He opened his trousers, shucking them. Samantha smacked her lips. He was the most delicious-looking man, and she did everything she could to get him to come to her short of full frontal attack. He ignored her. His big shoulders pushed her legs apart as he licked her inner thigh, her stomach, his mouth and tongue skating over her skin. But he never touched *there.*

It drove her insane with desire. She loved it.

She throbbed between her thighs, hot and wet with need. His warm breath slipped teasingly over her center. He kissed her everywhere else, leaning back to lift her foot and tease her instep, her calf, her knee. Lying on the ground, he pushed her thighs wider. Samantha held his gaze as he scooped her off the ground and brought her to his mouth.

"Oh. My. God."

She went boneless, his tongue sliding and dipping while

she looked on. Seeing his head between her thighs was more erotic than the feelings he created. And they were ripping through her like a spastic pinball.

She gasped for air, pleasure like a writhing animal in her. Then he drew back, his kiss letting her taste herself.

"Rick," she pleaded, sliding her fingers around his thickness.

She slickened a finger over the moist tip before he pushed her hands aside. "Oh, we are not even close to the prize."

"Yes, I am. I want you. Right now."

"No." The one word had a sinister sound as he pushed her onto her stomach, her body laid over the huge pack. It was a vulnerable position, helpless, but the instant he nipped the curve of her behind, delicious sensations crushed any misgivings.

He licked slowly, nipped, then soothed. She felt warm and soft and jungle sexy. His hands were no less busy, molding her breast, two fingers dipping into her heat to taunt her into madness. He whispered how beautiful she was, that he could smell her heat and it made him want to devour her again. But he didn't, teasing her till she was whimpering and buttery.

He spread her, his tongue plunging into her soft folds. She shrieked and he licked her like a whipped dessert. Just enough to bring her to the edge, to make the pleasure beyond unbearable. She trembled for him.

She begged.

He denied her.

Rick took his time at her spine, stripping her out of the shirt. His hands were strong and warm, massaging her sore muscles, and from behind, he cupped her breasts, then whispered in her ear, "I want you this way."

She twisted to meet his gaze. "Oh yeah."

He arched a brow. "Adventurous?" He slid one hand between her legs and stroked her wetly.

"I know what I want. And I trust you." She pushed back into him on his lap, his erection firm between her thighs. She slid back and forth on him. His grip on her hips tightened.

"I need a . . . I need . . ." Christ, he couldn't think! "Oh shit, baby, you're gonna make me lose it."

"We can't have that. Not yet," she said, half turning. She tore open the packet, teasing him with the condom. "I'm so glad you Marines are prepared for anything."

Her grin was she-cat dangerous, her fingers manipulating him till he was groaning like a mongrel dog. She bent, her mouth torturing him mercilessly.

He grasped her shoulders. "Put the damn thing on," he growled with a warning look. She was prim and adorable as she obeyed, sliding the tip of him just an inch inside her.

"Now who's begging?" she teased, rocking a little, taunting him.

He grabbed her to him, his expression dark and raw. "Yes, I'm begging."

"You don't have to."

His kissed her hard. "Let's be animals."

He positioned her in front of him, her back to his chest, his hands sliding roughly over her breasts, then diving between. He paid her back, circling the bead of her sex till he felt the first quiver of her climax. Then he stopped. She whimpered and thrust back against him, her hands braced on the pack. Rick pushed his erection down, spreading her. Then in one hard plunge, he filled her.

She moaned like a wild creature, her body tightly trapping his. "Oh my God, Rick."

"Oh yeah."

She moved, and he slid deeper. His gaze sketching her, her long, curly hair flipping back, the delicate curve of her spine, his erection sliding deep into her and back out.

She wouldn't be still or quiet.

She begged for speed, she demanded power. Slick and

driving. Rick gripped her hips, then reached around to flick his finger over her clit. She came in an explosion of panting cries and muddled words.

In grinding pushes and fused bodies.

His heart pounded like a sledgehammer. He shoved hard, and the rapture of it made him quake and roar her name. They pulsed like hot, raw wires and he trapped her to his chest and buried his face in the curve of her throat as throb after throb slammed into his body.

Her muscles quivered and fisted around him, draining him.

Then her arms rose, her hands cupping his head, and she twisted to kiss him.

Rick knew in that instant that he'd fallen hard for her.

Not for the sex, but he knew. She was *the one*.

This just made it better.

He wondered if it was all in his mind and in the haze of hot jungle sex. Or did she feel the same?

Rick woke at predawn in a state of readiness that had nothing to do with the U.S. Marines. A half-second later, he realized that Samantha had her head on his lap.

And she was going to town on him.

"Jesus H. Christ."

She laughed to herself, but never stopped. No woman had done this. No woman had given so freely.

He lay back and enjoyed it, but her lips tugging, her hands stroking in a long, hard pull made it impossible to think about anything but the explosion that was fast approaching liftoff.

"You little tiger."

She drew on him. He slammed his eyes shut and threw his head back. Then strong arms grabbed her legs and he yanked, pulling her so she was on top of him, her thighs spread.

"Rick, no, I wanted to—"

"I don't give a shit what you want right now except don't stop. Trust me—this will be more fun."

"It's that mutual satisfaction thing?"

"You couldn't fake a climax for me if you wanted—I already know you better."

"You think so?"

"I'll prove it."

He wrapped his lips around the tiny bead of her sex and sucked. She came instantly, and they held tight to each other, bucking like animals as he climaxed in her mouth.

It was several moments before they collapsed like rags, bodies slick with sweat and steam. She rolled off him and met his gaze, running her tongue over her lips.

He pulled her on top of him and kissed her, wrapping his arms around her. She lay softly on him, her head on his chest. Rick's hands rode up and down her spine.

"God, what a way to wake up!" he said, still breathing heavy.

Her arms propped on his chest, she smiled. "Revelee revelee," she said.

He chuckled. "Ooh-rahh."

They explored the area, finding enough fruit to last the next day. They'd needed it for the energy they were expending. She hadn't had such great sex in all her life.

Nothing will compare to the last three days, she thought. Not in memory, or in her heart. The more she got to know Rick, the harder she fell for him.

He was everything she thought she didn't want. The last thing in the world she'd expected was to fall hook, line, and sinker for a Marine. Out in the jungle. But then, she guessed, with no one else around, it was like dating for months. It wasn't like they hid anything from each other.

Well, except her dad's rank.

That he was Rick's commanding general.

And if anyone learned what they did out here, he'd suffer for it. She was used to the gossip and the treatment. But him?

Damn. She didn't want the helicopter to come get them. The closer the time came to making radio contact and leaving, the worse she felt.

Rick would find out and he'd be pissed. He'd walk away, and she was already hurting.

"What's up with you?"

"Nothing?"

He dropped what he was doing and came to her. "Sam, I know it's only been a few days, but I already know when something's bothering you."

It touched her that he could tell. She thought she'd covered it up rather well so far. "I'm actually reluctant about leaving."

He rubbed her shoulders, then drew her into his arms. "Me, too."

"Is it just that we've had some great sex alone in the jungle?"

He leaned back to meet her gaze and saw sadness there. "Christ, Sam. You really think I'm that shallow?"

"No."

"Then why say that?"

"Scared," she confessed.

He cupped her face in his broad hands. "Listen up, okay? I'm not those other people. And if you don't want me to find you after we get back, then say so. It will lay me out for about twenty years, but say so now."

She covered his hands, her eyes glossy. "I want you to come look for me."

He smiled tenderly and was about to kiss her when the radio crackled with call letters. Rick turned to it, speaking to base, then pulling out the map. "Roger that. Eleven hundred." He checked his watch. "White Knight out." He looked at her. "We have an hour. The chopper will land in a field, about a mile from here."

They'd already packed, all evidence of their stay erased.

"Let's get going, then."

He frowned at the sudden coolness in her tone. Rick nodded and led the way. It took a better part of the hour to make it to the landing zone. Rick was suited up much like she'd first seen him, full battle gear.

The sound of the chopper thrummed in the distance and she lifted her gaze to his. He was staring at her, frowning. Then he strode close and grabbed her by the arms.

"They'll see."

"You ashamed of me?" he said.

"No! That's just not possible."

"Then kiss me."

"Oh, darlin'," she said. "I want more than kisses." *I want forever.* She laid her mouth over his. The instant shock always got her; the hot, primal passion made her want to strip and lie down for whatever he had in mind. He devoured her mouth like he'd never have the chance again and didn't break the kiss till the chopper crested the rise.

"If it looks like I'm ignoring you, I'm not. I'm thinking of your reputation, not mine. You got that?"

"Aye-aye, Gunny."

Reluctantly, he stepped back.

The chopper descended, the door sliding open, a machine gunner poised on the threshold. His attention flicked to her for a second before turning to the terrain.

Rick helped her in, then climbed in beside her. His team was inside.

"What? You guys thought I needed help?"

"Hell, Gunny, we figured it was a free ride on a good day."

They glanced at Samantha. Rick eyed them hard. They were looking at her oddly. He didn't like it, and could only imagine what was going through their minds.

The chopper lifted off and headed home.

And Samantha dreaded every mile.

＊　＊　＊

They landed on a secure base in Venezuela, then were immediately transferred to a transport to Camp Lejeune. Samantha didn't even have time to change. Apparently her father wanted her on American soil as soon as possible. So much that she was on a cargo plane in a jump seat for the next couple of hours.

Rick was busy speaking with his men and on the radio to his commander, but every time he looked at her, Samantha felt that hard pull in her heart. He winked at her. She blushed and smiled.

When he got a second, he was right beside her, but because they were on a transport and surrounded by others, he didn't touch her. No public displays of affection. Plus you had to practically shout to be heard above the engines. But he let his leg brush hers and once he leaned close to whisper that he wished she was in his arms.

Naked.

It was the last thing he said to her before they set down on the airstrip. She had to tell him the truth before the door opened, and she grabbed his arm. He met her gaze.

"There's something I need to tell you."

The hydraulic doors opened, Marines hopping out, cars driving close.

He glanced at the others, backing her away. The engines were making a hard whine to shut down. "Me, too, but not here."

He inclined his head to the pilots who were coming out of the cockpit.

"But Rick, this is important. My father, well he's—"

"Gunnery Sergeant Cahill!" a voice boomed. "Front and center."

Rick gave her hand a quick squeeze. "I'll call you. That's my Sergeant Major." He was out the rear aircraft door.

Samantha stepped out onto the airstrip.

Rick stood at attention in front of Sergeant Major Stockwell. They saluted, and then there was a lot of back-slapping and handshaking. Samantha had known John Stockwell since she was a child. When "Uncle" John waved to her, she smiled and waved back.

Climbing into the van, Rick paused on the van step and glanced her way.

She stood on the airstrip, the sharp wind kicking at her hair. He smiled.

A dark sedan sped across the airstrip toward her.

That smile slowly fell, and the look on his face was crushing when he saw the two-star flags on the staff car's bumper. Then her father climbed out and came to her, swooping her in his arms and holding her tight. Her dad murmured something, but she wasn't listening.

Her attention was over his shoulder—on Rick. His blue eyes narrowed dangerously.

Her heart sank like a stone and silently pleaded for understanding.

Her father let her go, touching her face, kissing her cheek. She looked up at him, smiling, loving him so much, and wishing right now that he was a welder.

Eight

Rick spent the next hours getting cleaned up, a haircut, into a fresh uniform to be debriefed, then writing his report. He had a lot of time to think about Sam in the arms of Lieutenant General "Brickhouse" Bricker.

His daughter. Jesus.

He remembered every conversation they'd had in the jungle about her father, the "under the microscope" life she'd had, and the reasons she'd stayed away from Marines and her own father. He was beginning to understand it. Because the instant he was in the company offices it started, exactly as she'd predicted.

Staff Sergeant Parker braced his hip on the desk. "So Rick, you nail her out there?"

Rick glared at him. "You're really classy, you know that, Parker?"

"Hey, she's a babe, one hell of a hottie. Every man on this base has wet dreams about women like that."

"Obviously you don't have enough work to do. Because you're thinking too much. And get your ass off my desk."

Parker stood. "I guess the Ice Princess put you in a bad mood."

Ice Princess? The last thing he'd have thought about

Samantha was ice. Fire, heat, raw sensuality. And a grip on his heart so tight he could barely breathe when he thought about her. Rick kept typing. "Miss Previn was more courageous than you'd imagine."

"Normally she's a snob."

"Nah," a young sergeant said, dropping papers in Rick's in-box. "She's always nice. She just doesn't get near Marines. With a dad like 'Brickhouse' Bricker, I'm not surprised."

"Perhaps she's aloof because people treat her differently because she's the general's daughter."

It hit him again. The general's daughter. Now he knew why she was so upset about being stuck with a Marine, why she cut him off emotionally before they got in the chopper. And why the hell she knew the lingo and how to use a damn weapon.

Rick focused on the screen, but it was useless. He saved and stood, grabbing his cover and heading for the door. He never made it. The Sergeant Major caught him, motioning him into his offices. He stood before the man he respected most of all, waiting for the lecture.

"At ease, Rick—have a seat."

Rick dropped into the leather-upholstered chair beside the desk.

"Previn is her mother's maiden name," Stockwell said candidly.

"Yes, Sergeant Major. I figured it was something like that."

"She didn't tell you who her father was out there, did she?"

It was a moment before Rick answered. "There wasn't really any reason to." Except being honest. Rick ground his teeth.

Stockwell seemed to take that in for a second. "I've known Tom—General Bricker since he was a lieutenant. Samantha is my goddaughter."

Rick's eyes flared. "The snowball keeps getting bigger and bigger," he muttered.

"I've heard the gossip and know what she's been through. She has her reasons. She'd go out with her girlfriends and he'd know about it—hell, *I'd* know about it by oh-seven hundred the next morning because some dumbass NCO would shoot off his mouth that he'd danced with her or kissed her the night before. She couldn't do a thing without being watched."

"I don't really care about that, Sergeant Major."

"Yes, you do," Stockwell said with absolute finality. "She dated a captain once who didn't take her out unless her father was around."

Rick's brows shot up.

"It only took her about a week to figure that guy out. But he was just a repeat."

"What are you saying, Sergeant Major?"

Stockwell jotted something down on a slip of paper and slid it across the desk. "I have no doubt that you are up to the challenges that loving Samantha presents. Your toughest job will be convincing her it will work."

Rick stood, and picked up the paper. It was a phone number. "What makes you think I love her?"

"See these stripes, Gunny?" Stockwell pointed to the seven stripes on his sleeve. Three up, four down, with a star in the middle. "I got these because I know people. You're no exception. Now get out of my office."

The minute Rick was outside, he dialed the number on his cell phone. The general's quarters. The maid answered, but Sam wasn't taking any calls or visitors.

We'll just see about that.

At a special formation that afternoon, Rick got his first look at Samantha since they'd landed. She looked like a million bucks in a slim-fitting red suit and high heels—and standing next to her father. For a second, he felt like a sucker.

Yet when Rick was called front and center, a speaker read a citation for his rescue and safe return of one Samantha Bricker, Peace Corps nurse, all their conversations of how deeply she'd been hurt by men who thought of Daddy before they thought of her came rushing back.

"The Corps thanks you, but as a father I want to thank you for rescuing my little girl." The general held out his hand.

Rick shook it and nodded. "Miss Bricker was courageous and quick-thinking, sir. Give her the credit for her survival."

The general arched a brow, then glanced at his daughter. Samantha's attention was on Rick and he felt kicked by the look in her eyes. So much sadness. He realized right there that she thought he'd just dismiss her because of her father.

No way.

No fucking way in hell.

Although there was a reception in the staff club afterward—give a Marine a reason to pop a keg and they'd milk it till it was gone—Rick wasn't interested. He went looking for Samantha and found her alone in the parking lot beside a little black sports car. Before he got to her, a lieutenant got to him.

"Leave it alone, Gunny. It's going to hurt your career."

"How you figure . . . sir?"

"You'll never get a thing without someone questioning if the general's influence wasn't behind it."

"If it ever was, I'd call him on it, Lieutenant. And, sir?"

"Yes?"

"Butt the hell out." Rick strode across the lot. "Sam."

Samantha glanced up and her heart tumbled. "Rick." She wondered how she could draw a breath when he was near.

He stopped close. "Why?"

She didn't have to ask what he meant. "I didn't tell you

because I didn't expect to be in the jungle with you for days. I didn't expect to care for you so much."

"You think I'm just going to walk away because your father wears stars and I wear stripes?"

"You can't tell me you haven't felt the ribbing already."

"Oh yeah, I have—came close to punching a few guys in the face."

"See, that's why it won't work. The Marine Corps is small and—"

"Do you want it to work?" he cut in.

She was staring at her keys and now lifted her gaze to his. The tears in her eyes about killed him right there. "Yes."

He sighed, relieved.

"But you'll be miserable."

She opened the door and tried to get in. He stopped her, cupping the back of her head and kissing her like there was no tomorrow. She melted, whimpering against his mouth, clutching his shoulders. The area went wild with catcalls and shouts of "ooh-rah."

"See?"

Rick looked around and snarled at the Marines, then met her gaze. "Get in." He took her keys. "Get in," he said when she just stared.

She did, sliding over the console. He got behind the wheel, started the engine, and drove. "Rick?"

"Be quiet."

"Excuse me?"

"If you give me one more lame excuse about why we can't be together, we're going to have our first fight." He braked at a stoplight and leaned across, kissing her wildly. Till she was grabbing for him. Till he felt her melting for him. Then he drove, not saying a word, but they couldn't keep their hands off each other. He slipped his hand between her thighs, sliding up her stockinged legs. He moaned when he felt the lacy tops. She pushed his hand deeper, inching closer, and he pushed her panties aside and dipped and toyed with her. She molded him, shaping him. He jerked the car into the driveway of a house and got out, coming around to her side.

"My house," he said, pulling her up the walk.

It was darling, but she barely noticed. They were inside and he had her against the nearest wall, kissing her ferociously and stripping off her clothes.

They were savage and primal, tearing at each other like starved animals. She couldn't be still, nipping at his throat, his mouth, sliding her tongue over his skin. Immediately, he cupped her breasts and she pushed into his touch, begging for more as she shaped his erection trapped in his trousers. She made a little sound, of hunger and passion, her kiss growing stronger. Unstoppable. As if trying to devour him whole.

She opened his belt, flipped the buttons. Her jacket was open, and he tugged her bra down, her nipple spilling into the heat of his mouth.

She moaned.

He sucked, groaned, wanting her more than he did the first time.

Samantha's mind went blank to everything but Rick. His hands were under her skirt, his fist wrapping in her thong panties.

"You are not nearly naked enough." He yanked, snapping the delicate fabric. She smiled as he threw them over his shoulder, then he cupped her behind, pulling her into him.

"Now, Rick. Now."

"Bedroom—"

"Who cares!"

"Oh jeez," he groaned as she freed him into her palm. He wasn't going to make it. He braced one hand on the wall to catch his breath. But she stroked him, tortured him. He was rock-hard and as ready as she was. He lifted her against him and she wrapped her legs around his hips. His erection pushed against her heat. Rick thought he'd climax right then. He shoved away from the wall, staggering toward the back of the house, banging into the wall before rolling into the bedroom. They tumbled to the bed. And he was inside her, pushing.

"Oh hell. Condom," he gasped on a ragged breath, slapping blindly at the nightstand, knocking over the lamp as he yanked open the drawer. He grabbed one but she took it, tearing into the packet and putting it on him.

"I love it when you do that," he murmured, then plunged solidly into her.

"I love it when you do *that* . . . Oh Rick." They arched against each other, and he sat back on his calves, letting her ride him. She was like a tiger let loose, untamed and vibrant, tearing off the rest of her clothes. He palmed her breasts, leaned up to suck and kiss and nibble on her flesh as her hips surged wildly against him. He cupped her behind, pulling her harder.

She matched him. Wild jungle sexy. Sweat glistened, bodies pushing and pulling hotly.

"Oh Sam, oh God."

She held his gaze, thrusting sharply. "You are the best thing to happen to me, Rick."

"Me, too, baby."

She could feel him coming, the long, thick push of man inside her. She rocked, wanting him to remember this. Wanting him so deep in her life. But she was afraid. She'd take this and have him and love him. Because she was never sure. Of herself, of his heart.

She cupped his face. Her gaze locked on his and he bucked, his blue eyes intense and glazing as he climaxed with her. It was bone-chilling hard, leaving them breathless. She devoured him, riding the grinding pleasure with him, her little gasps tumbling into his mouth. When the frantic pulse settled to slow beats, Samantha clung to him, her heart loving and bleeding and hoping.

Hours later, Rick woke alone in the dark. Sam was nowhere around. And it was clear to him that he'd have to make a full frontal assault on the hardheaded woman.

The door opened, a maid smiling at him.

"Why, Gunnery Sergeant Cahill, come in. I'm sure the general will be glad to see you."

Rick scraped off his wedge-shaped Alpha cover. "I'm not here to see him, ma'am."

"Oh." The housekeeper smiled.

"Would you call Miss Bricker down, please?"

"I don't want to see you, Rick."

Rick sidestepped the housekeeper, staring up the twisting staircase. "That's really too bad, because we have to talk." She wore hip-hugging jeans and a frilly blouse that showed off her great cleavage. Her hair was a wild mass of red curls nearly to her waist, but when he looked at Sam, he'd always see her naked and open for him.

The library doors opened. "What is the meaning of this?" General Bricker stepped out of his study, his uniform collar undone.

Rick snapped to attention. "Begging the general's pardon, sir, but I've come to see your daughter."

"And if I won't allow it?"

"I'll improvise, sir, adapt, overcome. But I *am* going to see her."

"Just what exactly happened between you two in that jungle?"

Rick turned his head, his icy gaze landing on the general like a hammer. "With all due respect, sir, that's none of your business."

Bricker's bushy brows shot up into his forehead.

"This has nothing to do with the Corps," Rick said.

"It's between Samantha and me . . . sir." He turned his gaze to Sam.

His words riveted Samantha to the landing, almost choking her. That was the first and only time anyone had butted heads with her father, or had the guts to do it. And not care about the results.

"Rick . . . please don't do this."

He moved to the stairs, mounting them as he spoke.

"I love you, Samantha." She blinked. "I know it's crazy. I know how you feel about the Marine Corps, and believe me, now I understand why. But I know how you feel about me, too."

"Oh, do you?"

He loved that "make me" look she threw out. "Oh yeah," he said, smiling. "You survived in that jungle because you're your father's daughter. Because you know this life. No, shut yer yap and let me finish," he said when she opened her mouth.

Below in the foyer, her father smothered a laugh.

"It's in your blood. Because you were dragged all over the world with your father's tours of duty, you're stronger than most women. Hell, you're stronger than most men. If you hadn't lived this life, you wouldn't have survived the cliff, or had the guts to go help others in a hostile country."

"But your career—this is going to interfere. You know it already has."

"I can handle anything they throw at me. Jokes, teasing, I don't give a crap. My military career is mine. I'll get where I want on my own merit. I don't need his influence. I don't want it. But I need you."

Samantha stared up into his blue eyes, feeling her heart shimmer in her chest.

"Don't *not* love me because of the uniform I wear, Sam. Because I won't stop loving you because you have two stars watching over you."

"You really love me?" she choked.

"Oh yeah, baby. I'd die for you."

"Well, we won't have to take it that far." She looped her arms around his neck. "I love you, Rick Cahill. I mean, how could I not? You killed snakes for me." Her smile teased wider, and when he started to kiss her, she jerked back, eyeing him hard. "I still want to finish with the Peace Corps."

"Fine, whatever you want. If I can deploy, so can you. Besides, I already learned it would be impossible to talk you out of it."

Her eyes went bright. "So where do we go from here?"

"Marry me."

She blinked. Her mouth worked, but nothing came out.

"My God, she's speechless," the general said.

"Shut up, Daddy," she said without taking her gaze off Rick.

Rick twisted to look the general dead in the eye. "Begging your pardon, sir, but *do you mind?*" Rick inclined his head.

Smiling, the general strolled back into his library.

Rick faced Sam, and brought her hand to his lips, kissed them, then slipped a ring on her finger. "You left my house before I could give you this."

She gasped at the diamond. "Oh Rick, it's too much."

"It's never enough. Make me the happiest man alive and say yes."

She looked at him with teary eyes. "Oh yes."

"I love you, I love you," he said between deep kisses, his big hands mapping familiar contours. When someone cleared his throat, Rick decided the general was too damn nosy and he swept Samantha into his arms and trotted down the stairs to the door.

"Don't expect us back, sir," he said as he passed the general in the hall.

Samantha laughed, the stunned look on her father's face imprinted in her mind forever.

Rick really was a White Knight. He'd waged a battle, faced the dragon, but Sam was the one who'd gained the greatest prize. His heart.

Ooh-rah.

Please turn the page for an exciting preview of
MOUTH TO MOUTH
by Erin McCarthy.
Available in January 2005 from Brava.

Laurel had successfully lured Russ into her bedroom.

Not bad considering she hadn't known he was going to show up on her doorstep before she had finished formulating her plan for throwing herself naked at his feet. Figuratively, of course.

The e-mail from the con artist would give her an opportunity to bring up her quest for sex again. She'd try to be more subtle this time, but she was like a blind bat trying to fly through water. Seduction wasn't her area of expertise.

She wasn't exactly sure what was, unless it was directing a customer to the bin of chocolate Goobers.

That was going to be tough to eulogize someday.

Laurel bent over her computer and clicked on her e-mail. Russ stood behind her, looking large and denim in her frilly lace, girly-girl room. A glance back showed him kicking his boots off on her honey pine hardwood floor, like he was settling in. It stripped the situation of any business-like feeling that remained, and Laurel swallowed hard.

"Sorry, I was trailing snow on your carpets."

"It's okay." In fact, if he needed to take anything else off, she was fine with that, too.

He had on oatmeal-colored socks, the kind with the red

strip across the toe. Hunting socks, hiking socks, man socks. On her throw rug shaped like a fat white daisy with a lemon dot in the middle.

"Here's the first e-mail."

Russ leaned over her shoulder. She knew he was reading the message out loud—she could feel his breath teasing across the back of her neck. She reread it herself, drew in the masculine scent of Russ's aftershave, and shivered.

"He sounds so sincere apologizing, doesn't he?" Laurel mused. It was interesting to her, to read the message again, to wonder if she would have trusted the sincerity of it if Russ hadn't told her the truth first. She liked to think that sooner or later natural instincts would have kicked in and she would have sensed that something about the guy was off. But then again, it was just words on a screen, easy to interpret however you wanted to. Maybe in person she would have seen the lie in his eyes.

Russ's fingers touched her chin. She turned, startled, pulled out of her musings. His face was close enough so that she could see he had a chipped tooth on the bottom left—just a little point missing at the top. He looked frustrated, intense, like he was struggling to stay calm.

Laurel sucked in her breath and tried really hard not to want to kiss him. But her legs trembled, her shoulders shuddered, her breath caught. She wasn't very good at the not-wanting-him thing.

Too bad sex didn't seem to be the first thing on his mind.

"Don't believe him. Don't e-mail him. Change your address and stay clear of chat rooms. Do you understand me?"

Nope, she could tell he wasn't thinking sex. He was thinking *God save me from dumb blondes*. Laurel didn't want to hear another lecture, not now in her bedroom. She honestly hadn't been suggesting anything other than the fact that the guy was good at what he did. She wasn't such a sap as to still be taken in by him, despite what her mother thought. And she didn't really care one iota what Trevor Dean was doing, not when she had Russ Evans touching her. In a chin lock, but hey, she had to start somewhere.

Then move forward from there. She touched his lip with her thumb, gathered up her courage. "How did you chip your tooth?"

"You're changing the subject."

Absolutely. "I can see it . . . I was just wondering."

His eyes had gotten very dark, like melted chocolate. He hesitated, then said, "My buddy bumped me when I had a beer bottle in my mouth."

"Did it hurt?" Instead of dropping into her lap like a good little hand, her palm slid down his shoulder and held onto his bicep.

For balance, of course. Because she was in danger of falling flat on her ass, blown away by the rising desire she thought she could see in Russ's face.

Not that she was an expert on interpreting sexual interest, but she didn't think that under normal circumstances a man looked capable of tearing a woman's clothes off with his teeth. Russ was getting there fast, and she had the tight nipples to prove it.

"Yes, it hurt." He still had his hand under her chin, and he tilted her head a little, studied her. "So are you still planning on going wild and having casual sex?"

Yes. That eliminated the need for her to work sex into the conversation. He'd done it all on his own, and she was truly grateful. Now if she could just swallow her saliva and not her tongue, she'd be all set.

Laurel forced the words out, wondering if they slurred. "I'd like to. But not with just any man." He'd pretty much ruined that. She wasn't going to be interested in any man but him. "Not a stranger, either. But it's hard to meet people. I work in a candy store, and our clientele is not usu-

274 / *Erin McCarthy*

ally single men." She was babbling, saying too much. Just get to the damn point. "I would want it to be someone I could trust."

Russ took her hand, pulled her to a standing position, brushed her hair off her cheek, and she shivered when his callused hands swept her skin. "Why just an affair, Laurel? I don't understand."

Neither did she sometimes, so it was going to be tough to explain. She took a deep breath, captured his other hand with hers, and went over to the wild side. "I have a nice life, Russ. I do. But I'm lonely, that's all. I just want a man to touch me."

His eyes went dark, narrow, fierce. She almost forgot to look at his lips, almost imagined she could hear his thoughts in his deep rich eyes.

"I'd like to touch you, Laurel."

Good, they were completely in sync then. "I was hoping you'd say that."

"And I'd like to touch you now, everywhere, and tumble you back onto that prissy bed of yours."

Oh, my. Laurel glanced at her bed. She wasn't sure if she was ready right this second. It was just past noon on a weekday.

"But I'm on duty, so I can't."

Disappointment and relief collided like cymbals.

"But can I come back tonight? We can go out . . . see what happens."

"My mother is out of town," she said to avoid whimpering in acquiescence.

"Good." His hand went into her hair and his head bent down.

It took her a second to realize that he really and truly meant to kiss her. By the time she was clear on it, he was already there.

We don't think you will want to miss Alison Kent's
new five-episode series.
Here is a description of all five books.

Meet the men of the Smithson Group—five spies whose best work is done in the field and between the sheets. Smart, built, trained to do everything well—and that's everything—they're the guys you want on your side of the bed. Go deep undercover? No problem. Take out the bad guys? Done. Play by the rules? I don't think so. Indulge a woman's every fantasy? Happy to please, ma'am. Fall in love? Hey, even a secret agent's got his weak spots . . .

Bad boys. Good spies. Unforgettable lovers.

Episode One:
THE BANE AFFAIR
by
Alison Kent

"Smart, funny, exciting, touching, and *hot.*"—Cherry Adair

"Fast, dangerous, sexy."—Shannon McKenna

Get started with Christian Bane, SG–5

Christian Bane is a man of few words, so when he talks, people listen. One of the Smithson Group's elite force, Christian's also the walking wounded, haunted by his past. Something about being betrayed by a woman, then left to die in a Thai prison by the notorious crime syndicate Spectra IT gives a guy demons. But now,

Spectra has made a secret deal with a top scientist to crack a governmental encryption technology, and Christian has his orders: Pose as Spectra boss Peter Deacon. Going deep undercover as the slick womanizer will be tough for Christian. Getting cozy with the scientist's beautiful goddaughter, Natasha, to get information won't be. But the closer he gets to Natasha, the harder it gets to deceive her. She's so alluring, so trusting, so completely unexpected he suspects someone's been giving out faulty intel. If Natasha isn't the criminal he was led to believe, they're both being played for fools. Now, with Spectra closing in, Christian's best chance for survival is to confront his demons and trust the only one he can . . . Natasha . . .

Available from Brava in October 2004.

**Episode Two:
THE SHAUGHNESSEY ACCORD
by
Alison Kent**

Get hot and bothered with Tripp Shaughnessey, SG–5

When someone screams Tripp Shaughnessey's name, it's usually a woman in the throes of passion or one who's just caught him with his hand in the proverbial cookie jar. Sometimes it's both. Tripp is sarcastic, fun-loving, and funny, with a habit of seducing every woman he says hello to. But the one who really gets him hot and bothered is Glory Brighton, the curvaceous owner of his favorite sandwich shop. The nonstop banter between Glory and Tripp has been leading up to a full-body kiss in the back storeroom. And that's just where they are when all hell breaks loose. Glory's past includes some very bad men connected to Spectra, men convinced she may have important intel hidden in her place. Now, with the shop under siege, and gunmen holding customers hostage, Tripp shows Glory his true colors: He's no sweet, rumpled "engineer" from the Smithson Group, but a well-trained, hardcore covert op whose easy-going rep is about to be put to the test . . .

Available from Brava in November 2004.

Episode Three:
THE SAMMS AGENDA
by
Alison Kent

Get down and dirty with Julian Samms, SG–5

From his piercing blue eyes to his commanding presence, everything about Julian Samms says all-business and no bull. He expects a lot from his team—some say too much. But that's how you keep people alive, by running things smooth, clean, and quick. Under Julian's watch, that's how it plays. Except today. The mission was straightforward: Extract Katrina Flurry, ex-girlfriend of deposed Spectra frontman Peter Deacon, from her Miami condo before a hit man can silence her for good. But things didn't go according to plan, and Julian's suddenly on the run with a woman who gives new meaning to high maintenance. Stuck in a cheap motel with a force of nature who seems determined to get them killed, Julian can't believe his luck. Katrina is infuriating, unpredictable, adorable, and possibly the most exciting, sexy woman he's ever met. A woman who makes Julian want to forget his playbook and go wild, spending hours in bed. And on the off-chance that they don't get out alive, Julian's new live-for-today motto is starting right now . . .

Available from Brava in December 2004.

Episode Four:
THE BEACH ALIBI
by
Alison Kent

Get deep undercover with Kelly John Beach, SG–5

Kelly John Beach is a go-to guy known for covering all the bases and moving in the shadows like a ghost. But now, the ultimate spy is in big trouble: during his last mission, he was caught breaking into a Spectra IT high-rise on one of their video surveillance cameras. The SG–5 team has to make an alternate tape fast, one that proves K.J. was elsewhere at the time of the break-in. The plan is simple: Someone from Smithson will pose as K.J.'s lover, and SG–5's strategically placed cameras will record their every intimate, erotic encounter in elevators, restaurant hallways, and other daring forums. But Kelly John never expects that "alibi" to come in the form of Emma Webster, the sexy coworker who has starred in so many of his not-for-primetime fantasies. Getting his hands— and anything else he can—on Emma under the guise of work is a dream come true. Deceiving the good-hearted, trusting woman isn't. And when Spectra realizes that the way to K.J. is through Emma, the spy is ready to come in from the cold, and show her how far he'll go to protect the woman he loves . . .

Available from Brava in January 2005.

Episode Five:
THE MCKENZIE ARTIFACT
by
Alison Kent

Get what you came for with Eli McKenzie, SG–5

Five months ago, SG–5 operative Eli McKenzie was in
deep cover in Mexico, infiltrating a Spectra ring that
kidnaps young girls and sells them into a life beyond
imagining. Not being able to move on the Spectra scum
right away was torture for the tough-but-compassionate
superspy. But that wasn't the only problem—someone on
the inside was slowly poisoning Eli, clouding his
judgment and forcing him to make an abrupt trip back to
the Smithson Group's headquarters to heal. Now, Eli's
ready to return . . . with a vengeance. It seems his quick
departure left a private investigator named Stella Banks in
some hot water. Spectra operatives have nabbed the nosy
Stella and are awaiting word on how to handle her
disposal. Eli knows the only way to save her life and his
is to reveal himself to Stella and get her to trust him.
Seeing the way Stella takes care of the frightened girls
melts Eli's armor, and soon, they find that the best way to
survive this brutal assignment is to steal time in each
other's arms. It's a bliss Eli's intent on keeping, no matter
what he has to do to protect it. Because Eli McKenzie has
unfinished business with Spectra—and with the woman
who has renewed his heart—this is one man who always
finishes what he starts . . .

Available from Brava in February 2005.